The Unlikely Success of a
Copy-Paste Developer

IRIS CLASSON

Developmental editor: Cassie Jeans

ISBN: 978-91-527-1979-4

DEDICATION

I dedicate this book to my fellow programmers and
those that have to deal with us.

ACKNOWLEDGMENTS

To the programming community, thank you for giving
me a home, friends, and encouragement.
To my husband, thank you for being my number one
fan.
To my computer. Thank you for not blowing up the
battery until I finished the book.
To Loke and Tyr. Get back to bed.

PREFACE

Many years ago, I started writing down funny stories, situations, and characters I came across as a programmer. I did this secretly, as I'm sure some of my higher uppers would have been less than thrilled about it, even though they sure talk a lot about the importance of documentation. To be fair, I merely documented the bizarre and humorous aspects of a job often considered mundane.

Time passed and in 2020, I had survived my first year as a first-time parent to a baby that hated sleep (and still does) and was awarded a day at the spa from my dear husband. As you do, when you get some much-needed rest, I spent that time wisely and wrote an idea that would become the inspiration for this book. I essentially used my spa-day to work. Don't judge me. This was when the lazy sub-par consultant Leo was born! The stories and characters I had collected over the years became a part of Leo's life. After a much-needed day at the spa, I went back home and realized I still had a bullfrog baby (bullfrogs don't sleep) and the book, naturally, took longer to write than I had estimated. If you know anything about software developers, then you know we are the worst at estimating anything. And thus, the book was written with voice to text, on my phone, as I was walking for hours with my strong-personality child at night when he ought to be sleeping. This is great! I thought. And got myself another baby. Consequentially, the book was edited and rewritten during the frequent late-night feeding sessions newborns torture you with, while my dear husband wrangled the older one to sleep like a pro wrestler doing a final

comeback in his (almost) forties. And through the parental haze of emotional masochism, I managed to put together a book I'm immensely proud of and I'm obviously going to become filthy rich.

TLDR: All the situations, stories and characters are based on actual happenings, people, and stereotypes. Sleep deprivation was my fuel when caffeine wouldn't do, and this passion project has taken me years to complete. Please make me rich.

Je ne regrette rien!

1

It is said that you can tell a lot about a person by the way they live. Possessions, however many or few, are tied to one's identity like deliberate statements describing who you are. After all, no matter where your life takes you, home is where you return unless you are drunk and confused. It's a memory box, with bits and pieces sampled from your life - past and present - with your personality written on the walls. Metaphorically of course, unless you are a toddler with a pen, but no sane person would leave a toddler unattended with a pen. Some memory boxes are rather empty with white boring walls and the absence of memorabilia signifying either a person with a less-than-exciting life or a person that has yet to explore the wonders of life.

Leo Larsson lives in an apartment perfect for one, tiny for two.

An excuse or a choice? Maybe both.

It's located on the second floor of a beautiful traditional British apartment building in Kensington. A pale-yellow brick house from the Georgian era with a

square meter well-kept garden and slippery marble stairs. A breath-taking building for a visitor, breath-taking for other reasons if you were a resident. Let's just say that some period homes weren't damp proof and mold was to be considered a long-lived pet.

Nonetheless, the building was magnificent and full of personality, in contrast to Leo's apartment. Leo's hallway consisted of a plastic chair, the collapsible kind, a metal coat rack with two jackets (denim and rain jacket), and three pairs of shoes - all-white sneakers differing only by the number of scuff marks and dust. The living room, an extension of the hallway, was equally empty with a two-seat couch in sun-bleached grey linen, a square black coffee table with several cups of old coffee now resembling Petri dishes, a small LED TV on a white TV stand, blackout curtains in dark blue, and a framed map over London underground in the kitchen corner next to a tall closet where Leo's life was neatly folded consisting of a T-shirt and jeans combination for any event. Practical clothes that would make grandma proud.

The walls were dusty, but clean, white.

Wooden floor.

No wall-to-wall carpet -a criminal offense in Britain.

This was a part of Leo's personality. The boring bits. The other bits, rarely shared, was the pile of books in the corner, eagerly read, and deeply loved. The old wine fridge filled to the brim with fine wines, next to a sourdough starter waiting for its weekly bake. The cacti collection in the kitchen next to the hydroponic basil assortment and a pile of moving boxes containing personal diaries from Leo's life and therapy.

All of this could easily be overlooked and hidden in the sheer emptiness of the apartment. The few times Leo had visitors they would ask if Leo had recently moved in (and suggested places to buy furniture), but Leo had lived there for almost a decade, which sounds like a long time, but

apartments in London are hard to find and bloody expensive to move between, something you just don't do and besides, Leo was not the exploratory moving-around-type.

Interior design had never been Leo's strength, which was very likely the result of an utter lack of interest in all things concerning design. The apartment had arrived in flat packages, courtesy of IKEA - a tribute to Leo's motherland, Sweden. The Allen key puzzles had been assembled without instructions but with the help of 5 beers, a cat, and Indian takeaway, (the only edible British food there is).

Most of the apartment had been put together from a practical perspective, like a temporary home for an elderly person that would trip on carpets or get confused by decorative items.

There had been no parties, get-togethers, or late-night romances and consequently, the apartment was spotless, pure, and the perfect meditative retreat for a tired consultant - according to Leo. The only part of the apartment that didn't look like a successful office furniture yard sale was the corner in the living room.

Behold: The Home Office.

A majestic wild cherrywood desk with perfectly rounded corners polished to perfection and calmly reflecting the dim light from the living room window. Featured in the space, the magnificent, curved computer monitor framed with tropical plants resting their leaves against the silvery frame. A treasure hidden in a tropical forest. To match the screen, a beautiful backlit WASD keyboard intimately resting on the desk with its lights and shadows serenading the computer with clicks and clacks of love. The keys, Cherry MX, blue of course. The perfect sound, tactile feel, and resistance for a truly immersive experience for long nights creating metaphorical music, whispering commands in a dark editor (anything but VIM),

or CLI. The keyboards companion, a heavy but delicate and delightful gaming mouse. A magical wand for the magician for those rare occasions. In the corner, a wide selection of other keyboards and mice, for the collector that can never be truly satisfied.

Next to the desk, a silent and cool computer tower hard at work, an unbelievable ergonomic chair that required three YouTube videos to figure out how to use (totally worth it), and the lonely couch with one permanent empty seat reflecting its sadness on the wooden floor next to a coffee machine and a cat tower for the commander in chief.

And if one could measure how much a person loved their cat by the height of a cat tower, then Lion the cat was loved from floor to ceiling, regardless of his tenacity for asshole-like behavior exuding the stigma of cats everywhere. Assholery aside, cats were, according to Leo, smart, intuitive, independent, and graceful (often better company than human beings). Cats had all the desirable traits humans could possess but were rarely found combined. Unfortunately, Leo's workplace did not share the same appreciation for felines and the cat was not allowed in the office.

Thus, Lion watched on as Leo did an armpit check (scratch and sniff), confirmed the T-shirt could be worn another day and put on the jeans that had spent the night curled on the floor. With the questionable outfit assembled Leo marked all emails and messages as read, sans reading them, and let the team know Leo was almost there ignoring the time it would take to get to the train and then to work.

After verifying that no neighbors were in the stairwell, Leo snuck out like a pantless lover in the night rushing to the entrance where Mary's letterbox was waiting. Holding the wrinkly letters in one hand and laptop bag in the other Leo ran up the marble stairs – two at a time - all the way to

the top where the musty and dusty smell lingered by Mary's door.

The mail was dropped by the door where the senior citizen Rapunzel Mary was held captive by bad hips and evil marble stairs and Leo darted down the stairs silently celebrating successful, avoidant behavior. And just like that, Leo disappeared like a ninja in the night late for one of those rare trains to Peterborough. *Almost there. Yes, of course, I read the messages.* That, of course, was a lie.

2

It was an unexpectedly warm and humid day in the middle of May and Leo was sweating profusely on the train heading towards the cathedral city of Peterborough on the outskirts of London. Peterborough was a small city, and one could almost consider it a hamlet, if it wasn't for the damn cathedral. Everybody seemed to know about Peterborough, but for all the wrong reasons. It was a self-declared shithole, according to Leo, and The Sun. Voted the Biggest Dump in England in 2019. The best part about the city was the train station and the ability to leave quickly.

Leo had once rented a house on the main street (decades ago), between two friendly neighbors - one that traded bags of sketchy high-quality flour for cash (expensive stuff!), and a neighbor that enjoyed polyamory and had quite a few loud boyfriends visiting for 24/7 rendezvous. Love language: money, paid by the hour. The house Leo rented had a stable internet connection (a must for a programmer), low rent, and was close to the train station. Leo enjoyed a one-year lease for a one-month stay before making the wise escape to London.

While reminiscing, Leo's thoughts were interrupted by a colorful, "Excuse me, sir? Hello?"

A young boy leaned over the back of the train seat, waving with both hands and a beaming smile. He pointed at Leo's laptop. "Hi! Sir? Wow, mum look at those!"

Leo sighed and pulled off the headphones and placed the laptop on the empty seat. The laptop sparkled in the sun as the rays reflected the colorful stickers, some shiny, some worn out.

"Yes?" Leo murmured.

It was way too early for this kind of excitement, but one simply cannot ignore excited kids on the train. A tantrum has the potential to last a few stations.

"Where did you get those stickers? Is that a cat that looks like an octopus? Can I have some? I'll trade you!" He lifted his backpack. It was decorated with different stickers blending in with the Pokémon-themed pattern.

"It's mostly work stuff, and yes, it's an Octocat," Leo replied quietly, but audibly annoyed. "I don't have more of them."

He pouted and lowered his head. "But I want some! Mum…"

"Get back in your seat, Tim," the mother off-handedly commented. Tim persevered and Leo relented.

"Those are work stickers." Leo quietly replied.

The boy disappeared for a few minutes behind the seat before popping up again. "LOOK!" He pulled up two stickers, "Pokémon, Wigglytuff! You can have one!"

"Thanks, kiddo." Leo grabbed the sticker, unsure what to do with it.

"Look," he pointed at the laptop, "it fits in the corner."

There was indeed an empty corner that hadn't been stickerized.

"I had saved that spot for something special." Leo bit the inside of the lower lip, hesitating for a moment. "But okay."

Leo placed the sticker on the laptop, praying that it would be easy to remove and that this action would end the current interaction. Tim, however, was far from done.

He was leaning even further over the seat, legs almost lifting. His mom held onto his thigh, a mobile phone in the other hand.

"It looks like the one you have there. Is that a Pokémon?"

"No, that's the Go gopher."

"Did you draw it?" He jumped back in his seat. "Wait!" He pulled out a pen from the backpack, sending a second pen flying across the seat as he lunged forward. "Can you—"

"—No, didn't draw it. It's a mascot. For a language. A computer language, programming language." Leo was pretty shit with kids, but this wasn't the first time Leo had to explain the colorful animal stickers on an adult computer.

"Wow, mum! Computers can speak Pokémon! Can I have one?"

Leo grabbed one from the inner pocket of the bag. "Here."

"I trade stickers with my friends at school. They always have fun ones I don't have. And I have some from Spain. You can get really, really nice stickers in Spain. Do you trade with friends?"

"I don't have friends."

"Why not?"

"I like the stickers," Leo accentuated, "that *I* pick."

"But what if they have really, really nice ones?"

"Then they get to keep them." She gave a flat response.

"You should try!" He bounced in the seat as the train slowly came to a halt.

"Try other stickers?"

"No, friends! You can have some of mine! They are really, really nice."

Oof. What a slap. Leo cringed, "Nah, I'm good."

"This is our stop. Let's go honey." The boy's mother rolled her eyes as he kept digging in his backpack,

searching. He slid back in his seat until he was kneeling on the train floor.

"Sorry about that. He gets very excited about Pokémon." She pulled him towards the doors. "You really got to stop speaking to strangers, dear, even if they like the same toys as you."

"But muuummm…" His voice trailed off with a faint cry. Leo could see the boy bouncing up and down, trying to get a last glance at the laptop before the train doors closed, backpack by his side, his mum pulling on his shirt. *Train to Peterborough* scrolled on the platform screen.

Leo's stay in Peterborough had been short. The next-door bakery, also known as a local drug house, was particularly busy at night. In addition, the massage parlor's happy endings (the only happiness in Peterborough, apparently) were loud affairs. Leo admitted defeat, moved to London but kept the job.

And that is how Leo made the Guinness Book of Records as the only person in the world paying London rent and commuting to Peterborough.

A reverse shit-commute and today was just another shitty reminder.

Leo opened the laptop again, only to be met with, 'Don't worry, your files are exactly where you left them,' and blue background. *You know, I didn't worry until you told me that, Windows Updates.*

"Oh, my God!" a loud voice singingly echoed in the cart.

Leo dropped the laptop, leaned over, and hid her head between her knees.

"It's you! Ah! I told you we would meet again!" The Loud American threw himself in the seat across from Leo and leaned back, hands behind his head with a long sigh manspread like a cheerleader doing a split.

"Nice to see I'm not the only one escaping London traffic in the morning! How ARE YOU? And how are your teeth?"

Peterborough was the type of place that only had one dentist. In the city center, there was a sign that said, Dentist, and if you followed it, it would take you there. Shocking, yes.

In hindsight, it hadn't been a good sign.

The Loud American was one of the regular visitors at the dental office. He had found the place on Yelp. Leo found the dentist, Martin, by following the sign.

"Good. My teeth are fine."

"They sure are, you have a lovely smile!" Leo rarely smiled, so this was an inaccurate observation or a at best a social lie.

"Hey, is that your bike?" He wasn't done.

Leo's Brompton was packed away neatly next to the window.

"Yeah. I keep it there to avoid company."

"Hah! Funny!"

Nobody had ever described Leo as funny, although the bike, referred to as the circus bike, was a lot of fun to ride.

"Here is something funny," he continued, "You know why a bike can't stand on its own…"

"… yes, they can…"

"… because it's too tired. Man, you ruined the joke. Tire-d, get it?" He looked genuinely disappointed for a second before leaning forward. "Is it called tire in British? I'm from the US. It's called tire there. Although we don't bike much, hah!"

"I'm Swedish, but sure, tire. My bike must be beyond tired, it has collapsed from exhaustion." Leo glanced at the folded bike. It looked like it had been in an accident. Loud American laughed loudly, clapping excitedly and thus adding a seal to the current circus. There was nothing Leo hated more than being a part of a show. Yet somehow Leo

had managed to become a part of this particular train circus.

"I'm Neal, by the way."

"Leo, that's me," Leo smirked, *Neal the seal, that'll be an easy name to remember.*

"Is that a typical name in Switzerland?"

"I doubt it, and it's Sweden." Leo leaned back; arms crossed.

Neal was tall and lanky, just like Leo, but wore dressy clothes and had shiny shoes, not like Leo. He wore an old school Casio watch on his right wrist and had attempted a conversation at the dental office when he noticed Leo was wearing a smartwatch as well.

Leo had insisted his watch wasn't that smart. Leo soon realized neither was he, and let him insult the precious Pebble to kill the one-sided conversation.

Leo had purposely booked the dental appointments very early or late, after confirming with the receptionist that it was their least busy times. The plan had failed Leo, and Leo had been forced to socialize with Neal the seal.

"Leo. Cool, cool." He leaned back again, looked out the window, and gestured towards the filthy glass. "How did you end up here?"

"The UK? We moved here for my father's job." She replied with unexpected bitterness. It hadn't been the first time they had moved because of father's art program, but it had been the first time Leo had begged him to reconsider, scared to leave and start over again. A new life, a new therapist. Not tempting at all.

"Do you miss Sweden?"

"Not sure what there is to miss."

"Friends?"

Leo didn't reply. Moving around hadn't helped Leo's social life.

Neal persisted. "How did you end up in Peterborough? My girlfriend tells me it's a dump. She read it in the newspaper and wants me to find a new dentist. But I like

Martin. He wants to road trip in California next summer and he had good Yelp reviews."

"There's only one review."

"Yeah, but it's pretty good!"

"Still, just one." Leo insisted and tried to keep an eye roll at bay.

"Anyway, why Peterborough?" He interrupted cheerfully.

Leo sighed. Open-ended questions. The worst kind of questions. The laptop hadn't finished updating, and the fans were hard at work. Probably complaining about that extra sticker. Hopefully, the battery would last. "I work in PE, consultant at ConsultIt."

Neal seemed fascinated by the new sticker.

"Did you catch them all?" He laughed while applauding his own joke. Leo stared at him; eyebrows furrowed.

"Sorry." he abruptly stopped laughing. "What type of consultant?"

"Software developer."

"What? Really? Now that was unexpected!" Wide-eyed he continued, "been there long?"

"Probably too long. Tenth anniversary this week. Longest relationship of my life." The corner of Leo's mouth twitched slightly.

It was intended as a joke, but Leo realized by the empathetic look that it was a sad joke, and nobody likes sad jokes. It had been a lackluster relationship, straight from the start. Red flags galore. Leo would never forget the first day and the enthusiastic Julia from HR.

3

"Welcome, Leo!" A tall blonde woman wearing a black formal dress and cat socks had greeted Leo with a handshake. "My name is Julia. Have you been here before?" Leo had been there before. Four times, to be exact. And each time they had asked Leo the same thing.

Leo shook her hand briefly and blushed. "It's my fifth time here. We've met before."

Julia threw her head back and laughed. "Oh my, sorry about that! Many people, busy times, you know." Many people meant forty-two employees. A static number for the last two years.

"Designer? Project leader?" Julia asked, while gesturing for Leo to follow her to the kitchen. They made their way to the giant coffee machine. "You must be a designer! I can tell by your clothes. Simple, modern."

"Still a Software Developer, just another code monkey." Leo accepted the cup of coffee.

"Oh. Really?"

"I'm confident." Leo attempted.

"You probably want to add some extra water to that," Julia said.

Leo stared at the dark syrup in the cup. An attempt at swirling the coffee like a fine glass of red wine failed. The

liquid slowly licked the insides of the cup with its muddy texture.

"Frank likes to make the coffee extra strong; we usually mix it half and half with hot water," Julia continued and laughed, "here, try some vegan milk." The milk disappeared into the coffee as if it had been poured into a black hole. The coffee remained a dark shade of brown. A vegan magic trick.

"Just the way I like it." Leo took a sip, smiled, and handed back the milk. "It can double as food spread."

Julia laughed but questioned for a minute if Leo would do that. *Software developers are a strange bunch. And they'd go to great lengths to obtain their daily caffeine*, she thought to herself.

"Fantastic! You will fit right in! You are going to LOVE it here. Our employees are very," Julia crossed her hands firmly against her chest, paused for a dramatic second with her eyes closed, before continuing, "important to us. And we would like to welcome you as part of the team," Julia leaned forward and winked, "with a minor challenge." She glanced away, recharging her theatrical skills, and then locked eyes with Leo as if telling a secret. "If you go to your desk, you'll see a box there. It contains what will become your chair but… it is not assembled yet! Because we are a T.E.A.M., and we build things together. TEAMbuilding! Get it?"

Julia was struggling to contain herself and Leo took a step back to give her more space for the dramatic gestures.

Julia continued. "I love this part of the welcoming process! Anyway, the chair. You will build it and you will need help. The team will be there for you, even for tricky chairs like the one you've got- a wonderful chair by the way. We can build the chair together, but no YouTube Just your chosen work family." Julia started walking. "Let's welcome you to the family and let's build that chair!"

Julia's phone rang, and she glanced with an abrupt stop, "Sorry, it's the ping-pong table delivery. I got to go help the guys with this. But you got this! Go build that chair!"

Leo, momentarily stunned, scanned the room, looking for the team. Julia waved from the far end of the room.

"And no shoes indoors! Unless indoor shoes!" she yelled and pointed at her socks. "Love cats! Family!"

Leo sighed, remove the sneakers, and walked to the team corner with the shoes in one hand, coffee in the other.

Leo's colleagues were busy, but a blonde, well-dressed guy spun around in his chair, playing with a pen. "Hi Leo, how's it goin'?"

Leo blushed. "… good, I -" Leo looked at the empty desk. There was no box. However, there was a chair. And somebody had assembled it.

"Oh, yeah, that…" He turned towards the chair and rolled his eyes. "This happens a lot. Julia gets excited about HR stuff. But they always deliver the chairs in one piece. But it's a fun idea, isn't it? We probably should tell her. Have a seat."

Leo still had the same chair, ten years later. It was an alright chair.

Neal was staring at Leo, unaware of the flashback that had run through Leo's mind. "You like it then? Your workplace?"

Leo paused and rubbed the blue ConsultIt! Sticker on the laptop. A cartoon cowboy was the mascot, but instead of guns, he had two keyboards, fingers on the enter key. "Because we deliver twice as fast," according to the product manager. "That's not how it works," they had explained many times. "That's not how any of it works."

"It's okay, I guess," Leo replied. The update had finished. The laptop was suspiciously quiet. Windows updates had left a burn mark on Leo's shin.

"You Swiss people are not the emotional type." He smiled and raised an eyebrow before grabbing his bag quickly. "Wow, time goes fast when you're having fun! This is my stop, one stop early, selling a beautiful house

today- you should have a look!" He pulled out a business card and held it out as an altar sacrifice.

"Is this paper?" Leo held it against the window. "How retro."

"HAH! I'll make sure to say hi to dental Martin King, unless you beat me to it!" Neal cheerfully said, placing a hand on Leo's shoulder to help himself up.

Leo pulled back. "Uhm, please don't," Leo replied dryly, and straightened the denim jacket as soon as he let go.

He danced out the open train door, turned his head, and offered a thumbs up, "Best dentist in town!"

"The only dentist in town!" Leo shouted back as the doors closed.

Leo had gotten 50% off on the annual check-up for that review. Neal danced on the platform, waving with his whole body. It had definitely not been worth it.

4

The bike ride to the office was uneventful but warm and Leo was a hot mess when she arrived at the office. From a distance, you'd think she was the sporty type, slim and tall, balancing on two tiny wheels like a professional. Close up, you could hear her struggling breaths and a few chosen words cursing the heat. She had gotten the bike when she started her reverse commute to blend in with the Londoners and the rest of the balancing monkeys. Unnecessary public transportation meant less random human interaction, something she considered a win. Besides the occasional sticker-interrogation by kids, she mostly sat alone, enjoying the tranquility of the mind-numbing happy hardcore beats and the occasional (weekly) Windows Update.

As Leo was making her way through the parking lot, she considered her alternatives if Neal was going to become a regular on the train. She didn't have the stamina, or the willpower, to bike more than a few kilometers, and there was no way she would drive on the wrong side of the road. Not a fan of learning new skills or changes, she was uncomfortable with both options.

The bike scraped the entrance door as she dragged it in half-folded. A dead body ready for the morgue. She scanned her card at the second entrance, leaving the folded bike in a corner looking sad and abandoned, and ran up the stairs to the conference room. She had barely rounded the corner when her watch lit up, "@channel Scrum!" *Late for Scrum again. Great.* She pushed the door open to the conference room and scanned the empty room. *Yes. First again. Not late if you are first.*

The room remained empty, except for Leo, for a few more minutes until it was twenty past ten. Down the hallway, a verbal ping-pong of passive-aggressive remarks echoed as James and David closed in.

".. maybe we should move Scrum to 11…" David suggested as they entered the room. He paused and looked at Leo sitting on a FatBoy in the corner. Phone in hand, biting her nails, headphones on.

"Too early," James replied. "After lunch sounds more reasonable."

Leo put her phone down and pulled out her laptop from her backpack. "Ten is early?" She raised her eyebrows. The only morning person at the office, including those that had little ones.

"Yeah, for a developer it is," David stated, grabbing a chair. He sat down with his hands behind his head, heels together, knees spread wide apart. "Plus, we were here ten minutes ago but went for a walk waiting for you."

"Jesus. David, you are NOT a developer. Also, it's not called Scrum." James shook his head, palms pressed against each other. A silent prayer for the agile sins that had been committed. "You've copy-pasted code twice and we've spent two weeks trying to figure out what the hell you were trying to do. Embrace your role as project leader and leave the code to us."

"Can we embrace the fifteen-minute rule for stand-up?" Leo interrupted. "We can talk about our feelings and

hug it out afterwards. And by the way, it's called stand-up or daily scrum, not just Scrum."

"I'd say stand-up is pretty offensive if we had somebody on the team that can't stand up." David placed his hands on his hips, pleased with his inclusiveness.

"But we don't, do we?"

"What if we did?" David continued. "You could get hit by a car when looking the wrong way before crossing the road. You know, you - a Swede, driving on the right side of the road?"

"The right side. That's right. The RIGHT side. And are you saying I should get hit by a car? Making friends with HR again, are we?"

James flicked some water at David from his glass. "Can we get started now, kids?"

Leo shot James a look, *don't you dare do that to me*. She plugged in her laptop and projected the Kanban board on the conference monitor. "Let's walk the board with the Swede. I'm going to need caffeine via an IV if we don't start soon and it's insanely hot. James, can you fix the aircon?"

James jumped up and out the door, opened the door to the storage room on the other side, pulled out a dusty scraggly fan, and placed it in the hallway between the two rooms. The stand-up could now start, albeit, sitting down. He had done this many times before and could now do the setup in less than three minutes.

PetSockShop was one of the biggest clients they had. An international distributor of shoes and socks for pets. They had revamped their online presence so they could sell directly to customers, besides business to business. Leo's team had been tasked with improving the webshop, with James as an intern junior developer and David, who wasn't supposed to code, as a project leader of sorts.

The project had turned into a shitshow for a variety of reasons, but the biggest problem they were having now was the horrendous performance. Back in the day, when

the team was larger with a pool of thrifty third-party consultants, somebody had gotten the brilliant idea to implement their own cache.

How hard can it be?

Turns out, it's *really* hard.

There are two truly difficult problems in Computer Science. Naming things, cache invalidation, and off by-one errors.

For the last few months, they had tried to figure out how to fix the slow and inconsistent cache, but they had made little progress.

David had decided, against his better judgment, to give programming a go, and copy-pasted some code he found online. The fix caused a substantial memory leak that took a month to locate. The incident had earned David a poster on the wall with a picture of him with a bandit mask on and the text, *Hide your cache registers, ladies.* David liked the poster and had made extra copies and placed one in every room.

He was now sitting next to one of the many posters in the conference room and pointed at it with a satisfied smile. "How are we doing with the cache, ladies?"

"Honestly, it's not going well. I'm still looking into ways we can patch this, but other requests have gotten in the way."

"As in HTTP requests?" James grinned.

Leo pointed at the board. Most issues had a red tag, 'bugsbunny,', and a 'prio1' tag. "Our lanes are drowning in bugs and support requests, or as you like to call them David, *features and Easter eggs*. We can barely swim from one side to the other, from backlog to deployed."

David sighed. "Why don't you guys prioritize better?"

After some talking to from HR, David had started alternating between calling them 'guys' and 'ladies.' However, with the recent preferred-pronouns-talk and

wheel of identities, he wasn't sure what to use anymore. He had added *people* to his repertoire, but it just didn't have the same feel to it.

"This wouldn't be happening if we had more tests…" James looked straight at Leo "… or testers."

"We test every time we use the system, don't we? The clients are the best testers!" David twirled with his hands out, palms up, like a princess showing off her dress. "Nah?"

"I'm pretty sure they haven't signed up for that," James replied. "Anyway, the way I see it, we need to rewrite the cache. Preferably the whole site, but definitely the cache. And when we do that, we can implement proper testing."

"We'll have to save that for a future sprint." David looked out the window.

"How far in the future are we talking? Before I graduate? Maybe a doctorate later?" James looked at Leo and was met with a shrug.

"I have added the two of you to the support team. We've got less time to work on this." David dropped the comment like it had no weight to it at all.

Leo looked up; mouth open, suddenly cold albeit the heat. She held up an index finger. "What did you say?"

"All developers must help support. We decided this last week. Didn't you read the email?"

"You know I don't do random human interaction. I. DON'T. DO. SUPPORT. As a matter of fact, I am very unsupportive."

"You will do support." David kept his stance, a blank yet slightly combative stare.

"I'm a software engineer. Not support." Leo replied, reeling inside, trying to figure out how to make this clearer.

"You are a data consultant and according to the internal resume clients will consult you regarding data stuff."

"Are you saying all engineers have to do support?" Slight panic rose in her voice.

"Not the architects. But the rest, yes. The data consultants," David replied flatly.

"How do architects differ from devs here?" James looked genuinely confused.

David hesitated as Leo looked keenly at him, dying for a bullshit reply. "Architects formulate the vision," David cleared his throat, "the grand plan at a high level. Developers are worker bees — they carry out the vision, they do the grunt work." Pleased with his reply, he punctuated the last sentence with his hands on his hips and a nod.

"Formulate the vision? We can do that. We aren't blind," Leo replied with sarcasm laced words.

"It's not that easy and you know that. The vision considers the business and the domain aspect. Last time I checked, you had no interest in that." *Touché!* David gave himself a mental pat on the back.

"True that. But what if I changed my mind?"

"We can't afford more architects —"

Leo wasn't having it. "Everybody knows architects are just developers who think they are too good to code; therefore, they just tell others how to code. Like prophets who can communicate the revelations of the binary father — and mother. Are you saying we are mere disciples?"

"What would that make David?" James asked.

"An Apostle. Sent by PetSockShop." Leo retorted.

"Look," David huffed, "we can't afford over two. And we currently have … let's see … TWO."

"I'll trade the paycut for the title."

David looked at the ceiling with a long exhale, "The title requires specific skills—"

"The bar is on the floor. Mikael set it there—"

"That you don't have. I'm not having this discussion now." David did a timeout sign and looked at James for help.

James leaned in. "Hey, it's not a death sentence, Leo. It can be fun! And a learning opportunity."

She looked at James. He was so young and hopeful. Barely half a year of experience from the harsh reality of working as a consultant. He'll get there.

"I'm done learning. I want to code. What about the technical debt?" Leo asked..

"It's frankly not our problem. Besides, they already decided on continuing with Web Forms. Their fate is sealed. We should be happy they don't use blink tags on their submit buttons." David laughed. "And I believe they still use XP on their terminal server."

"David, YOU like XP?" Leo questioned.

"Of course I don't, but it's still funny," he replied.

"How was the workshop?"

"Shut up."

"Fuck, it's hot in here." Leo stood up and looked at the wet spot on the FatBoy. Her t-shirt, *Stuck in VIM, please send help!* was stuck to her back like a candy wrapper in the heat. "I swear to God, if we bring in more servers in this office, somebody is going to die from heatstroke. Got to join another meeting; I have a meeting with the meeting customer. David, are you joining?"

Temporarily moving on from the convo, Leo was now focused on trying to remember the customer's name. Although she had been on that project for half a year, she had yet to memorize the names of the people involved.

"Alright, I'll have a look at the cache. Maybe I'll rewrite it." James triangled his fingers.

"James, don't!" Leo said seriously with a slight tone.

"Can't get worse, can it?" Famous last words.

"You do you, but do it on a different branch, ok?"

"Oh, NOW you want best practices?!" James laughed and grabbed his computer and walked backward out of the room, colliding with the fan. "God damnit! I'll leave the fan for your meeting about meetings. I've got to prepare the Meetup for tonight. The user group is discussing another awesome library. It's pretty… awesome…" James' voice trailed off down the hallway.

David fiddled with the projector cable, trying to connect his Mac, searching through the mammoth box of dongles and adapters.

Devices were modernized years ago to only require one - possibly two - ports. A sleek and elegant design, promoting simplicity in a complex world that could only ever be useful when paired with a colossal box of dongle Lego pieces, so one could make the device useful. And because the binary father hates the ordinary, he made sure to always alternate which dongle would fail to work, just to keep people on their toes.

Never forget, Apple started it.

Every few weeks, they, Leo, and David, would do a remote call with a client to discuss when to have the next meeting. Half a year in, and nothing had been done or decided. This was the type of meeting where everybody was invited. "Just in case!" as they said. A new PowerPoint slideshow would be prepared to re-iterate the same vague things, but nothing in it would be actionable.

This is a known meeting ritual seen among the great corporations. If there are no slides, then it's not a real meeting.

David was happy if they could keep billing. Leo, on the other hand, hated meetings with a deep and unexplainable passion, although her calendar was as empty as the snack drawer in the communal kitchen. She could absolutely afford a pointless meeting or two for that much needed human interaction.

"Alright, we are in!" David claimed victory as the call loaded and they could see the other participants.

"Hello?" a voice cut through the speakers.

"Can you hear me?" An unfamiliar voice echoed.

"Can somebody mute?" Leo gave David a paper under the desk and whispered, "I think somebody is in the bathroom and forgot to mute." David looked down, *Conference Call Bingo.*

"Oh, I'm in." He giggled and scanned the bingo sheet discreetly. Each bingo slot had a common conference call phrase or situation. He already had three. He just needed awkward silence and somebody asking, "can anybody see my screen?"

"What's the apple for?" Two apples took up two squares on the sheet. Recent addition. Nice.

"It's when Bernie gets flustered."

"He gets flustered easily."

"You kidding me? He looks like he is ready to explode every few sentences!"

Bernie would gasp for air regularly. It could be an impressively unhealthy lifestyle, or it could be tight pants. Leo didn't know. She had never seen Bernie in real life. The many meetings they had forced Leo to attend, all with the topic of *more meetings*, had been remote. She had no desire to see Bernie's pants, nor attend more meetings about meetings, regardless of how gorgeous the PowerPoint slides would be. Animations and all.

David kicked Leo under the table and whispered, "Bingo."

"You cheated; no chance you got that so quick. Grab another one."

"Sure, but you owe me a coffee. Not the shit Frank makes in the kitchen. That stuff nearly gave me a heart attack last week. I think he is using beans only and no water."

Leo nodded and pretended to pay attention to the meeting. They were showing the second slide, which listed the company's values. *Fast, but made to last.* Paradoxically, the meeting progressed slowly. Almost as slow as the PetSockShop cache.

She had no idea how to fix the cache without a rewrite and they didn't have the time or resources for that. They had promised the client the delivery estimates today at the latest, and David had booked in a meeting to discuss the cache with James and her at the end of the day.

Considering how the conversation went earlier, she wasn't looking forward to it. But then again, she hadn't been terribly excited about anything at work for years. Sometimes she envied James and the innocence and enthusiasm that came with a lack of consultancy experience.

"Can you check if you got the invite?" David leaned over Leo and glared at her screen.

"No can do." Leo looked at the empty calendar. "I'm busy all week."

"Looks empty to me." David pointed out.

"Look, there's an appointment there." Leo pointed out a tiny green block. *Dentist.*

"That's just sad, you know," David chimed.

"I like it sad." Leo closed the lid and turned around, making David jump back.

"Aren't Swedes supposed to be cheerful?" he asked.

"This is my cheerful face," Leo replied, unmoved.

"Doesn't quite look the part there, Leo."

"And that's why we had to leave Sweden." Leo said smugly.

"You have to be friendlier when doing support, you know, Leo." Leo's less than cheerful face dropped even more. There's no way I'm doing support, she thought.

5

David had sushi for lunch. About half a kilometer from
the office, in the middle of a rehabbed
transitional neighborhood, a food court had opened two
years ago with an expanding offer of cuisines. He would
frequent the vicinity and eat there with colleagues, not Leo
though. She always brought her own lunch and ate at her
desk. He had always assumed it was a Swedish thing, but
James had told him it was so she could leave early and
avoid a busy train. James would sometimes join, but not
for sushi. If you had sushi, then you were on your own.
Raw fish in Peterborough wasn't recommended. This
wasn't a city where you'd expect fine dining or fresh
produce of any kind.

   David didn't mind being alone. It had been a rough
couple of weeks with the divorce being finalized and all
the heated custody discussions. Thinking about it now, it
had been a few rough years, not just weeks, and food
poisoning would fit right into the mix. He had gained
weight from the stress and poor eating habits, and maybe
some food poisoning would give him a proper cleanse.
The weight gain was a poor fit. Physically and mentally. He
had always considered himself an athlete without specific
accomplishments, with clothes tailored with little leeway

for an ongoing divorce. He was fit, considering his age anyway. His blonde hair and year-round tan, which was a novelty in pale Britain with its stark shades of pink, had made him feel like a Tour du France team member in his bike clothes. He felt more like a stuffed Danish sausage nowadays, but the sushi was supposedly either healthy or health risk and he couldn't stomach more salads.

David used an old photo for the dating app, Tinder, with a few layers of creative editing and some status symbols cleverly placed. He was posing in front of a black helicopter with a cowboy hat on his head. The hat was his. The helicopter was not. Like a professional influencer. Sans makeup and ass-selfies.

Waiting for his sushi, he swiped through the female profiles in Peterborough. Five swipes in and he was back where he started. How sad, he thought as the sushi arrived. *I've swiped through Peterborough while hoping for food poisoning to help me drop some weight.*

For each piece that he balanced sandwiched between his chopsticks, he recited his worries. Number eight and nine were the kids, especially the two-year-old, when he had them solo for a full week every two weeks. Ten was PetSockShop, eleven was his career if they couldn't fix the cache delay. The list didn't kill his appetite, though. Nothing did.

The last piece sat forlornly on his plate as the waiter approached timidly. "Do you want to take it with you?"

David was caught off guard. "Where? Like on a date? Or a long walk on the beach?" The words were out of his mouth before his mind could stop him.

The waiter pointed at the spongy sashimi piece. "Doggy bag, then?"

The piece mentioned barely held it together, soy sauce ungluing the rice. The seaweed was soggy, and the sesame seeds he had sprinkled made it look diseased. Herpes sushi.

David tried to make up for his abrupt humor earlier. "I don't think my non-existent dog wants this, but thanks anyway, kid."

The waiter removed the plate swiftly with a full body turn, looking over his shoulder with furrowed eyebrows as he walked towards the kitchen. They had a strange obsession with their guests finishing their plates at the sushi place. He usually had no problem ignoring it and would purposefully leave a piece just to mess with them. But today was different.

The last piece reminded him of his life, slowly falling apart. It looked how David felt. He couldn't afford to lose his biggest client with a late delivery. He'd be royally fucked if he didn't deliver, and not the good kind of fuck.

He hurried back to the office on his black racing bike, sweating profusely under the sizzling sun with the cars passing him too close for comfort.

His stomach was bubbling, and for a second he regretted the lunch, but by the time he made it to the office, covered in sweat, his stomach had calmed down.

He looked sick.

This stress is going to kill me unless this weather finishes me first.

6

David clicked and clacked his way to the elevator, hoping to close the door without Frank as company. He failed.

Frank joined him and eyed David up and down before resting his eyes on David's crotch.

"Do you wear the bike clothes everywhere, ball-pad included? Just to bike around the corner to the food court?" He nodded towards David's crotch, a moose knuckle on display. He straightened his checkered flannel shirt and readjusted his gray ponytail. "Can your balls breathe in that?"

David glanced at the ponytail in the elevator mirror, a silvery snake down Frank's back. It's a well-known fact you must have at least one guy with a ponytail if you have Linux servers and in-house IT support. Frank was that guy.

David wiped his forehead, thrust his hips confidently, and pointed with both hands, finger guns ready. "What can I say Frank? It's pretty comfortable, you should try it."

"Doesn't look like it. I mean, is that sweat or tears? Your balls are trying to escape, crying for help!"

The elevator stopped at a floor, but nobody was there. Frank groaned and pushed the button to close the doors.

"What did you eat anyway, didn't see you at the Fish and Chips?"

"Sushi."

"Again?" Frank grimaced and stepped out of the elevator. "You have got to stop eating that shit. Not good for you, David."

"If anything, Frank, it's the coffee you make that would give anybody the shits within minutes."

"Doubt anything could strain through your eighties Lycra wrap."

"I look good though, don't I?" David winked. He exhaled and held his breath as he bent down to undo his bike shoes, replacing them with slippers.

James and a few more colleagues came out of the other elevator, takeaway in their hand. "Hi David, meeting time?"

David eyed their matching Birkenstocks. "No outdoor shoes indoor," he said matter-of-factly.

"They're indoor shoes. Bircks!" They gestured while pointing at their brown sandals.

"Fancy cork with leather straps, I see. But you are wearing them to the food court, outdoors… that makes them outdoor shoes," David replied with a slight raise of the eyebrow.

"Yeah, but it's indoor shoes worn outdoor, not outdoor shoes worn indoor." They were trying to plead the case with confusion.

"And the difference is…?"

Leo walked by, having overheard the entire conversation. "Arguing about shoes again, are we? Let's go. The conference room with aircon is free. I'm dying. I'd like to have this meeting before my funeral."

They were back in the conference room they had used earlier. The fan had been humming all day. David connected his laptop to the projector with a combination

of adapters that fanned out from his one port, glitching occasionally.

"Alright." David cleared his throat and clicked his pen a few times, "Refinement time. And honestly there is only one thing I care about today as Scrum Master and Product Owner, and that is WHEN we will have the performance problem fixed for the shop."

"You are a Scrum Master now? Weren't you project leader last meeting?" Leo chuckled and shook her head. James let out a singular laugh before returning to his salad.

"I have many roles. This is one of them." David had a shit-eating grin on his face.

"When did you become Scrum Master?" Leo retorted.

James put his food aside and leaned in with a big grin. "After the conference. You know, the one with the workshop?"

"Let's do the refinement…" David hastily replied, with a sudden damp forehead, beads forming like cheap necklaces decorating a slippery piece of skin.

"… oh noes, I want to refine this," Leo interrupted.

David had attended a conference a few weeks ago, an Agile conference.

You might not know but being Agile is a must for software developer companies. You don't have to be Agile, claiming that you are is good enough. It's like the participation trophies you get as a kid, or golden stars for doing shit you should do without golden stars, it's just something you must do to be considered a good boy. Or girl. We don't collect golden stars, instead we collect fancy words and abbreviations, and those can be traded in for real currency. Extra valuable if you are a consultant because you only trade with make-believe words when getting hired for a project.

David, although a limber and athletic cycling enthusiast in his late thirties, was not Agile. He was the opposite of Agile. A Waterfall master in fact. And his Un-Agile self

had not attended many conferences as he preferred networking events, where there was less focus on attending sessions and workshops and more focus on fancy dinners and parties. However, the conference had an XP workshop and since they had to maintain several systems hosted with Windows XP; he thought that would be very useful and they could sell in more hours with that expertise.

Microsoft officially stopped supporting the operating system in 2014, but it didn't stop him from loving XP and refusing to give up while pushing clients to upgrade. True love can never be forgotten. For the few clients that were using XP, the help from him had been immensely valuable, as no other consultancy firms wanted to deliver work on an unsupported operating system. He had been extraordinarily thrilled about the workshop and immediately booked tickets, hotel, and travel to Norway. In addition, he made sure everybody at the company knew he would return as an expert. However, the workshop didn't go as intended. As always, he had made several assumptions and couldn't be bothered with details. He showed up on that Monday in his best suit ready to rock, only to learn that the workshop was not about Windows XP. As you'd expect, an Agile conference weren't too concerned with operating systems, and offered workshops on Agile methodologies instead. XP being one of those, XP for Extreme Programming.

Too embarrassed to return home early, he wandered mournfully around for the three days the conference lasted, occasionally eating extremely expensive Norwegian food (the Vikings seemed to know how to pillage modern time foreigners) and attended one session on the topic of Scrum. When he came back home, met by colleagues wanting to know the details of his XP adventures, he couldn't handle the embarrassment and somehow put together a story about him going there to become a Scrum Master. He spent a day searching online and reading Scrum

for Dummies to get a general idea, and at the end of that day, he felt confident in his new role, courtesy of Dunning Kruger.

James leaned back "… and that is the story. You really should join us for lunch Leo, you are missing out on the office gossip. David, I believe in you - scrum away!"

David excused himself and went to get coffee and when he returned everybody seemed ready to get started with the refinement. Or backlog grooming as they sometimes called it. Truthfully, the grooming would be more akin to putting lipstick on a pig. The word *grooming* had gone out of fashion in 2013 because of its connotations with child exploitation, but David was happy to exploit developers and therefore found the word fitting. David groomed, James and Leo refined. HR was very unhappy with the former.

David sat down and stared at the computer. They had changed the screensaver to the Windows XP logo, and James and Leo were giggling like drunk teenagers in the park. He sighed. "You people are so immature."

"Alright Master of the Scrums, tell us what to do!" James bowed. *Scrotums,* Leo thought, and hid behind a slight smile. David glared at them.

"You can call me Master any time you like. But let's get to work. I want an estimate for the PetSockShop delivery. The last item in the backlog is the performance problem. When? I need a deadline." He spit the words out, all business in his tone.

Leo exhaled slowly and looked out the window. "How long is a string?"

"String? I need an estimate. Give me a number. Not a string. Integer. Don't forget to include time for support."

"No floats, I assume then." James winked at Leo.

"He said estimate, not accurate estimate. Floats are fine," Leo replied without emotion.

James paused. "Honestly, I don't know. Besides, I thought we weren't doing deadlines- or *'estimates'* as you

call them. You know, scrum and all. The best we can do is a guestimate," James replied, "and that depends on how we fix it. Sorry."

"Obviously," Leo wasn't sorry and therefore continued, "if James gets to decide, then we'll rewrite this until we retire and the robots take over, using a plethora of hipster libraries he heard about at a user group. It'll be the most performant webshop in the world, but we'll deploy on our deathbed. And equally, I'm not doing support, obviously." Nailing that one home.

"I don't care how it gets fixed, just get it done. And give me an estimate. Or guestimate. Whatever you want to call it. Leo, unless you are an architect, you will do support," David added, not missing a beat.

Leo swallowed dry air. "Nope. No support for me. No chance." Leo continued before David could reply, "and the estimate? I don't know. And If I don't know, James certainly doesn't know."

"Can you do a walk to measure?" David threw out a hand. "Here?"

"Ah, David. Sorry. It's a great idea, a fantastic idea. But this room isn't big enough!" James pressed his lips together into a tight smile and slowly shook his head.

"Can't we go back to T-shirt sizes? Do we have to make up a new estimate scale each time? Sort of defeats the purpose." Leo groaned.

"Leo is right, David. HR doesn't have to know." James stated.

"Look, I'm not being accused of body-shaming again. And if we add all the extended sizes HR required…" David air quoted "… for inclusiveness, the scale won't make sense anymore."

"That's a great point David, good thinking. Let's do the walk before HR finds another problem with our scales." James peeked out the hallway, came back, and moved the aircon out of the way.

Leo stood up, lips pressed firmly against each other, and looked down the hallway. "If this is the initial story, which was creating the whole darn shop…" Leo walked two steps and pointed at James' bare feet followed by a gesture towards the end of the hallway, "… then I might as well go to the end of the hallway and use the bathroom there." Leo started walking, accompanied by a muffled shuffling sound from the jeans that were slightly too big on the lean frame. She gestured for James to follow. He smiled big and with small, quick steps, caught up.

"For real? I…" David looked at his phone. A slightly paler David frowned and looked away. "… God damn it." He closed the email app.

Subject: Papers. Sender: Sarah.

"You alright David?" James waved slowly.

"No. But I'll be once I get an estimate. Let's blow their minds. Can we do that?"

"I don't want to blow anything." James chuckled.

Leo caught David's eyes. He looked away, the light reflecting on a tear. *Fuck it, he needs this.* Leo walked a few more steps down the hallway, hesitated, but stopped.

"I can fix this," Leo shouted back.

James looked wide-eyed at the black hole at the end of the hallway and threw out his hands. "Really, Leo? You got a magic programmer in China ready to fix this for us?" He was referring to a programmer that had hired a programmer in China to do his work for years and nobody ever noticed because he had done such a good job. They had discussed at length how awesome that would be, jokingly, of course. But secretly they had researched whether it would be doable.

David pumped his fist in the air. "That's what I'm talking about! Hope you are not pulling my leg - this would be splendid." He measured the length by counting steps. "3 meters, assuming a 90 cm stride."

"… not with your legs," Leo drawled back.

"Ignore Leo, David, your legs are great! All that hiking is paying off!" James offered a thumbs up. Leo's eyes did a roll.

"If Leo says it can be done, it will be done!"

"And assuming a week per meter and multiplying by Pi like you always do, James, that gives us…" his voice faded as he pulled up his phone and found the calculator shortcut, "… something between 2 and 2.5 months." He was all smiles. "Let's go with 1.5 months. We have a deadline!"

"I don't remember giving an estimate, nor do I remember giving a deadline." Leo looked intensely at David, but he avoided eye contact and walked back to the room.

"I'll let the client know!" David shouted as his shadow followed him as mantel into his cave. The supervillain had left the measure. The heroes moaned in defeat.

"Sneaky bastard," Leo murmured with a glare. She worked her lower lip before continuing on her thumb.

James slapped Leo's back as he walked by. "This is going to be a lot of fun! I LOVE profiling. Performance is fun!"

"Can you be less enthusiastic, James? Please! We are consultants, we don't do enthusiasm, nor do we do fun." Leo recoiled, trying to avoid the enthusiast.

"Nope, never!" He spun around loosely, almost floating, with a big grin as he disappeared around the corner.

2,147,483,647, Leo thought, *that's how long a string is.*

7

The evening had settled in, and the office buzz fizzed out as the options to leave Peterborough became sparser. The last bus had left, and the train took half an hour longer. Public transportation had made it clear that Peterborough was not the place to be after dark.

David had tefloned his way through traffic and made it home, Leo had caught the last fast train, and HR had paused the surveillance equipment for the day.

James grabbed a cold beer from the communal fridge in the office and went to the printer room. The only sounds he could hear were a few colleagues in the Caribbean corner, the printers, and the industrial fans. The warm afternoon had left a thick and moist air lingering in the building and James had strategically placed the industrial fans in an attempt to improve the airflow.

"I like what you've done with the place." Mikael popped his head through the open door, the light reflecting on his overly waxed hair.

"Oh. Wow. That's really something Mikael…" James' mouth remained open as a shirtless Mikael glided in, his chest as shiny as his hair.

"Ah yes, this stuff?" Mikael drummed his chest. "Furiously hot in here, so some of us went sans shirt as

soon as HR left the building!" His shirt was tucked in his back pocket, but he made no attempt at putting it on. "Working hard, you know. Architecting architecture stuff. Not sure you did stuff like that in school?"

James collected the printouts and stacked them neatly. "We had some courses. But you're the expert. I've heard about the work you've done with the SaaS system. How is the Message Broker going?"

Mikael placed his hands on his hips and dug his thumbs in under his belt that barely held together the pressure from his gut. Sweat had collected in his belly button like a well filled to the brim.

"Going great! Half the time it works every time!" Mikael winked.

"You mean 60%? Anchorman?"

Mikael rubbed his chin. "Maybe it is 60%. It's been a while since I saw the movie. But yes, most of the time it works every time."

"50% is not a majority." James smiled politely. "That's great Mikael, great work!"

"Stop staring at my nipples dude." Mikael covered his nipples with his hands.

"It's hard not to. They are aggressively staring at me!" James laughed.

"So, user group again? Talking about open-source stuff?"

"Yes! It's the first one at the office, huge turnout expected."

"I've never understood that stuff. Open source?" Mikael leaned against the door with a suction noise as his moist skin met the glass. "Why? Like why bother?"

James let out an exasperated sigh and rubbed his forehead. "You use though, don't you?"

"Open source? Nah, not my thing." Mikael casually replied.

"RabbitMQ?"

"Ah, The Rabbit?"

"Yes, *The Rabbit.* It's not like you could or would write that yourself," James replied.

"I could if I wanted to. But that's boring stuff. I have better things to do. Look, well, not at my nipples, hah! I know you are passionate about the open-source stuff. The entire office *knows*. I just don't share the same view as you on that stuff." Mikael said, sweat still visible on his exposed midriff.

James clenched his teeth behind a forced smile. There was no point arguing with slippery Mikael. "Let's agree to disagree. I got to prepare for this evening, ok?"

"Is Leo coming?"

"No—" James paused mid-turn. "Is that why you are shirtless?"

"No, NO. Of course not." Mikael grabbed his shirt and pulled it over his head, fighting to birth his head through the narrow opening. "Pumped for support?"

James turned off the light and walked past Mikael out the door. "Yeah, I like our customers." He gave a thumbs-up to Mikael without turning around, while Mikael stayed behind in the printer room.

"I'm not doing support, you know," he yelled from the room as the distance grew. "Architect. Busy with other stuff."

"I know, you already said that!" James yelled back.

"Ah yes, I did!"

With freshly printed stickers in his hand and a colorful poster that said Welcome to the New.Lib.JS User Group, James waited by the door, ready to welcome new and old members.

He had ordered vegetarian pizza, with vegan and gluten-free options, beer, and sodas, and, of course, some snacks. He had styled his short curly dark hair and put on a clean *T-shirt with the text Mechanical Keyboards – Making Sure Everybody Can Hear Me Working!* He had gotten the t-shirt from Leo on his birthday. The gesture had surprised him

as they weren't friends and they seemed to disagree with most things. The only thing they had in common was their sense of humor and not liking David. They didn't hate him, but they certainly didn't love him. He was unexplainably annoying, arrogant, and smug and he wasn't a very good listener, nor did he show respect for their professional opinion. Besides that, he was OK.

David had never attended the user group, and neither had Leo, but she seemed to be anxious. It could just be a Swedish trait. After all, they are known to be exceptionally good at social distancing.

The first few people arrived, and the stickers were going fast. That was a good sign. The app that they used for signing up for the event would list where people were from, and he had noticed that people would travel far to make it to the user group. Consequentially, some giveaways such as the stickers and free food were very much appreciated.

When he was still in uni, he couldn't find sponsors for food, and he quickly learned that hungry developers aren't fun. He didn't have kids, but according to David, there were similarities between hungry developers and toddlers. Thus, based on experience and not advice from his know-it-all colleague, there was an abundance of food sponsored by Microsoft. He had vaguely promised to mention their cloud services and more (which seemed like a fair deal). As a result, he had received a box with stickers, food, and trial subscriptions for Azure that would make sure to charge you your firstborn if (when) you forgot to delete orphaned disks.

"Hi James!" Meron was first to arrive and awkwardly offered his hand for a handshake 50 meters before contact.

He had a frayed backpack slowly slipping off his right shoulder, barely held together at the seams. He sandwiched the laptop in his armpit, probably because the

backpack had given up on its only mission in life to carry things.

"Nice to see you, Meron. I knew you'd be early." James smiled and finally shook his hand after stretching in the last two uncomfortable meters. Meron held his hand a tad too long. "Ready for your session?" James pulled away, pretending to fix the stickers that lay on the tall table next to him at the entry.

"Yes, I am!" Meron lit up, his eyes sparkling. "My professor just graded the project, and I got an A! Can you believe it? My parents are very proud!"

Meron and James had met at the previous user group meeting when James had embarrassingly tried to speak French to him after he overheard he was from Eritrea. It didn't matter that all James could say was *les clés sont sur la table* (the keys are on the table) and *Bonjour, comment allez-vous* (hello, how are you doing). The stuff school thinks will help you on your next travel. Meron had taken it well and explained that he didn't speak French, he could only speak English and a tad of German from school. His younger brother Yonas, still in high school and tagging along, was not as polite, and jokingly called him the colonist.

Meron was a prodigy and had several popular open-source libraries and websites, and today he was going to talk about YouJShouldKnow. A website that listed all the new JavaScript libraries since a user-selected start date and time, with summaries of what they did and why they were hot right now. Although that was the primary use, a secondary use would be to generate a heart attack.

"Where is Yonas?" James looked around as more members of the group made their way in, some saying hello, and some going straight for the food or beer.

It was easy to tell students apart from non-students. The students would always go for the food first and stay behind so they could bring home leftovers. James had hidden a pizza for David and Leo for tomorrow's lunch.

"He is not joining today. He failed another test, and they ground him until he can improve his grades in math. We've given up on sports," he laughed. Yonas was slower than an old snail. "I wish there was something I could do, but he doesn't want to listen to his big brother, you know." Meron shrugged and popped his lips.

James motioned for Meron to follow him to the conference room. They started setting up the projector as the room filled with people and the smell of pizza and beer. "I totally get it; I have a little sister and she thinks I'm an annoying show-off." James shrugged. Meron nodded and looked nervously at the crowd. It felt different from presenting at uni.

"I guess it's time," Meron whispered, barely audible as though the rusty fans.

"We can't hear you!" Somebody shouted from the back.

"Can we turn off the fans?" A voice asked.

"Look," James went to the front, "it's either the fans or death. I'm not a fan of the fans, but right now they are keeping us alive. Meron might have to yell his way through this presentation, but I cannot have any casualties during my internship. I'm not moving back to Bristol."

"Hey what's wrong with Bristol?"

"Peterborough is slightly better. That's what's wrong with it!"

8

"You are late again." Sarah looked like a collapsed souffle. "The kids are already asleep."

David scratched his arm and looked at everything except Sarah's eyes. Moist but sharp, her eyes pierced through the thick air between them.

"Oh," was all he could mutter. "I'm sorry. I had to wrap things up at work. Deployed new features. You know."

"I know. Deployments are never quick," she spat the words out. "I've done plenty for you, remember?"

David nodded and looked down at his shoes. Sarah had helped him many times, although she had her own work to attend to. And their children.

"You can get them tomorrow morning, before work," she continued, and grabbed the door. "I got in trouble at work again for leaving early to get Samuel, you know."

"Sarah… I'm sorry about that. I got my calendar mixed up."

"Oh? I thought it was the deployment?" with eyebrows raised Sarah shook her head. "But I guess, as always, my time is less valuable." She took a step back to close the door, "And don't forget Samuel has mini league soccer tomorrow."

"I won't forget."

Sarah paused and stepped forward again. "And I won't be available to fix your screwups tomorrow. My phone will be off."

"There is nothing to fix! You think I can't even get Samuel to his soccer practice?" David's voice was crisp and loud, but his eyes remained avoidant.

"Last time was a fucking disaster, wasn't it?" Sarah shot back.

"What? No?"

"You dropped him off and left!" Her usually calm voice cracked.

"What did you expect me to do? Join his team?"

"He is two and a half, David! You can't just drop him off!"

"Then what are we paying for?"

"He is TWO years old! You can't leave him alone!"

"What happened to the half?"

"Bye David. Get your shit together, because I'm not your project leader anymore."

Sarah slammed the door shut. David stood there for a second. An elderly man walked by, glaring shamelessly.

"Broken door won't close unless given a good push!" David explained with a shaky smile.

"Looks like an irate woman slammed it shut in your face."

"Yeah, I guess it did. Just a broken door!"

"Are you sure it's not a broken woman?"

"Hey fucking Freud, maybe mind your own business?" David huffed down the stairs and the man disappeared quickly around a corner, as if he had never been there at all. David was relieved. He had never won a physical fight, and his face was too precious to be banged up.

He wiped his face and inhaled slowly. He had hoped she would let him in, show him her new place. Seemed rather unlikely.

He shuffled slowly to his bike and looked at the empty carrier. A teddy bear and a red card inside. He biked down the narrow street, leaving behind two shadows in the window upstairs, breathing fog against the glass.

9

Sautéed from the sun, Leo sought shade in the dental office, closing her eyes and letting the recycled air undo the damage from the heat. She had an uneasy feeling after the guestimate. She wasn't sure she could deliver, but oddly, she felt compelled to promise something that would push her out of her comfort zone.

Leo had pulled David aside at the end of the day. He had switched to his shiny bike-skins and looked overly compressed in his *functional clothes* as he called them. "Is the function supposed to be slow death by compression?" Leo had asked.

"What do you want Leo? I got to pick up the kids or Sarah is going to rip me a new one."

Leo shifted her weight from one foot to another and scratched the back of her head. "Support. I can't do that. You know I hate it."

"It doesn't matter, we all have to do it. Well, not *all* of us, but the developers must."

"Isn't that a waste of resources?" Leo asked.

"We can afford it. You are not that expensive," David locked eyes with her, "nor irreplaceable, sadly."

Leo furrowed her eyebrows underneath the fringe. A single bead of sweat escaped, and she rubbed it away. "But Mikael is?"

"Yes, he is. We only have two architects. And soon we'll only have one. That's a big problem for us."

"Have you seen his work? For real?" Leo hoped she could talk her way out of support.

"I'm not the one to judge and I don't make the rules. We are one short, and we can't have just one in-house architect."

Leo looked at the open landscape. Mikael was talking loudly in a corner by a whiteboard. A diagram and two penises had been drawn.

"Leo, it sucks. I know. But I got to go." David could see she wasn't happy with the situation at all.

"Wait!" Leo grabbed his arm but let go immediately as he turned around. "What if…" she looked around "…I do more senior work?"

"You are a senior developer, that's what you are supposed to do. You can help us find a replacement for Melvin and help with the interview like you did with Mikael."

"That didn't go so well." Leo moaned.

"He is here, that's a positive result." David grabbed the bike and pushed it through the open doors. "I got to run. Check with Melvin or Mikael if they can help with the performance problem, we don't have a lot of time."

The doors closed behind him and Leo stood there for a long time fiddling with the strap on her backpack. It had frayed from its abuse, but she carried on with her dry fingers and ripped nails unable to stop. Shallow breathing echoed in the hallway and she felt dizzy. Mikael waved. *Fuck support.*

At the dental office the only thing she could think about was that conversation. Maybe she wasn't cut out to be a developer if she couldn't even stomach support or be

valuable enough to avoid it. "Dear, we just don't think it's the right path for you. Our family aren't engineers. We create art, passion". Her parents' voices echoed in her head, a conversation they had had one too many times before she went low contact.

The clock on the walk ticked out of sync with the second clock in the hallway. She had never noticed how many clocks there were in the dental office. One on each wall. Almost like they had been put up today, to highlight her obsessive thoughts. Ironically, Martin, the dentist was late. Four clocks that she could count, there in vain mocking her for being on time. Martin had agreed to see her later in the day, close to closing time. She was due for a cleaning and in contrast to most people she didn't mind going to the dentist. And Martin was alright. Strange, but alright.

A young petite blonde woman rounded the corner and gently welcomed Leo, "Larsson, I assume?"

Leo stood up, not sure whether she should offer her a sweaty palm.

The assistant waved for her to follow her. "I assume you've been here before. My name is Helen, I'm new at the clinic." There was no handshake, thankfully. "Martin has requested he does the cleaning today as it's late but I might come in to have a look before I leave. Here, take a seat and he'll be right with you."

The white, sterile room was comforting. It reminded her of her apartment, but a tad cleaner, and a whole lot less cat hair.

Martin walked slowly in, looking intensely at her, "Hi Leo, it has been a while."

"Sorry about that. Promise I've flossed."

"Mmm, we'll see." he sat down on what she assumed was an ergonomic chair of sorts, although it looked like it was missing a few parts. Maybe his team didn't help him build it. She giggled and blushed when she noticed he was staring at her.

"Have you been working out?"

Leo hadn't. Ever. In her life. "No. It's the heat, I biked here." She had done so at an embarrassingly leisurely pace.

Martin kept staring intensely at her, head titled forward, chin down, not blinking. Similar to how Lion does to show his disapproval of humans. He tilted his head to the side and attempted a smile. "Alright, let's do some late spring cleaning." He masked up, covered her face from below the eyes to her chin, with a slot for the mouth. He was sweating profusely, generating beads of moisture on his forehead, threatening to rain on her. "We use ultrasound now," he mumbled and started cleaning. "It's called an ultrasonic tooth scaler. The electricity is converted to mechanical energy, 50,000 vibrations per second. It's amazing. Tiny bubbles are created and they help clean," he excitedly continued. Leo excitedly kept sleeping. "Leo?" He removed the protective sheet and raised the back of the chair. "Have a final rinse."

Leo came to and immediately turned red. *Can't believe I fell asleep again. The only person to always fall asleep at the dentist.*

"You have incredibly white teeth." Martin leaned forward and admired her teeth. Leo felt forced to show them, let them get the compliment.

She gave a forced smile, full teeth - making Colgate proud. "Thanks?"

"Although, I'm not sure you've noticed. But you have plough-shaped teeth."

Leo looked at him, raising her eyebrows and crossing her arms. *What the…*

"Can I take a dental mold?" Martin didn't wait for a reply and disappeared quickly. She waited and quickly searched online for the word plow to examine the shape. There were many different plows, none of them looked like her pearly whites. He came back and caught her doing mouth gymnastics in front of the mirror.

"Ah, you are stretching, that is good. Here, let us put on some balm so we don't crack those fine lips. It's a big

mold, and it's tricky to get it in. Once it's in though, then it's fine. You'll hold it for a minute or two and then we are done for today."

He applied the balm, a tad too happily, and she reluctantly opened her mouth as wide as she could and bit into the mold. It reminded her of when she had eaten playdough as a kid. Even the smell was the same. She missed playdough. Maybe she'd get some.

"There." Martin wiggled the dental impression back and forward, letting go of the suction.

"Perfect!" He held it up against the light, like a precious diamond of considerable size. "I'm going to do magic with this!"

Helen came in and had an inaudible conversation with Martin in the corner. She left and came back just as quickly as she had arrived. With a large digital camera, the professional kind.

"I need some photos of your gorgeous teeth," Martin explained and switched on extra lights.

Leo followed Helen's and Martin's instructions, feeling like a glamour model. Teeth glamour model. Maybe a new career?

Tired from smiling, and the bizarre experience, Leo offered more pictures next time and excused herself. She had to go home and feed her cat, she explained. "Yes of course," Martin had replied. Helen had already left but left the camera with Martin. He put it in his laptop bag. It barely fit. The mold was next to it, in a transparent box. "I should get a proper camera bag." They walked out together.

"You should consider braces, you could get Invisalign. Wouldn't be visible and would perfect your smile." Martin locked and alarmed the office. She nodded and beelined for the stairs.

"My car is parked in the garage, see you soon Leo!"

She walked down the stairs. *Plough shaped*. But very white. The story of Ploughwhite and the Dentist. She

would write about this later. Her jaw ached. Somewhere out there, there was a dentist with a dental mold and a photo album of her teeth. And with that thought plowwhite biked home, amused, intrigued, and a little bit worried.

10

Lion was sitting by the window lazily gazing at the tall chestnut trees and the leaves quivering in the wind. The sun had hidden behind the usual grey and moody sky and given Lion a much-needed break by the window. Leo was at her desk and had pushed Lion away from her keyboard several times before spraying him with water. She had no patience for him, she had a toothache from the cleaning, and the root of her teeth at the front felt sharp against her tongue. She couldn't stop feeling the room between her teeth and investigating them in a small handheld mirror.

"Are you there, Leo?" James' voice made her put the mirror down and looked at the monitor.

"Yes, yes. I'm here."

"So, how do you want to proceed. Do you want to drive?"

They were supposed to pair program and write the cache solution together. Having said that, neither of them were good at collaboration. For the most part they preferred solo work. Neither of them wanted to drive if somebody else was going to be the navigator. David had bought into the Extreme Programming ideas after the

famous workshop and subsequently was enforcing parts of the method. Only the parts that didn't directly affect him.

"I really wish there was a copy and paste solution for this." Leo sighed and tried to get Lion's attention for a quick cuddle.

"We've tried that before, remember?" James stopped screen sharing and turned on his camera. His living room was behind him and was astonishingly stylish. An art wall behind the cognac leather couch showcased a variety of interesting and thought-provoking pieces. She recognized Banksy and wondered if it was an original. For a second, she wished her home was equally elegant.

"There should be some library that we can pull in to fix this quickly. Don't you have a user group dedicated to new libraries?"

James smiled, "It's JavaScript, though, not much use for our services. Unless, of course, you'd like to use…"

"…never mind." Leo grabbed Lion, and he hissed as she forced him to sit on her lap. "He is such a prince," she remarked.

"Looks more like a king."

Leo paused. Lion jumped down and ran to the kitchen. King. Holy shit. CacheIsKing.

"Zoning out again, Leo? Maybe you should take an Advil and get some sleep instead. I'll try to rewrite and see if I can calculate an estimate for how long it would take." James suggested.

"What if we just clear the cache?" Leo held her breath. It was the most stupid, or brilliant thing, she had suggested that week.

"Like a clear cache button?" James laughed.

"Yes, but automated, and by defining a set of rules. We have the metrics from the profiling. We could use them to find a good middle ground or use machine learning."

Leo beamed and rubbed her hands. She was feeling much better and hadn't licked her teeth for at least ten minutes. Her coffee was sitting lonely on the table, and she

hesitantly took a sip, waiting for James' reaction. She spent the time thinking about Martin and how he had commented on her white teeth. Just in case, she added more milk to her coffee. She needed a caffeine kick and some good beats. She felt inspired to code. An unusual feeling. "Come on, James, what do you think?"

"Well, I do like machine learning, but we don't do any, and I doubt we have time for such an intricate solution. I do, however, like you're thinking. Except for the cheapness of emptying the cache."

Leo laughed, genuinely and wide-eyed, "Is that a yes? Are we agreeing on something?" She leaned back and spun around with a playful and devious facial expression. With the dark room behind her, the monitor being the only light source besides the window covered with the dark green leaves from the trees, one could only see her face floating in the dark like a mime or magic trick. She was wearing her favorite black t-shirt with a large 1 in white, and the subtext *just one bit off*.

"You seem very excited. And scary. You are scaring me, Leo." James pretended to bite his nails.

"Don't be an ass!"

"I'm just kidding. What is your evil plan?"

"Give me a minute."

"Alright. I'll play the ukulele meanwhile." James pulled out what looked like a mini guitar from out of frame and started playing. She turned off the sound and searched through her email for her Bitucket login. She went to the website and tried one of her three usual passwords and succeeded on her third attempt. *I really should update my passwords.* She logged in. There it was. The CacheIsKing repository.

She hadn't looked at the code for five years, which was when she had migrated it to the latest version of C#. She would have to do that again and set up some automated builds. But it was doable. She hadn't been this excited in years.

She waved at the web camera but could not get James' attention. He was playing with his eyes closed. After turning on the living room ceiling light, which was as bright as an evening construction site since she didn't check the WATT/lumen conversion. It worked. James stopped playing, and she turned on the sound again.

"Oh, did you move? New place?"

"No?"

"It looks very empty."

"I like it empty!" she defended herself.

"Like your unit tests." he winked

Well, fuck you too.

"Watch this." Leo shared her screen. "I wrote a library at uni, and it is almost up to date. It does what I suggested."

"No way!" He leaned forward, like he was trying to lean into her apartment. He requested control and Leo accepted.

"It was my final assignment at uni"

James read the README file. "A library that lets you easily, with the help of a wide selection of adapters, plug in a cache, internal or external, clear the cache regardless of implementation. It supports custom rules but has a default setting that uses machine learning to optimize continuous cache clearing."

He smiled. "This sounds very promising, Leo! Do a spell check on the README file, but this is…" his voice trailed off as he leaned in and kept reading with his mouth open. He spent a long time looking around in the code, attentive and mesmerized. He would make supportive sounds*, ah, oh, I see, nice.* Her favorite was: *clever!*

"Hey, can't believe I'm saying this, but this is some really advanced stuff. I'm impressed."

"You think?" She fished for more.

"I mean, there are no tests as I can see, but it's from school and back then, when dinosaurs walked the earth and Cobol was the shit, one didn't do tests. That's what I

read in the history books, anyway." He paused and apologized. "Sorry, I'm just joking with you. Tests would be nice, but it looks good. We might use this. Fuck it. Let's try it."

Lion was mewing, trying to get her attention, but Leo was busy dancing in her chair. Fuck yes! "Houston, we have a solution! I'm going to prematurely celebrate with a beer." She ran to the fridge, remembered she doesn't drink beer at home and grabbed some wine instead.

"Wine o'clock?"

"Yes, it is! I need this. My teeth are hurting."

"What would Martin say?"

She looked at the red wine and laughed. James and David welcomed her stories about the dentist.

"He would probably say something strange." she chuckled and thought about the photo session. "Anyway, come on, let's do this! I'm finding my Balmer's peak right here." she pointed at her glass.

"Okay, okay, I guess you are the driver and navigator. You know, you can go solo. I won't tell on you."

"Thanks. I'll let you know when the pull request is up. I'm going to need heaps of code reviews on this. It's some old shit I put some lipstick on a few years ago."

"Have fun!" James ended the call.

Leo grabbed some cheese from the fridge and some more wine. I should order some food; I'm going to be up all night doing this, she thought with a smile.

Guess who just made herself irreplaceable now?

Leo finished filling up her glass and gave her reflection a toast. *Architect this, Mikael.*

11

A perfect day of programming would look like this for Leo.

She wakes up early in the morning after a long night of deep sleep filled with dreams where she solved all her programming problems. Calm, well-rested, and full of ideas that didn't vanish as soon as she opened her eyes, she stretches in bed with a horizontal yoga routine she didn't know she knew. Birds can be heard through the open window and a gentle breeze strokes her body as she glides out of bed and into the kitchen after getting dressed in her soft fleece hoodie and slacks. Miraculously washed and dried overnight. A true miracle as she hasn't done laundry for a few months and bought new t-shirts instead.

She grinds freshly bought beans, fair trade, of course, and lets the smell spread in the apartment - the perfect air freshener. Not that the apartment needs it, her apartment is sparkly clean, not a dust bunny in sight, and no old leftover pizza by the sink and a mountain of paper waiting to be recycled.

She makes herself coffee and feeds all her senses with the sweet but bitter taste. The buttery smell, warmth against her fingers, and the sound of steam escaping the coffee machine. A love song for her adrenal glands.

Two perfectly toasted croissants and scrambled eggs for breakfast, melting on her tongue and leaving her full, but not fat-feeling. She is ready to start her day of amazing code and dances to her desk for a spin in the chair.

The computer has finished all its updates, even Windows and Visual Studio (without running out of disk space), and everything works as expected. The files are indeed exactly where she left them, and the computer might even be faster and with more disk space after the updates during the night.

She sits down, full of ideas and passion, dims the light by closing the curtains, and puts on her headphones, fully charged, no Bluetooth issues, and her favorite playlist. With dubstep in her ears, coffee by her side, she becomes an explosion of ideas and solutions, typing fast on her WASD, never having to leave the keys to use the mouse.

None of the editors get stuck, no processes are killed. The only killing is done by her, because she is totally killing it. When her stomach rumbles, half the day has passed, and she orders some pizza for lunch and dinner.

A slice in hand, not sticky or buttery, and certainly not dripping on her precious keyboard, she eats while continuing to write that sweet, sweet code with some ice-cold Coke to cool down. The computer needs no cooling and even with 100 Chrome tabs the computer purrs as happily as her cat Lion, who has entertained himself without a problem all day.

As the night progresses, she pours herself some wine and immediately finds her Balmer's Peak and hits level 1000 celebrated with long-lasting adrenaline high.

A bottomless bag of assorted candy and salt and vinegar chips helps her focus on her taste buds while she collaborates with her gray matter to put together the greatest puzzle she has ever put together. And right before midnight, before her constant flow of energy ebbs out, she does a pull, and a rebase. There is no conflict and everything she wrote that day just works. Not a single

conflict, no failing tests, no red builds. And yes, the builds are automated. She can now go to bed after a long hot shower and enjoy falling asleep immediately and waking up without a hangover or an aching body.

Her masterpiece finished. Her Mona Lisa.

Leo finished migrating the library and added it to the client project. It didn't quite happen as described above, as there was more cursing, sweating and aching involved. But we can all dream, can't we? The apartment might not have been cool and clean, but cleanliness is subjective anyway, right? Lion absolutely had a few cat-tantrums, but it was very close to a perfect day of programming. Leo excitedly let James and David know she had a first version ready for testing. She collapsed in her bed, clothes on, pizza on her nightstand, Lion resting his butt on her face, leaving his usual anal print of dominance.

12

The hangover was a fact. The peak had dropped, and Leo had resurfaced on the other side of the night, penalized by her body and liver. With the world slightly spinning, she had made it to the train, and painfully biked to the office. She fantasized about swimming. Feeling the cold-water glide through her fingers, silky smooth and cooling, she would float in a crystal-clear lake. Instead, she was swimming in her own sweat. Her body profusely refused the leftovers from last night. She used to be able to drink a fair bit, but something happened after 25 and she could get hungover by thinking about a glass of wine. It had been worth it, though. Never again, she promised herself again.

"You okay, Leo?" David walked past her but had to take a second look. "You look awful."

"Thanks," she muttered and wiped her fringe to the side so she could pat her face with a tissue.

"James told me you have exciting news. See you in a bit?" He ran off after the fantastic compliments. She pulled out her phone and started the camera app in selfie mode, a harsh mirror. She did indeed look horrible. There are no filters saving this.

"LEO!" James came skipping down the hallway, two iced coffees in his hand, and a bag of donuts tucked under

his arm. Her stomach rumbled excitedly. The donuts looked delicious through the little window in the bag. The bottom of the bag was stained from the grease and had left a mark on James' shirt.

"You are my hero!" He gave her the coffee. "Come, come! Let's celebrate!" He went in the first door and opened the bag. "Green frosting are the ones with lime, pink is strawberry."

He leaned back in the chair, feet up. "I saw the commits, fantastic stuff! Clean and well organized. Didn't know you had it in you." He laughed.

The truth was, she had spent several hours redoing everything just to make sure that it looked like she had done everything in the right order, with the perfect commit messages for each change. She had rebased the shit out of the code. The first version had been an iterative of mangled mess, but James didn't have to know that. James was obsessed with commits and making sure that each change is small, structured, and chronological. Preferably with plenty of tests verifying the logic. Luckily for her, he hadn't noticed the lack of tests he had remarked about on their last call.

"There is one little thing though," he interrupted her thoughts. *Oh no.* She grabbed another donut, divided it into four pieces, and laid them out on her napkin. One sip of coffee between each was her plan.

"I couldn't help but notice that the namespace of the library is *MachineLearningAssigmentTest1.*"

Leo pinched between her eyebrows and looked down, shaking her head. "Yeah, I was a tad tired." They both laughed. "Not again, heh?"

When she had published her first Apple application in her first year as a developer, she had screwed up her configuration file for the application, and published the app named as FirstApp1. She hadn't noticed, and the app had gotten several reviews and gained popularity by the time she noticed.

"I couldn't access the repository for the code. I get a 404, not found."

"Did you go to the right place? It's on Bitbucket." Leo asked.

"Ah. We use that as well?"

"No, it's where my university made us open accounts, but yeah…" her voice faded, she was thinking. She would need to fix that. "I should move it to GitHub and have a dependency on the package instead of cloning the repo."

"Coolio. Let's do some mob programming," he said.

"We are just two. That's not a mob," Leo replied cheekily.

"Pair programming, but its sounds more fun to mob. I don't have anything to do right now. I triggered a build, and that's going to take half the day if we are lucky. It's Mikael's setup. I wish we had gotten Melvin." He grabbed the mouse and connected it to the Wi-Fi Wu Tang LAN. "Did you change the name again?"

Leo squinted her eyes and threw her hands up. "Maybe?" She finished the coffee and her final donut piece, wiped her hands on her jeans, and grabbed the keyboard. She was feeling better.

"How was the user group?" Leo asked, as she located the repository. She logged in to GitHub and created a repository, "CacheClear or CacheIsKing?"

"CleverCacheClear- CCC? It went well, the speaker Meron is impressive. We've discussed hosting a youth group to help younger students out. His brother is struggling, but the user group is not really for beginners."

"How do you find time for everything? Here, you can do the namespace renaming." She pushed the keyboard towards him and he grabbed it. The code repository was opened in a dark editor and he was squinting, trying to see it.

"I do the planning in-between builds and during long meetings. Or when you are all playing table tennis or

PlayStation." It took him a few seconds to make the changes. "There! It's ready for the cloud."

She grabbed the keyboard back and for the first time, it felt natural to go back and forth working on something together. Usually, they would bicker, or one would go solo and hijack the keyboard. She pushed the code to its new location, ready to create a package.

"Ah, fuck." She zoomed in on the documentation. "Look: GitHub Packages is not available for private repositories owned by accounts using legacy per-repository plans." That was disappointing. "Fuck it. I'll make the repository public."

"You sure about that? I mean, it's your code. And it looks alright. I guess I would be too self-conscious to do that."

She shrugged and deployed. "Yeah, but who is going to see this?"

13

David ran up the stairs to his apartment, barely touching the steps, his voice echoing in the stairwell as he hummed a victory song. It's a rare sight in Cambridge on an exceptionally wet afternoon. He must be doing drugs again; the neighbors concluded and quickly hid before he danced past their door. David reached the top and flung open the red door and threw himself into the apartment. A millisecond later, he had magically removed jacket, shoes, and laptop bag all in one move like an escape artist at the circus.

He pulled out his phone, connected his headphones, and without hesitation, called Brian. He paced back and forth, stopping occasionally to admire himself in the mirror in the hallway. *Hey you! Yes, you!* David pointed at himself in the mirror and gave a wink. *Looking good, man! Keep that tan going!*

A faint, "Hello?" Pulled him away from the mirror. *God damn Bluetooth shit keeps disconnecting.* He tossed his AirPods on the table like two bald electronic toothbrush heads. The charger looked like a dental floss container. Funny, huh?

"Brian? Hi Brian! It's David from ConsultIt!" David was quiet for a minute and took a sip of water before he continued. It had been on the table for a day or a month,

enough to let little bubbles form, and half of it had vaporized in the lingering heat. Several cups with moldy coffee kept the questionable glass of water company, as did some used plates, a noodle container, two nuggets, and a half-eaten sausage. "I have fantastic news for you! I have solved the performance problem and I'll make sure we deliver early on the shop!" David returned to the mirror and gave his hair some attention.

White spots on the mirror gave way to his morning routine - brushing his teeth in the hallway while making his way out the door. The spots created a snowy landscape on the mirror and every second week the kids would scrape off a snowflake or two while they waited for him to get ready.

"Yes, I personally made sure we fixed the performance problem." David's face turned a slight shade of red. "Well, yes, I do code. I'm a developer as well, you know, a man of many hats!"

David didn't own a single hat unless you counted his collection of bike helmets and that one Tinder helicopter-cowboy hat. "It wasn't easy. I had to fix some messed up old code - copy-paste stuff, but it's done."

They wouldn't have gotten this done if I hadn't pushed for a deadline and faster delivery. Anybody can code, not everybody can motivate and lead a project.

"Give or take two-three weeks, max. Yes. I know. But this deadline is a real deadline. I'm sorry the team has let you down. However, this is a unique situation, and I'm personally more involved. Keeping my eyes on them. Like a hawk." David made a squealing attempt at a hawk-like sound, quickly discovering that he, in fact, was not a good hawk imitator. He was far better at lion sounds. And cats. Cats are easy. Any meow would do. David's son Samuel loved his lion sounds.

"Of course, let's do that. I'll send a meeting invite for next week. Got to pick up my kids from kindergarten now."

They ended the conversation, and he quickly changed clothes from stylish business casual to dad clothes and hid his laptop and other electronics on the top shelf so the youngest wouldn't find them - *little kleptomaniac fucker*. And just like that, he ran down the stairs as quickly as he had arrived. Like a magician, he came home one person, and left like another.

Dad-David found an empty seat at the back of the bus, nodded to the elderly neighbor, and pulled out his phone.

"Hi James, just letting you know I've let Brian know the performance problem is fixed and that we'll be delivering early." He covered the phone and mouthed *sorry* to the lady. She pressed her lips together and turned away with glazy eyes fixated on the passing world outside. "Yes, yes. I know you guys didn't set a new deadline, but it's obvious that we have a fix and therefore we should be done early. Just make it happen then. I'll help with testing." The phone vibrated, and he saw Leo was calling. *Darn it.* He added her to the call.

"David. What. Did. You. Say to Brian?"

James sighed, "Apparently we are delivering early…"

"Wait a minute!" David shot up. "EXCUSE ME! Stop! This is my stop!" The bus screeched and came to a sudden halt with a thud. David got off the bus. "Are the two of you in the same room?"

"Yes…" Leo hissed, "but I want the option to leave the room but remain on the call, in case I need to scream."

James laughed, "I guess I'll be fine regardless, as an intern. I can always run back to school and hide in the study bubble for a few more years." He lowered his voice, "But David, we don't have enough time as is, let alone the new promise you made on behalf of the team."

"Just make it happen." David replied.

"If you remove me from the support rooster…"

"…Leo, only architects. The architect gets an exemption." Exasperated and ready to move on, David was prepping to get back into Dad-mode.

"I'm an architect now, aren't I, for fuck's sake? It's more than Mikael has done with his little failing rabbit. The broken broker." Leo not letting up pressed further.

"If you get this up and running and in production, I might consider you for Melvin's position if the dev manager agrees. But you have to have something to show. In production."

James cleared his throat. "Ehm, we only have production. It's our machines and then production."

"And that's where I want to see it working." David said.

"I fix, and no support? Right?" Leo wanted assurance.

"You heard me the first time."

The two of them continued bantering back and forth until David nearly missed his stop. "Ciao!" He hung up and got off the bus. An email notification grabbed his attention. Brian was excited about the call earlier and wanted David to send some new performance metrics. *Things are looking good again.* He waved to Samuel, who stumbled towards him on the other side of the fence. *I might get a raise this year. I really need that.*

"Hi, mister Manning!" A soft and squishy lady in a flowery dress with a pink apron opened the gate and let Samuel through like a prisoner finally set free. "He has been eating sand again." She nodded in Samuel's direction with a loving smile framed with tiny little lines. Life tattoos, one for each toddler at the kindergarten. Samuel wiped his mouth and looked sheepishly at his dad, face covered in dirt like a poorly spread-out facial mask.

"I can tell. Come here Samuel, let's get your brother." He was definitely going to need a pay raise. Chances were, his youngest was a special case.

14

Frank's viscous syrup refused to blend with the hot water. It was an impossible task. Leo forced a spoon through the layers and watched as bits of the syrup floated to the surface. Driven by desperation, she tried a spoon.

Frank jumped in front of her, hands out, fingers wiggling. "Congratulations!"

Leo swallowed, but the coffee grasped her throat like a piece of gum on the sole of a shoe. The taste and consistency reminded her of mold and old leather. She and coughed and wheezed. "I'm not pregnant," she finally replied with a red face.

"No, not that. I know you're not pregnant. You're not the type to do that solo." Frank grabbed a cup and scraped coffee into his cup. "Congrats on the shop. I'm surprised you let David code again. After last time, you know. So many support calls that day."

Leo swallowed another spoonful and cringed from the taste, "David isn't allowed to code. We've been successfully preventing his contribution for…" she opened the notes app on her phone "…61 days and counting."

Frank scratched his chin, "Hmm…David said he wrote the code. That he fixed the performance problem by himself."

Leo's eyes widened, pupils the size of Oreo cookies, "He said what?!"

"That he wrote the code. Nights in agony writing the code and so on. You know David, the usual dramatic monologue. I stopped listening halfway through and he didn't even notice." Frank shrugged.

"What the hell?!" Leo raised her voice to a volume she rarely used. "David is taking cred for my work! He seems to forget or pretends to, that he has professionals and capable human adults on his team. Nothing I'll ever do will be good enough!" Leo's eyes were blank, and she blinked away a tear as she slammed the cup down on the counter. "I bet I'll be stuck with support until the robots take over and I'll keep hating my job and my life and I'll probably end up old and alone. And fuck David." She finished, anger not subsiding.

"Ouch. That's a lot. Never mind, my job is your worst scenario…" Frank held up his hands. "Easy on the catastrophizing though, miss." He looked behind Leo, waved to somebody, and slapped her on the shoulder as he walked by, "I got to go, support call. Nice work on the site. And take a breather before you confront David." He disappeared around the corner, the coffee cup left behind.

Leo stomped to her safe space like a soldier returning from a lost battle. Defeated, angry but thankful that the handicap accessible bathroom was free. She went in and took an hour-long breather and did some work on her laptop which mainly consisted of copy-pasting the *EmailUserPassword* from a different project. The login had caused a lot of problems and Frank had complained that the users would call with error messages. She added the *IgnoreError* method with a comment *'Ignores login error'*.

She pulled out her phone. The lockscreen hadn't been activated and the phone had generated an impressive amount of heat. She held it against her chin, probably getting cancer or implanting a 5G chip. The messaging app

glowed in the dim bathroom lights. An empty *Read* was waiting for a reply.

Leonarda dear, I understand you are busy, any chance our emails are not coming through?

We miss you.

- Dad

She put away her phone, scrubbed her hands, and sighed at her reflection before dragging herself out from the therapy-handicap-accessible bathroom where all-important-thinking was done.

15

Leo had snuck out hoping nobody would notice she had spent a significant amount of time in the toilet, with her laptop. Not that she was the only one; she had noticed candy wrappers on the floor, and a notebook with amateur drawings of what looked like a cat. Unfortunately, with the toilets facing the open office and it being the end of the day, it was going to be difficult. It didn't help that James yelled out her name.

"Leo! There you are! I thought we had lost you! Did you drink Frank's coffee again? Or maybe a little Sushi?"

Replying shyly, "No. I'm good. Just needed some personal time."

James wrinkled his nose, "Your face is red, kind of sweaty."

Who points that stuff out? Leo thought before answering, "Thanks for remarking that, James. It's a new look I'm going for. I'm glowing."

"Anyways, I was looking for you as I'm heading to the pub with a few guys from support. I know you don't like the pub but it would be nice to have you join us after

work. And we should celebrate the nice work you've been doing, sincerely."

"Yeah, thanks. I don't know." She bit her lip and gripped the laptop as it nearly slipped from her hands. She scanned the office space. Little worker ants busy doing their thing, building the stack. "Is Mikael joining?"

"I don't think so? Do you want him to join?" James asked.

"God no. He would probably just give unsolicited advice regarding the performance library. I don't want to deal with an," she air quoted, "an *architect* right now."

James did a second scan of the office with Leo. No Mikael in sight.

"I know what you mean." James raised an eyebrow and continued looking. "He isn't exactly the right person to discuss performance problems with."

Leo giggled and shook her head.

"Does that mean you're coming?" James mirrored her smile.

"I dunno. Social stuff. You know me." She shrugged.

"No pressure, but it'll be fun. There's this guy, Meron, you know? The guy from the user group I told you about. He wants to meet you. He was jumping up and down when he found out I worked with you. And he is pretty bad at social situations, so you'd have that in common."

"Great. That's just odd. You aren't selling this to me you know." Leo responded.

"We could use your help with planning the next youth group meeting...the first meeting was a disaster. I made a complete ass of myself." James commented.

Leo brushed away the hair from her face and gave a half-smile, "Oh, I'd love to hear more about that!"

"I bet you do! I guess you'll have to meet your fan to hear more about that. He was there and he is not happy about it." James added.

"Am I a peace offering?" Smirking still.

"Yes, you are. The best kind." James replied with a smile.

The elevator pinged and they all squeezed in to avoid going down the 15 stairsteps to ground level. This was the second time she had joined an after-work event. If post-interview after-work counts. It had been after the technical interview with Mikael. This happened a few years ago. Around the time the front-end team had migrated the front-end for the third time in two months as it had gotten 'old'. From Angular to React, to Rectangular to Compact. Something like that. James had recently joined the team, early internship at the beginning of his education, and had assisted Leo with the interview.

"Welcome…" David had inserted himself into every interview, total of five. This was the final interview.

"…David, you don't have to join the technical interview," Leo told David as soon as he entered. "More chefs results in worse soup and all that."

David raised his eyebrows, "I'm the master chef. You are line cooks."

Leo rolled her eyes and nodded towards the empty chair. She gestured towards David, "You've met this guy before, right? Project leader turned project manager and product owner. Honestly, nobody knows the difference between the two."

Mikael was sweating profusely with a shaky grin slapped on his face. It was the fifth interview at the end of the day and somehow, they had forgotten to feed him.

"Do you need a break?" Leo filled a glass with water and pushed it towards Mikael.

"I'm good. Good. Just, it's a lot. I slept poorly last night, nightmares." He swallowed excess sweat from his upper lip.

"Oh?" Nobody was interested in his dreams but an inquisitive 'oh' was offered.

"I," he laughed nervously, "dreamt that you gave me another call, David."

"That would indeed be a nightmare." Leo hid her smile behind a glass of water, accidentally magnifying the grin into a caricature.

"… and told me there were two more interviews. I was, like, noooo." He pretended to pull his hair.

"I understand," David replied flat, unamused. "The big companies all do it, multiple interviews."

Despite an office bar and a PlayStation, they weren't Google or Microsoft. The marathon interviews were one of the few things ConsultIT had in common with the big ones.

"Just a joke, I'm good. Let's go." Mikael took a big sip. "Foot in mouth disease," he chuckled.

"You're sick?" David rolled back his chair.

Leo sighed slowly. "It's an idiomatic expression David…"

"Are you calling me an idiot?"

"It's an expression, idiomatic expression. He is not sick; he just talks a lot. Let's move on." Leo explained. Wrote the code my ass, she thought to herself.

David nodded and rolled back in.

Leo pulled up a colorful editor on the external monitor and spent a few minutes trying to figure out the resolution versus font size. The code zoomed in and out, a dizzy intro, before settling with a large font for the code and tiny everything else. "Windows never plays nice with font sizes," Leo mumbled and chewed on her lower lip as she navigated 10 levels deep into a folder with managers and helpers, and a few utility classes. "Here we go, this is some of our older code. Legacy or vintage as I like to call it."

James laughed, "Vintage, I like that."

"Yeah," Leo continued, "or retro. Depends on its reuse and age but generally it's just old shit regardless of what we call it. But vintage is my favorite, as we certainly try hard to preserve it in its original state."

"There's some retro though." James pointed at the top of the screen. The URL for a pasted section from

StackOverflow was left as a comment, no shame in sight. "That yours, Leo?"

Leo kicked James under the table and turned to Mikael sliding the mouse and keyboard in his direction. They had seen Mikael's code before. As a matter of fact, Mikael's assignment had already been added to the admin platform, like the rest. The patchwork the admin platform had turned into was questionable but hey it's free, if time is of no value to you.

"Have a read and give some feedback." Leo gestured towards the monitor.

Silence.

"Oh." Mikael frowned. "I see. Oh no. Oh oh." Like an owl he'd repeat 'oh' 'oh' for a few minutes before scrunching up his face. "Very smelly stuff."

"Which part?" Leo waited for his face to iron out, but he kept the expression for a few more painful seconds.

Mikael waved in the direction of the screen, a big circle, framing it with his manicured hands, "Static. I see a lot of static. That's a code smell."

"How come?" Leo enquired.

"It just is. Everybody knows that." Steady reply.

"Please elaborate," Leo continued.

Mikael was quiet, scrolling up and down looking busy, "I just, wouldn't do that. It's smelly."

"Could you think of any reasons why one would sometimes use static?" James asked.

Mikael violently shook his head, "I would never allow it. I'd just remove it."

"Could there be consequences?" Leo leaned back with her coffee.

"Yeah, the code would be better." Mikael snarled.

James opened his mouth but didn't say anything and moved his legs as far away as possible from Leo's potential kicks.

Leo took over and scrolled to the top. "Alright, let's move onto this section here. The constructor."

"Yeah, that's a code smell." Mikael crossed his arms.

"Which part?"

"The constructor. Too many parameters. Smelly." He waved his hand in front of his nose waving away the smell.

"What would you do?" Another question from Leo.

"Not that."

That's not very helpful, she thought. "Any suggestions?"

"Don't do it." Arrogant reply.

"Okay. Let's step away from the smelly for a moment and let you breathe." Leo nodded in James' direction, inviting him to ask questions.

Mikael filled his chest and blew out hot air through pursed lips, "Thank God!"

"Let's talk performance," James suggested.

"That's important!" Mikael exclaimed.

No shit Sherlock, Leo thought. "Yes, indeed it is. How do you profile performance problems?"

"How do I what?" Mikael retorted.

"How do you evaluate and measure performance?" Leo repeated the question with emphasis.

"I experience it. If it feels slow it's slow.? He replied matter-of-factly.

"Measure? Benchmark?" Leo needed some mathematics.

"I compare how it feels like before and after." Mikael tapped his head. Leo was pretty sure she heard the knock echo in what she assumed was an empty chamber aside from a broken record titled, *Smelly Code.*

"No tooling?" She asked.

"I've used the stopwatch on my phone sometimes."

James and Leo exchanged glances.

"Okay. Okay. Debugging then. How do you debug?" Leo pressed further.

"I just don't write them." Mikael said.

"What?"

"Bugs."

After the interview David was incredibly happy. "That went exceptionally well! A perfect consultant!"

"Is it due to the level of bullshit?" Leo closed the lid on her laptop and looked at her notes before curling them up and throwing them in the bin.

"So, roman style, thumbs up or down?" An enthusiastic David-thumb gave away his vote.

James and Leo synced two thumbs down. "That's a no go for me." Leo added a second thumb and shook her head. James nodded. "No go, quadruple no."

A week later Mikael was hired, as an architect with an unexplainable infatuation for Leo. *She was definitely flirting;* he had told James who vigorously shook his head in response and insisted that no, she certainly wasn't.

16

The pub was dark with a distinct smell of mildew and old beer. The yellow ceiling spotlights were dimmed to hide the past-due date of the surfaces and the people that were hiding in the dark corners. The floors were sticky, making sure you'd stick around, and the local fruit flies kept a respectful distance from the group as they entered.

Leo had never been to a pub in Peterborough before. When they left the office, they had been a medium-sized group, ten people chatting about their day and the weather the last few weeks. But every time they rounded a corner, somebody else dropped off and by the time they arrived at the pub they were only four. Leo, Stefan the UX guy, Amanda from accounting, and of course James. Amanda was waiting for her husband to finish work so she could catch a ride with him, and Stefan was mostly quiet and skittish. User experience was probably his only social experience.

James was the only one talking but Leo wasn't paying attention. They lined up at the bar, doing their best not to make any direct contact with the tacky surface, and shouted their orders to the bartender. The fruity aroma produced by yeast cells was what fruit flies found particularly attractive Stefan shared. A specific gene that

produces acetate esters, found in fermented beverages, created the smell that attracted them. The taste is what kept them there. The preferred booze strength: 6%, half the strength Leo preferred. Facts were Stefan's go-to for starting or maintaining conversations with strangers. When Leo waved away some flies Stefan saw an opportunity to provide unnecessary facts. From one socially awkward to another.

"What are you having, Leo?" James shouted.

"Just one beer, for solidarity and more fun facts. I'm assuming the wine here is in the bad-old, not the good-old category." The wines on the top shelf seemed depressed and slightly suicidal as they balanced close to the edge covered in dust ready for a fairy dust goodbye and shattered dreams. "We are certainly reducing the average age here." Leo scanned the room squinting. The guests were mostly men, probably 70 and older.

Stefan nodded, "It's the only place where the guests are somewhat well-behaved. Very few brawls here, compared to other places in Peterborough."

Probably because they are too tired. Leo balanced the tray with beers and followed James further in. A young guy was sitting by a table, face lit up by his phone like a dim halo around his hair. His face was all she saw clearly, as his dark clothes, oversized blazer, and dark denim trousers, combined with his dark skin and features, hid him well in the gloomy pub. He was staring intently at his phone, rubbing his chin slowly. He jumped up as soon as he heard James' voice, gave a lazy but warm smile, and held out his hand. Leo could tell he had already had a beer or three.

"Presenting, Meron, the youngest customer this pub has ever had," James chuckled. Meron jokingly punched his shoulder.

They took turns shaking his hand and shouting their names.

"Hi, I'm Leo." Leo shook his hand and he leaned in and put his other hand to his chest locking eyes with her.

He was wearing a bright yellow t-shirt under the blazer. *What an odd combination. "*Pleasure to meet you, James has told me a lot about you." James had told her he was shy and asked that she tried to speak to him since he seemed to be so eager to meet her. *Not romantically!* James had promised.

"Leo! Larsson!" His eyes widened. He held on to her hand while the rest of the group betrayed her and silently stood by and watched the awkwardness unfold. Leo looked disapprovingly at James, raising her eyebrows where sweat had accumulated and betrayed the *je me sais quoi* impression she was going for. If this was a blind date attempt, with what looked like a minor, she might have to kill James. This was indeed an exercise in futility and none of them were great athletes.

"Hey, hey! People grab a seat! Should we order some chips? Nuts?" James pushed Meron in and he reluctantly let go of Leo's hand as he lost balance and fell in his chair. Leo massaged her hand and sat down.

"Food maybe?" Leo looked at the crumbled menu on the table.

"We don't usually eat after work, we drink instead," James laughed, "besides, I wouldn't recommend eating the food here."

Amanda who had been texting on her phone stood up, "My husband is here, got to go. I can grab a waiter on the way out and send him to the table if you want to… Leo?" Nobody seemed to care, and Amanda disappeared in the darkness of the pub as she waved and walked away.

Leo ordered the Parma Chicken while Meron was staring at her trying to make eye contact. Leo lived a pedestrian life, she wasn't used to attention, and discomfort filled the air around her to the point where she felt she could barely breathe. Alcohol seemed to help a little bit and she downed her beer before the food arrived. She excused herself and went to get another one. She took her time, read the news, checked her emails, and drank half

her beer by the bar until she saw her food being brought
out to the table.

"I thought you had left!" Meron scooted closer to Leo.
He had moved to the chair Amanda had right next to Leo.

Leo looked at her chicken. It looked like it had died a
thousand times over, like a sad phoenix rising only to be
baked again at a scorching temperature for three hours. It
was hard as a brick, sweaty, and inexplicably pale. The fries
dripped tears made out of rancid oil and the salad was
pushed to the side, limp and colorless, as a warning. You
are next.

"Yeah, I guess I'm not eating. Does anybody want
this?"

"I'll take it back to the kitchen for you" Meron grabbed
the plate.

"Hell no, that's just weird. Is that a joke?" She asked.

"Sorry…" He sat down, plate shoved to the side, "I'm
just a fan."

"Fan of what?" Puzzled look on her face.

"You." Meron stated.

The table went quiet. Somewhere in the background,
two elderly men were arguing. The kitchen sounded like
they were smashing things and the speakers were crackling.

Leo was about to evaporate from the heat generated by
her cheeks, "I…I genuinely have no idea what you are
talking about."

James offered help, "Are you a fan of the Swedes
Meron, is that what you are saying?"

"No! I mean, Swedes are okay." He rubbed his right
cheek and returned to picking at the tiny invincible crack
on the table. "Nothing wrong with Swedes! It's the library.
I maintain a lot of projects myself, and the stuff you write
is so cool. I thought James was joking when he told me
you had written it. Everybody is trying to find out who the
maintainer is."

"What library?"

"Cache Is King." He said with a hint of, *how do you not know mixed with admiration?*

Leo looked at James, shrugged and seemed just as confused as her.

Meron gave his phone a push, sliding it to Leo, "This one, it's yours, right?"

Leo was looking at her repository. It was hers, but not the way she left it. It had hundreds of followers, a gazillion issues, forks, and pull requests. She grabbed the side of the table to steady herself, her breath turning shallow and short, face getting warm.

A voice behind her made her jump. The guy sounded worried, "Is something wrong?"

"I, no I…I'm just having a mild panic attack, that's all." Leo hastily replied, regretting the personal information.

"Oh…because of the chicken?" Meron asked confused.

Leo turned around convincing herself that nobody could see her red face in the dim lights. The guy was wearing the pub t-shirt in a vomit green color, with mustard text. The colorblind person that designed the t-shirt must have thought it was a lovely brown t-shirt. *Everybody looks great in brown. Or vomit green.*

James chuckled, "The chicken does look like it had a panic attack, but Leo here is just a shy superstar we are learning".

Stefan pulled the plate towards himself "I'll eat the fries then. The chicken is mummified and one shouldn't disturb the afterlife." The waiter walked away silently and Leo hid her head in her hands. "The Egyptian way, mummification, took over two months, did you know?"

"An Egyptian chicken then. It certainly spent at least two months in the frying pan." Leo sent the phone back to Meron and the plate to Stefan.

James pulled on her arm, "You got to see this." he was staring wide-eyed at his phone. Leo took a peak between her fingers. "I don't think I want to see more…"

"You positively want to see this!" James exclaimed.

James had done some investigation when he had seen the repository's popularity and a quick search online showed that the library was indeed very popular on StackOverflow. Somebody had asked how to deal with a performance cache problem and the top answer, the one approved and upvoted thousands of times, was one showing how to use Leo's library with a link to the library. Further down somebody else had linked a blogpost with examples and a fork (and pending PR by the look of it) with detailed documentation. The question had made it to the top questions and answers list that week and was a contender for the top of the month. Leo was staring in disbelief at the ranking and mumbled, "I never turn on notifications…"

"You never read your email anyway," James added. And that was true. *If I don't read and reply to emails fast, then people won't be bothered sending me them. Voila. No support for me!* Leo had replied when questioned about her email habits.

Meron hadn't said anything for a while but hadn't moved his gaze from Leo for a minute and Stefan was concerned that he was forgetting to blink. Can't be good for your eyes.

Meron cleared his throat and continued where he had left. "This is very exciting for me. I rarely meet other maintainers in real life. It's also really cool that you are a girl —"

"Woman, thank you—" Leo corrected.

"Woman. There aren't many in the open-source community. But don't worry, your secret is safe with me."

"It's hardly a secret that I'm a woman," Leo replied.

For a second Leo questioned her style and whether jeans and T-shirts with sneakers were doing her a disfavor. Then she remembered she didn't care and that she had this discussion many times with her father. He had always been concerned with her choices or lack of them. Her apathy in certain areas of life was how he phrased it. Mom-jeans

(considered a respectable choice among fashionable youngsters) and fitted T-shirts with clever messages were conscious and practical choices. The sneakers, not so practical color, but comfy and passed most dress codes although borderline for fancy events - which she never got invited to anyway. Maybe she would now. Some sort of awards for stupid libraries becoming famous for stupid reasons.

She checked her email, could she have missed something? She was pretty sure she hadn't enabled notifications on GitHub but she hadn't checked her email for a few days. James leaned over her and giggled when he saw her open her email.

The only emails she had, besides the odd newsletter and an unopened email from her father asking for, 'Just a coffee at least?', was from the dentist.

"Oh!! Is that from Martin the Dentist?" James clapped, "please tell me there is another bizarre story for us."

"It's probably nothing." Leo realized that might be a good way to distract from the newly found fandom. Meron was creeping her out and they were all getting a bit tipsy. Before she even opened the email her phone vibrated and she let out a yelp.

Did you see my emails? -M.J.

"No way…" Leo's voice faded. She held up the phone, "He just messaged me. Asking me if I had read his emails. It's 9:16PM!"

James gasped, Stefan shook his head, Meron looked at Stefan and mouthed *what happened?* Stefan gave Meron a quick update on the dentist stories that had amused everybody at work. They usually didn't come directly from Leo, it usually was secondhand information from James, who loved office gossip. Martin had gotten quite a few new customers this way. Everybody was curious who this strange dentist was. Leo didn't like office gossip but had

kept sharing the incidents with James and David as she didn't have much else to share from her life. She looked at the first email.

Hi Leo, hope your teeth are having a fantastic day!

I scanned the beautiful mold we made, and I've adjusted the teeth to show you your full potential (if you were to choose to straighten them a little bit).

He had attached three photos with what looked like dentures. The email was sent from his personal email. martin_the_man_81@freeemail.com. In the second email, he asked if she had seen the previous email, and not to feel pressured. She had a lovely smile, perfect whiteness. But the shape could be improved. A new image was attached, of her smiling wide and awkwardly, with the smile adjusted to be broader and more even. It was a terrifying smile.

"Holy shit!" James covered his mouth and pointed at her phone. "What even is that? Is that from the modeling session you told me about?" He was laughing hard and accidentally tipped over a beer. Everybody pulled away from the table as the beer spread everywhere, while the group laughed at the absurd situation. The same waiter came back to the table and removed the chicken. Leo was laughing with tears down her cheeks.

"He took the fucking chicken! It has left for the museum!"

"Let's cheer to that! I'll go get us another round!" James stumbled to the bar and the rest moved to the table next to them.

I'm going to regret this tomorrow, Leo told herself as she accepted the new beer and leaned in to cheer with the group.

17

Leo woke up with a pit in her stomach. A horrible feeling that something was wrong, that a disaster had happened. Twisting and turning in her bed trying to escape the dampness from her overnight sweat lingering on her bedsheets she forced her eyes open and scanned the room.

The room was quiet, the sharp smell of alcohol hauntingly in the air, a stark reminder that she had a rough night. She hated hungover anxiety with a passion. There were no black holes or missing memories, it had been a fantastic evening. The best evening she had had in years.

They had stayed at the pub until closing time taking turns buying rounds, playing cards, and talking shit. Meron had stopped being creepy (although he did ask for a selfie with her) and Stefan became increasingly social and talkative as he kept drinking.

She hadn't noticed him around the office, she generally tried to stay away from support and anything that had to do with design, frontend, and user experience and therefore their paths rarely crossed. It could have been the alcohol clouding her mind, but she remembered him as charismatic and entertaining. They had spent a considerable amount of time talking about Martin's emails

and Stefan had booked a dental cleaning to see if he would get an equally intriguing experience.

They ended the evening with a feast at McDonald's, with the Peterborough teenagers, and it had been the best meal she had ever had. She had ordered a second meal and brought it home. She peaked over the edge of the bed and smelled the meal before she saw it, it didn't look or smell nearly as yummy as she recalled.

She stumbled out of bed in search of precious water. Her clothes were on the floor by the kitchen, except the t-shirt, underwear, and socks that she had worn to bed. She caught her reflection in the microwave. Horrible. When people talked about bed hair they didn't talk about her hair. It looked like a raccoon had searched for food there and it had been a successful hunt.

As drunk as she had been when she got home, oddly enough safe and sound on her bike, a raccoon could have hosted a party and she wouldn't have noticed.

She gulped down two glasses of water and threw herself down on the couch. An expected migraine was brewing and the light from the early morning sun was terrorizing her. She was late for work, again.

She made a double-strength coffee, inspired by Frank's coffee, and alternated drinking the coffee with the lukewarm diet coke from last night's meal. The burger didn't make it, but she did eat the fries, hiding in a corner hoping nobody would ever find out about this humiliating moment where she sat on the floor of her living room eating stale fries in her underwear.

Head buzzing, stairs moving, Leo made the usual run down and up the stairs with Old Mary's mail. She paused at the top, leaned forward, and hurled into the emptiness of the stairwell. This would not be a good time to meet Mary, she'd rather not give away her identity, especially not like this. The top floor was quiet and oddly breezy. Mary's mail from yesterday had made it to the other side. Leo dropped a newspaper, two bills and a postcard in front of

the door dried her forehead with the back of her hand and looked around quickly before she tiptoed down the stairs hurling quietly on repeat.

She biked from the station feeling slightly better. A shower and some fresh air had helped but she couldn't shake that hangover anxiety greatly amplified by the sudden popularity of the library. She was terrified people would find out she had written the library and given into Meron's excitement to meet his hero, she was certain he would tell somebody, his little brother or other classmates, and word would spread. The more she thought about it the more confident she was that she had to remove the library to preserve her traffic-free life. She was content with the status quo and didn't like change.

She made it to her desk without meeting anybody and leaned back in her chair for a quick nap. James had come in mid-nap and amused himself by watching her drool and snore before waking her up with a coffee and donuts.

"Oh God, sugar. I need this." Her voice broke into a whisper. They had been shout-talking all night due to the loud horrendous music. "Is this going to be a new habit of yours? Bringing coffee and donuts? I like it!"

James sat down on the chair next to hers and leaned back, "Dunno about you but considering how I feel and how much we all drank I just assumed you needed this as much as I did. Stefan didn't even make it today. We lost a good man. They say never leave a person behind but in this case, he begged for a sick day."

David's fast footsteps could be heard down the corridor. He peaked in the conference room, "Is it time for Scrum?" he cheerfully asked.

"You are too energetic for us right now, David. We are dying here. Look at Leo, I don't even know if she is alive." James pointed at Leo. She was sitting leaning forward resting her forehead on the edge of the table, eating the donut by the edge of the table. Hangover relapse.

David bent over and looked under the table. "We are always dying James, it's human nature" He took off his blazer, "Can you fix the aircon, James?"

James exaggerated his heavy breathing and shook his head slowly, "No sir. I want to end this quickly but painfully. The heat will have to take us out."

Leo pulled herself up and drank the rest of the coffee, "Maybe. Just maybe, we can skip daily scrum today. We've been working on the same things the last few weeks. There's nothing new. Let's go home early."

"What's up with you guys? And why are you eating donuts for breakfast again, is something going on?" David asked.

"Are we having an HR issue again, David?" Leo grimaced.

"Jesus. Guys, people, ladies. What do you want me to say?" David threw his hands up.

"Why not just say, everyone?" James suggested.

David had never considered that. He rubbed his chin and looked up at the ceiling, trying out different sentences mentally. *That might work.*

"Let me try, what is up with everyone? Nope. That's not going to do it for me."

"That's all we had David. Let's go home." Leo got up, raised her hands, and dramatically let them fall.

"Hilarious. Jokes aside, my comedic duo, I come bearing great news today. I've bought a license for an app." David added.

"That's amazing!" James replied wide-eyed with a big grin, "Tell us more about this app." He grabbed another donut and took a big bite and leaned back waiting.

Leo stood by the door leaning against the frame, scrolling on her phone, and biting her lip. "I can't believe how many emails GitHub is sending me. What on earth is happening? I have to pull the repo."

David plugged in his computer and opened up the browser and started looking through his tabs, "Can I

please have your attention, everyone? I'm just going to try to find it…it should be here somewhere…there!" He showed a website with a giant shiny tomato. "We are going to start using a technique called, Pomodoro."

"Oh no." James sighed loudly to which Leo raised her eyebrows and put her phone away. She wondered what David had come up with this time around. Once every few weeks, he would come across an article or have lunch with somebody and excitedly announce at work the next day that he had a brilliant new idea that would change everything. It rarely did as he would lose interest just as quickly as he had found it. James referred to it as *conference-driven development*. Attend a conference, watch a session on something, get smitten and *have* to use said thing.

Ironically, James was the same way with his love for new and sexy libraries and frameworks. David just took it a step further and came up with the wildest ideas and seemed unable to predict problems.

Leo looked at James. He was always up to date with the latest in tech and she'd rather get his version first. "It's a so-called technique where you're working in short bursts, usually by using a timer for example, a kitchen timer. It's called Pomodoro because the guy who invented the technique used a kitchen timer that looked like a tomato. It's fancy time boxing and David here is going to force us to do this."

Leo was genuinely impressed, "Thanks James, don't know how you always know all the latest things."

"Not to burst your bubble, but this has been around since before I was born." James replied.

"Sounds stressful…"

David leaned in "…or a great way to light some fire under our assess and get shit done."

"You rarely mean your ass, David." Leo added slyly.

"Well, I'm not a programmer, am I?"

"You were one not long ago. According to Frank and our customer." Leo rolled her eyes.

Silence filled the room. Leo stared at David, but he quickly began avoiding eye contact. James collected the empty coffee cups and donut papers and threw them in the bin. He sat back down and sighed from the effort. "Tell us then, which tomato is deciding our programming fate this month?"

David cleared his throat and summoned some leftover energy. "When I was at the agile conference…"

"…accidentally…"

"…I did some networking. You know me, I like to make friends. I spoke to one of the presenters and he had this amazing application that has been shown to improve focus, throughput, and output. I've been emailing him since, and yesterday I ran into him after spin class. We bonded over our shared interests, obviously staying fit and being devoted biking enthusiasts, and we talked about how important performance is to us. Performing as a professional, like an athlete. Even if you aren't an athlete, you can think and be an athlete." David paused and hoped they wouldn't correct him on the last sentence.

Leo looked half-sleep and James was staring at the ceiling with his arms crossed and legs spread out wide. "I got a discount and bought a license for us! Now let me fill you in on what is magical about the app." He gave a quick drumroll on the table but neither of his colleagues moved. "Come on, can I get some excitement?"

"No!" they replied in unison.

"Fine. I'll show you instead." He navigated to a website decorated with fancy tomatoes and downloaded a file after logging in.

"You haven't changed your password, I see," James remarked. David ran the installer file.

"Unlike the two of you, and I don't know how you've bypassed this policy, I'm forced to update my password every 6 months."

"Seems to me like you are just incrementing the last number on your default password."

"It's a new password for the system, same old but new for me. A win for them, win for me. Here we go, the app is now installed!" He opened *Settings* and configured the tomato for 15-minute bursts. "Obviously we'll use the default recommendation for 25. The way this works is like this. You install the app, start the timer, and when the time is up it will lock your computer for a set amount of time."

Leo furrowed her eyebrows nearly making them high-five into an angry unibrow. "What if I'm in the middle of something?"

"You pause that something. See? That's the beauty, you have to take a break. And that will make you more efficient…"

This is crazy, Leo thought to herself, "…or stressed. This seems like a bad idea. I don't have any work items that can be split into tiny bits like this. It takes me a minimum of 30 minutes to remember what I did before I went to the toilet. James, help me out here."

James shook his head. "I don't know if I want to. Sounds to me like we are going to get more breaks than we usually get." he grinned. Leo was not amused and looked at him pleadingly. "Okay, jokes aside. We work in an open office; we are going to be distracted and disturbed every few minutes anyway."

David pointed at James, "I have a solution for that, hah!" He turned and faced his computer and tried to look something up, but the computer was locked. "You got to be shitting me."

James and Leo laughed, "Guess it works. Enjoy the break!"

David held down the power button and rebooted his computer, face flushed. "Anyway, we can tweak the settings. I've bought hats. When working you wear a hat, and when somebody wears a hat, you are not allowed to disturb the person."

"Doesn't that violate the dress code?" Leo asked.

"We are exempt. Software developers can wear what they want. Within reason!"

"Better get that aircon project started then, no way I'm wearing a hat 8 hours a day in 40C."

David looked at his watch, "I got to go into a meeting. James, can you help me uninstall this, so it doesn't lock up during the meeting?"

"No chance. This should be an excellent opportunity to learn to do concise meetings. Plus, it's karma for taking cred for our work." Leo said in a flat tone and made eye contact with David again. "Have fun with the tomato. I'm sure you can fix it yourself, as a faux stack developer."

"I'll help you, this one time. Bring me the tomato." James grabbed David's computer.

"Thanks, James," David muttered and looked down. "Leo, do you have an hour or so? We need to talk."

Leo raises her eyebrows nearly brushing up against the ceiling. "I'm not sure David. Do I? Do I have the time? Life at support is busy you know."

"It's about that. See you in five."

18

Melvin was in perfect shape. A perfect circle. He was the office Pac-Man, munching his way through the day happy as a baby. He was sitting next to David on the couch in the lobby waving his hands and laughing. "Leo! Hello, hello! You got to hear this story!" Before Leo had the chance to say hi or sit down Melvin shared one of his epic stories. Every time he laughed his whole body would laugh and jiggle like Santa on happy drugs. She sat next to him, barely squeezing in on the last few inches on the couch and waited for him to finish.

David sat on Melvin's left side, quiet, and avoidant, while Melvin dried his forehead with his sleeve, gasping for air between laughs. "And that is how we DDOS'ed ourselves. The Distributed Denial of Service attack, by us for us!"

Melvin's laughter was as contagious as measles but somehow David had built an immunity. Leo's face broke into tiny lines, and she laughed. "Doesn't sound very distributed though. Wouldn't that be a CDOS? Centralized Denial of Service attack?"

"Yes! Ha! Yes indeed!" Melvin cackled and slapped himself on the knees nearly knocking David off the couch.

Melvin turned and looked at Leo, a tad too close. "Didn't you write that code, Leo?"

Leo blushed and shrugged. "Maybe I did, maybe I didn't." Endless retries in a loop. She had never forgotten. Maybe the *IgnoreError* was a bad idea. Maybe.

David cleared his throat, "I requested this meeting because Melvin, as you know Leo, is leaving us."

"Geee David, I'm not dying, you know!" Melvin chuckled.

"Might as well be," David replied.

"David, it's parental leave." Melvin chuckled once more.

Leo leaned back and looked at Melvin. "I actually thought you were dying, based on how everybody talked about it. *'Can't believe he only has two months left.' 'It' so sad! We'll miss him.'* Everyone kept going on and on." Leo continued in a high-pitched voice. She had never been good at impersonating.

"David, come on. You got kids." Melvin elbowed David.

"Didn't take any parental leave though. And I saw what happened to my wife. After a couple of years with the kids she stopped talking like an adult. It's like a disease. Changes you forever."

Melvin let go of a smile, "Leanne prefers to work, and I prefer to be at home with the baby once he arrives. Who wouldn't, babies are frickin' adorable! Wouldn't you?"

Leo and David remained silent.

"Nonetheless," David cleared his throat again, "we'll need another architect. If Mikael gets hit by a bus, we'll be down to zero architects and the developers will panic and start running in circles."

"I'm pretty sure we won't, David. We can code without them. Even you can code, right?" Leo glared at David.

David ignored Leo and looked at Pac-Man instead, "I'm considering Leo for the role. Nothing decided, just a

thought. Melvin, would you mind doing a handover for the authentication migration?"

Leo froze. Unrecognizable happiness, comparable to a thousand kitties with bowties being hugged, erupted inside her. She hugged all of them. All the cats. A smile bubbled up and across her face. Big and bright, no poker face insight. Melvin beamed and gripped Leo sideways by her shoulders. "My new little architect friend! Yes of course! I'll certainly try!" He winked. "And retry…and retry. Wait for it. And…Retry."

19

Leo waited for James in the corridor. Pacing back and forward she kept thinking about the library. At the pub, it had seemed a little bit funny, but the thought of somebody discovering who wrote it filled her now with dread and anxiety. Her hands were literary shaking as she scrolled through the notifications, too anxious to read them.

"Hi! Waiting for me or David? He might be in there a while." James brushed some leftover donut pieces from his Manchester pants and watched them land on the floor. "The ants will get them." He smiled and waited for a reply from Leo. She was staring at her phone and quickly put it away.

"Yes, you. I sort of need to ask a favor. If you don't mind."

"Sure. Of course. How can I help?"

Leo took a deep breath and stroked her right arm. Her fingernails were badly chewed and scratched against the T-shirt sleeve when she stroked her arm. "Remember last night? The stuff we found out about the library. I haven't looked at it in depth yet, but I should. I just seem unable to make myself do it. It's my anxiety, I haven't mentioned it before, but I have some problems, anxiety problems, and

…" she took another deep breath and looked down at her feet, her white sneakers glared back. James stood silently by the closed door fiddling with his laptop cord. He was trying to make eye contact with Leo. She looked up briefly. He nodded in the direction of the other conference room, and they slowly walked together. It felt oddly intimate and her senses seemed heightened as she noticed the shuffling sounds James' shoes made and the muffled sound of her socks against the wood flooring. In the background, she could hear the rest of the office, busy working, talking, typing. Somewhere in the open kitchen, somebody was grinding coffee beans. Probably Frank. "… and I need some help going through them as I have no idea what to do," she continued, "I need some handholding, metaphorically."

"Sure, sure. Happy to help. Sorry about that, by the way, anxiety sucks. And it's a big thing, I get it, so much attention pretty much overnight. You've mentioned it before though, the social anxiety."

"I have?"

"You talk about it a lot, for a self-proclaimed nervous wreck with social anxiety." James bumped her shoulder with his fist and laughed.

Leo smiled back and rubbed the shoulder, "Maybe I'm a social individual with social anxiety."

"Maybe. Or a social introvert. But I'm not your therapist. Just saying that you seem fine, I doubt anybody in the office would think you are an anxious wreck." He opened the door to one of the smaller conference rooms and she walked in and sat down at the table." At least this room is a little bit cooler. Want me to get the fan or is this okay?" James closed the door.

"It's good." She smiled.

"Alright, let's have a look at the repo then. Hand me the adapter?"

"Can we not use the big screen? I don't think I'm ready to see it projected on a large screen." Leo requested.

"Okay. Well, get closer then. Let's get cozy and have a little read." James suggested.

He found the repository on GitHub scarily fast. Just a quick search and it had made the top three ranking for .NET. Some Microsoft repositories cried further down the page.

"Ranking well Leo!"

Leo didn't reply. Her heart was pounding, and her fringe was sticking to her forehead again, cheeks glistening with nervous sweat. She brushed the fringe to the side and dried her face with her hand. "It's the hangover," she pointed at her forehead, "the sweat." James nodded understandingly.

"Are you ready, Leo? Maybe start with a small issue and then work our way through them?" His voice was warm and empathic, head tilted, hands resting on the keyboard.

"Let's do this." She looked nervously at the door and rubbed her hands under the table.

He got up and closed the door and let her look at the screen, letting her take her time and not interrupting. He stood by the corner of the table for a while, waiting for her to invite him back to the duo preview.

"Sam00 seems to be a fan or a critic," Leo commented as she scrolled. "Not sure if he loves or hates this library. But he certainly has a lot of opinions."

James sat down and rolled his chair closer to hers and let her show him the user's profile.

"Just because they have a lot to say doesn't mean it's something you have to listen to. There is a bunch of passive-aggressive change requests for grammatical errors, hardly worth the effort if you ask me."

"I know, I won't blindly merge in PR's. It's like buying the pig in the bag."

"Is that a direct translation? It's *a pig in a poke*."

"What's a poke?" She asked.

"It's a bag."

"So…basically the same thing?"

James shrugged and smiled. "I just like your Swedish idioms. They're cute."

"Oh no you didn't, never call a female developer cute," Leo replied more playfully than she intended.

"I didn't. You are not cute. The idioms are. Promise, Leo Larsson is absolutely not cute." James replied with that same sincere smile Leo was becoming accustomed to.

"You are being an ass, James." Leo pinched his arm.

"But you are not hyperventilating anymore, are you? So, a little bit of ass seems to do the trick." James winked.

Leo laughed. Maybe she didn't mind a little bit of ass. Her breathing had indeed almost returned to normal, but every few breaths she would force herself to take more slow and long breaths to avoid triggering shallow breathing. She pointed at the laptop, "But this Sam person seems to have more than grammar to comment on. Half the issues tagged with feature requests come from him. He seems pissed off for some reason."

"Well, screw him then. It's not his library." James added, "I have to say though, that's an impressive number of typos." James had sorted by the typo tag.

"You know how they say naming is hard?" Leo suddenly smiled as if she just remembered something. James nodded yes and turned towards her waiting for a story.

"When I did the project, I really struggled with what to name things. Classes, variables, you know how it is. We were under time pressure and there were a lot of late nights. I decided to name everything poop-related. Childish? Yes, very much so. But I was stressed, and it gave me the comic relief I needed to keep working on the library once the caffeine wore off. When the deadline started closing in, I completely forgot what I had done as I had gotten used to it by then. I even had a poop-name generator app I used in the background to automagically generate these names. One hour before the deadline I

realized I had forgotten to change the names and I had an hour to scan the hundreds and hundreds of files for these stupid names and change them. It wasn't pretty. But I got it done. But the traces remained like skid marks in stark white underwear. I managed to upload the unedited version as I had used Dropbox as source control. Thankfully, the teacher never downloaded any assignments and just approved everybody's work. Including one guy that went for a month-long Thailand stay and never handed in anything."

"Good farts linger in the air." James continued and laughed. "I like you even more now Leo, and you must share that app of yours. Who knows, it might get bigger than this library! Nonetheless, we should use it. Maybe we can convince David it's the latest thing to do and maybe that architect position will be yours and you can look down on us simple developers as we cry between support tickets."

"Nah, I don't want a networking lunch with him. Besides, this will do. The cache solution is my escape ticket."

They sat there for an hour, walking through the pull requests, issues, and forks. Although it had started awkwardly, she felt better after a while, physically and mentally. If she hadn't deleted the Bitbucket account she could have downloaded the name generator, but it would be easy to make another one, maybe even one that was less childish and one that added manager, utility, or helper at the end of each suggested class name. Last time she had checked their code they had 50+ helpers, utility classes, managers, and alike. Each time James had reviewed her pull requests and saw another helper class he had commented on it. "Can we be more specific? What exactly does it do?" She would always reply, "It helps." He would sigh and reply, like a broken record playing the same song repeatedly, "All code helps. That's the point of code." She was certain he would appreciate the naming app. Though,

there was an inherent risk that he would give her a harsh review. According to the many comments she had gotten on the library she had a lot to work on.

At eleven somebody knocked, and David could be seen waving outside through the glass wall by the door. He pointed at the clock and then at Leo and gestured for her to come out.

"Ah shit. Another meeting about meetings." Cue eyeroll from Leo.

"Sounds fun." James smiled and collected his things that he had spread out on the table, "I'll go hide somewhere in the office, got to prepare the youth group meeting tonight. Hopefully, it goes better this time."

Leo pointed at her clock and showed five fingers to David through the glass wall. *Five minutes.* She turned and faced James and helped him pack away the tray with adapters. "I never got around to asking, what happened last time?"

James stopped and seemed embarrassed. He was looking at his shoes and kicking some invisible dust bunny. "Meron thinks that I went overboard by starting the whole thing by talking about continuous integration and deployment. The kids were struggling with the concept and some of them left during the first break. One of them was his brother, so obviously that wasn't what I intended."

"To be fair, that seems like more of an advanced topic for beginners. Not everybody is like you James, staying on top of things and eager to learn the latest. Plus, they are teenagers. Pretty sure they are doing console apps or something and not anything requiring a pipeline."

"Maybe. But I wanted to cover what the school doesn't cover. What I wish I had learned." He said sincerely.

"Couldn't you start smaller though? Maybe ask them what they would like to know?" Leo added thoughtfully.

"Maybe. Maybe. I've already planned tonight's topic but if it doesn't go well, I might try your suggestion." Another smile.

Leo wanted to ask what they had planned tonight but five minutes had passed, and she was crossing 'fashionably late' territory. Not that she would miss out on anything, but it wouldn't look good if she came halfway through the meeting and interrupted the power point presentation. A deadly sin.

"Let's talk later or Monday if I don't see you after lunch. Sincerely appreciate the help." She said.

"Nemo problemo."

Leo hastily walked back to the conference room she had been in earlier and found David sitting at the end of the table talking to the external screen.

"Sorry I'm late," she whispered, "is the camera on?"

"No problem, we finally got audio issues fixed so we haven't started yet." David replied.

"Hello? Ah, I see I was muted, Alright, with everybody here, let's talk about the previous meeting, the plan for today's meeting, and plans for the next meeting!"

Leo looked at David and shook her head in disbelief, "I guess we are still just talking about meetings."

"Just play along, they pay well." David gave a thumbs up and opened his email. "We can hear you loud and clear. The famous Leo is also here. Go ahead!"

Leo's heart jumped a beat and she immediately started sweating. *I hope David doesn't know about the library and what happened. If he does there is no chance, I'll be able to keep my identity a secret.* David hadn't mentioned anything, and it would be highly unlikely that he would pass on an opportunity to have a little fun with that. She opened her laptop and angled it so he wouldn't see her screen and found the repository. She had 10 new notifications and it had been less than 15 minutes since she last looked at it. She looked over at David again, he seemed busy with his laptop, probably emails. She logged in on Reddit and went looking for some therapy in the form of cute kittens. *One issue per cute kitten.*

"Leo? Leo!"

Leo's face turned red as she realized David had been trying to make contact.

"Did you print any bingos? I've finished my emails and this meeting is scheduled for another hour. I'm not going to make it out alive without your help."

She looked down at her laptop, issues on half the screen, cats on the other. "I didn't prep any, but I can fix one. Give me five."

Another notification popped up and Leo froze. *What the hell.* Sam00 again. David was looking at her intently. Leo ran the bingo generator, another weekend project, and sent a few versions to the printer. *Fuck this.* She went to settings for the library. *Make Repository Private.* She wasn't sure this was a good idea and had a bad feeling about it. David was pretending to beg. Hands together in prayer, looking at the ceiling, slowly sliding down the chair onto the floor on his knees. "Save me," he whispered, "get the bingo, my architect in the making."

Leo's heart skipped a bit. *Architect in the making. Are we bargaining?*

She whispered back, "Bingo is printing…" she looked at the screen. *I'm doing it. Private it is. I can look at it later.* She clicked the button, closed her laptop, and went to grab the printouts. In the background, David was celebrating on his knees on the floor, conference camera still off, hopefully.

20

It had been an intense day for Leo, and she was worn out and ready to call it a day. The office was buzzing and even with her headphones on she couldn't escape the constant noise as she archived the last of the notifications for the library. Only the emails from Martin were left unanswered and unarchived in her inbox. She honestly didn't know what to reply and had looked at the photos several times.

Twice she had gone to the bathroom, with her laptop, to take a closer look at her smile and compare it with the photos he had sent. Julia had looked disapprovingly at her each time she snuck in or out of the handicap bathroom like a thief in the night. *They shouldn't have made the bathroom so inviting*, she bargained with her conscience. The bathroom with the dude or dudette on wheels was spacious, had a button for help (which she would hopefully never use), and it had slightly better connectivity than the other two toilets further down the hallway and lastly - it was soundproof enough to hide those afternoon bombs. A coffee machine would've made it heaven on earth. No need to ever leave.

The tomato situation had not been resolved and on her desk, she had a stack of hats David had dropped off after lunch with a kind reminder to install the app. James had

promised her the app could be removed from startup processes without notifying David, but she would have to wear a hat. The sparkly tiara, resting royally on the top of the stack of peculiar hats. Last in, first out. She put the tiara on and sank in her chair. Fake eyelashes and a velvet tracksuit would have completed the look. Housewife of Peterborough offices. Another reality show in the making.

Quick deployment to production awaited. Quick meant half a day, but at least the pipeline was short. Computer to production was hardly a pipe. More of a hole a rat chewed through a wall. James had left for the day to prepare the venue for the youth group but had warned her on Slack "Do not deploy on a Friday. I don't want to spend the weekend cleaning up our shit." A beautiful contrast to David's, "Fridays is the best day to deploy! Customers love new features on a Monday!" In case things went to shit there were no firefighters on call to put out the fires, but David loved leaving the candles burning overnight for that extra thrill.

"You think this will float?" Leo had asked James before the deployment. They had clicked around, monkey testing style, and nothing broke.

James had checked the error log for new lines, "I think we are good. Let's do this!"

'*Doings this*' meant copy-pasting the files to production while hoping nobody would visit the webshop while the old files were being replaced. And that's exactly what Leo did for a few hours until she got bored and packed up her things. If she didn't leave now, she would be late for the dentist, the highlight of her day.

As she unpacked her bike outside the main entrance the sky rumbled like an empty stomach in a deli shop and dark clouds were crowding the sky. A few drops tapped her arms. Tap. Tap. *Here comes the rain. The deployment is probably done by now.* She put her phone in her back pocket and with a last look at the ominous sky, she pedaled to her monthly social visit with Martin.

David always had a spinning class on Friday, but it had been canceled he learned as he stood outside the spinning room in his flamboyant, but very functional, bike clothes and new spinning shoes. He didn't want his new outfit to go to waste on a fantastic Friday like this one and found himself a bike at the front of the cardio room. He was ecstatic that Leo had deployed the latest version with the performance fix, and he couldn't wait to let the client know. He kept looking at his phone waiting for a notification that it had been successfully deployed. Two songs in and at a moderate heart rate the notification came. He called Brian.

"Brian! It's David!" David stopped spinning and took a sip of water, "I'm at the gym, biking." He inhaled slowly and exhaled with a cough. "Not a medical emergency. Anyways…" David was indeed out of breath, "…I have personally deployed the performance fix and the site is now live! I promised I would deliver on time and there is no better day than a Friday to share fantastic news!"

He looked around to see if people were listening in. An elderly man locked eyes with him and squinted with lowered brows as he grabbed his towel and hurried to the furthest corner.

David slid the front zipper as far down as it would go, sparkly little sweat drops like oil on a hairy frying pan popped out for a second before he slowly wiped them away. *I don't sweat, I sparkle.* "Well, of course, I couldn't have done it without some help, but I want you to know that I've personally spent evenings and weekends on this to make sure you get the very best. Yes. Yes! We should absolutely celebrate!"

He jumped off the bike and paced the connecting hallway. "I gave the site a quick spin and everything looks great. There shouldn't be any problems. Alright, I'll talk to you later! And don't forget you've promised me lunch!"

He ended the call and skipped back to the bikes, a wet towel claiming his spot.

David opened a window next to the bikes and noticed the clouds hiding behind the building next door. Murky and gloomy, threatening downpour. Thankfully, he had taken the car and it was his week without the kids. He could stay at the gym biking for as long as he wanted to. He put on Barbra Streisand, *Don't Rain on My Parade,* zipped up, and biked to Paris.

As the gloomy clouds were crowding the Sky, James stood outside the gray and rundown library in Peterborough. He wasn't the type of guy to go to the library. As a matter of fact, he didn't even know that Peterborough had a library if it hadn't been for Meron suggesting they use the library for the youth group. Somewhere in Peterborough, there was a lone sign with worn-out letters that barely spelled 'Library'. James had never seen it. "Where else would you go to print something on paper." David had told him when James expressed his surprise that there was a library. They had removed the environmentally friendly message, *Save a Tree. Don't hit Print.,* a few years back when David started biking to work and David's youngest was born. Technically though, a tree on average produces 20, 000 sheets of A4 papers, so that would be one hell of an email, Leo had told James when they discussed the mandatory email flair.

Monday morning James had called the library and a cheerful librarian had replied, delighted to receive a phone call to break the month-long silence. He had asked, after half an hour of one-sided chitchat from Monica who felt a need to share her life story before letting him talk if he could use a communal room to teach a group of young students programming. Monica had replied yes with the

only condition that they do not serve alcoholic beverages, trash the place, or look at porn. Considering that the kids were on average 14-year-old nerds he could absolutely guarantee they wouldn't be throwing a party there or trash the place. Thinking about it, if you have enough teenagers they will find a way to trash the place. He had to double-check the attendee number. He hadn't set a max for attendees. Whilst verifying the attendees a voice approached him from the side.

"Hey man, you want some medical marijuana?" A young man, long unwashed curly hair, lumberjack shirt, and torn jeans. It was either a homeless person or a hipster, James couldn't tell.

"Wrong country, we don't do medical marijuana here," James sighed with a smile. Just a typical day in Peterborough. "Besides, you don't look much like a doctor."

"It can be medical if you want it to be. I'll be your doctor," the guy grinned, "besides, why you hanging out here in the parking lot."

"I'm using the library for something."

"The library?" He looked confused, turned around, and looked at the building behind them. "Ah yeah, this is indeed a library. Nobody uses the library man. This is an outdoor shop, Fridays are mine. You are not trying to sell on my day, are you?" He looked genuinely worried. A small business owner just trying to get by."

"I'm not selling anything or buying. Please, do you mind giving me some space?"

"Sure." The guy takes a step to the side and scans the parking lot next to James who nervously looks at him as he sees Meron cross the road. James was concerned the guy would scare away Meron.

Meron was easily recognizable from afar by his peculiar gait. It was a one-fourth limp, half a slow stroll, and the rest nervous ticks. He crossed the parking lot hastily as to avoid the looming rain behind him while occasionally

looking shyly up in the direction of James and what looked like a hipster friend. He was never sure when the right moment to make eye contact was. If you make eye contact too early, do you have to maintain eye contact until you are close enough to talk to the person? Or do you have to yell, *hi,* before getting there? On the other hand, he couldn't pretend that he hadn't seen James. He pretended instead that he was busy with his phone. As he approached, he reached his hand out, a tad too early which forced them both to walk towards each other with the right arm waiting for a handshake.

"Hope we are not *over-booked*." he laughed nervously and looked at the guy next to James. "Julian! Taken up programming?"

"Nah, here working you know," Julian grinned.

James looked at Meron, who didn't seem like a likely friend, "You know this guy?"

"Yes. He sells drugs, mostly marijuana…" Meron shrugged.

Julian leaned in and winked "…but I can get a hold of other things as well!"

"No doubt you can. Is he a friend of yours?" James turned towards Meron, "You use?"

"No no no!" Meron held his hands up. "But we've met before. It's Peterborough, it's a small place. Julian, we got a thing planned for tonight, would you mind moving your business to the next lot? I'll let people looking for you know."

Julian nodded, gave a fist bump, and elegantly turned on his heels, and walked away whistling. They watched him set up camp in the next lot by the hotdog place, waving happily back.

Meron looked at his clock. It was time. "Ready to make shit happen?" He held his index finger over his lips.

James rolled his eyes and laughed, "Where did you come up with the library puns?"

"Internet, maybe?" Meron replied sheepishly. He had indeed spent several hours looking up library puns he could use as ice breakers. He had heard humor was a great way to make friends but unfortunately, he had none. But as we all know, Google makes you an expert in any field or situation.

Chatter and footsteps interfered with their conversation. On the other side of the parking lot, a group of kids was heading in their direction, stopping twice to check their phones, looking around. They looked like a flock of confused geese trying to find shelter before a storm caught them.

"Reckon they are ours?" James squinted. It was getting darker, and their age wasn't obvious from a distance, "Drugs or code?"

"I think my little brother is one of them, so it could be both or either," Meron whispered. He shifted his weight back and forward, hands in his pocket, looking at the flock getting closer.

"Did you see the poster?" James handed Meron a rolled piece of paper, white on the outside, colorful inside. "I didn't have time to email it to you as I got Stefan to finalize it around lunch- he did it for free- but I reckon it looks good!"

"What is this?" Meron pointed at the title, visibly upset.

"Today's topic! *Deadlocks, threads, and parallelism,* my favorite topics.*"*

"They are 14 years old James!" Meron threw the poster back at James.

"Well, they should start early with good practices" James quietly replied.

"The closest they've gotten to a thread was when they learned embroidery in kindergarten!" Meron dropped his bag and shook his head. "Console apps, that's the most they've done."

"There's a thread there isn't there?"

Meron pointed at the approaching flock, "Not one they are aware of, or care about."

The geese had made their way to the entrance and the flock leader greeted James meekly. Head down, staring at his shoes with his peers hiding behind him. "We are here for the youth group…" he mumbled almost to himself.

"Welcome!" James opened the door for them, and they hesitantly walked in as if they might be kidnapped by a hipster and an exotic nerd. Meron was wearing his finest shirt, gifted by his mother, blue with red roses on it. The shirt matched James' flower tattoos. They looked as intimidating as a pension gardener with an interest in IT.

"Hey, by the way, how much do you guys know about threads?" James made eye contact with the leader.

"Well," a tall kid in the back scratched his head and turned to face Meron, "as in thread count?"

"See!" James threw his hands out and gave Meron a big smile, "they know about threads."

"How come? Why do you ask us about threads?" The group looked puzzled.

Meron looked at James, at the kid, and back at James. The other kids had returned to hear the conversation and crowded the entrance. On the other side of the parking lot Julian was waving sloppy, clearly having sampled his goods.

"What exactly do YOU know about threads?" Meron continued.

The tall lanky kid kept scratching his head as if inhabited by lice or drugs and stuttered "My mum says 300-500 thread count is ideal for good-quality bedding."

"I guess you don't know about deadlocks either?" Meron interrupted.

"Is that something we should get for our door at home? We already have three locks, but only because we live next to the main street. Shady area you know. Mum doesn't like that I bike to school. She didn't want me to go

here after school today unless we went together as a group. I'll look into that lock though."

"Just go inside, we'll be there in a second," Meron stared at James, hands on his hips, his dark eyes matching the now turbulent sky, "you promised me, James. This is not cool."

"Sorry. I was going to ask Leo to talk about the cache library, but she was having a rough day."

"That wouldn't be appropriate either. Nonetheless, with the library removed there isn't any code for them to play around with." Meron sighed.

James grabbed Meron's sleeve and turned him to face him, "What do you mean?"

"They are kids, as I've said several times, and they don't know about caches either. They aren't there yet. They need help with the basic stuff! Loops. Data structures. Basics!" Meron pulled free and started walking.

"No, you said the library was removed?" James stuttered.

"Yes? Didn't she tell you?"

Monica came running out the door, heels announcing her arrival by frantic little clicks against the floor. Flustered, she threw herself out the door and pulled her hair away from her face while flailing with her other arm.

"You can't leave them alone in here! You can't leave me alone with 70 kids!" She straightened her dress, took two deep breaths, and gestured for them to hurry inside.

"70? Those are not ours. We just let in seven kids!"

"You know this is not the main entrance, right?" Monica pulled James in while pushing Meron with her other arm, surprisingly strong for her short stature.

"There's another entrance?" James blurted.

"Three other entrances!" Monica replied with a trembling voice.

"Three?!" James and Meron looked at each other before Monica guided them to the lobby as the teenagers poured in from all entrances.

James' phone could barely be heard in the noise but it vibrated perseverant in his pocket and he pulled it out and hid in a corner to answer.

"James? Is that you? Fuck! I've tried to message you several times. We are fucked! The deployment is fucked. And I can't get a fucking hold of fucking Leo. What.The.Fuck…" James couldn't hear everything David was saying, only intermittent *fucks* and *fucking*. Meron was panicking and trying to gather the crowd and move them to the community room as Monica was waving, pushing, and yelling. "…the site is down! I can't fix it; you have to fix it! Fuck James, I'm…"

"I'LL FIX IT," James yelled in the phone; a tad louder than he had intended. The room went silent and everybody was looking at him.

"Hi…welcome. Grab a seat in the community room and we'll get started! We have a slight change of plans regarding today's topic. Instead of threading, I thought I'd rather show you how we do deploy and do rollbacks, with some Sherlock Holmes bug hunting. Sound fun?"

The silence was palpable. Meron stood in the middle of the group, glaring at James, mouth wide open, hands shaking. Outside the rain had started pouring down and the heavy drops echoed down the hallway as they drummed on the large windows.

21

"Hello, Leo!" Martin rounded the corner and greeted a glum-looking Leo with a contrasting broad smile. "I see we have a princess here with us today." He bowed slowly and exaggerated. The rain was pounding on the windows. Leo had not escaped the rain, as evident by her drenched clothes clinging to her body and wet bike tire marks on the floor as she has insisted on bringing the bike up to the waiting area.

"Princess?"

Martin pointed at his head, then at her. Leo looked in the window reflection, first focusing on the rain scratching the glass, trying to get in, secondly her reflection. Her fringe was licked to her forehead like a headband. Decorated with something sparkly on top.

The tiara. I'm still wearing the fucking tiara. She removed the tiara quickly and threw it in her backpack.

"Work thing," she mumbled, totally embarrassed.

"No need to be embarrassed, it's not often we have regal visit here in tiny Peterborough. But please let us know next time you are late." As if reading her mind, Martin waved a finger at her.

"Sorry about that, I got caught in the rain and my phone got drenched." she held out her phone, providing evidence to free herself from the criminal allegations. "I can't turn it on, couldn't call."

Helen magically appeared from behind the wall she had been hiding behind.
"I can fix that! You need rice. It'll dry it up for you. We have heaps of it at the back."

"Rice?" Leo stared at the phone, then back at Helen.

"You don't have toddlers, I'm assuming. You'd know if you did, they love dropping things in the loo." She grabbed Leo's phone and disappeared around the corner.

"We have a long session ahead of us Leo, come on in." She followed Martin to his office, feeling naked without her phone, cold, and wet. A miserable princess, on a miserable rainy day.

"Have a seat." Martin nodded in the direction of the chair as he straightened his pants before sitting down. They were slightly too short and made him look like a child that only ever wore hand-me-downs. A pair of colorful socks revealed themselves with what seemed to be a combination of cats and flowers. A poor kitty was trying to escape the shoe. *Business, but also a little bit fun.* That's how Leo's dad used to describe his style, which was conservative and dressy, but always with some random crazy and colorful socks to match.

The cat socks must have been purchased the same place Julia in HR had gotten hers. The kitten contorted by the fold made her think about the PetSockShop. Hopefully, the launch had gone well after she rushed deployment as there hadn't been any testing after the deployment. The build was green, the services had a heartbeat and the surgeon, Leo, was pleased. And NO ERRORS. A dream come true. Everything worked on her machine. Why wouldn't it work on the work servers? She sat down, her t-shirt clinging to her chest, a puntastic look.

iceberg{ *position: fixed;* } *.titanic*{ *float: none;* } One of her favorite pun T-shirts.

"I like cats. My niece picked this pair for me." Martin pulled the socks up, straightening the kitten. "By the way, if you are cold, would you like a tunic from us?"

"A what?"

"Tunic," he tugged his shirt showing it off before continuing, "we have a closet full. It's not a problem. You'll be here for 3-4 hours, and you look cold." He pointed at her. Leo was rubbing her left arm, goosebumps decorating her arms like a Braille book. "I don't think we have extra pants, but we do have a tunic. Shirt if you prefer." He got up and within milliseconds presented a neatly folded blue tunic in plastic wrapping. "Here, for you. You can use the room at the back." It was almost like he had done this before, a thought that was too disturbing to consider and consequently, Leo accepted the odd gift with a slow outreach of her hands where he placed the tunic-like an offering to the dentist gods. Leo quickly left to change. As she curled of the wet t-shirt and folded her bra inside it, she stood there bare-chested for a second and looked at her reflection in the window against the heavy rain. *I'm half-naked in my dentist's office.* His computer monitor had a web cam mounted on top - it didn't have a cover for the lens. A knock scared her, and she pulled the tunic over her head and crossed her arms to hide her nipple tents.

"Good fit?" He seemed to be staring at her crossed arms where her nipples threatened to escape the embrace. Leo avoided eye contact and rubbed her arm, nodded, and whispered, "thanks." She sat down, demurely crossed her ankles, and leaned back, looking like a mummy with her arms crossed.

Martin looked at her with a delighted smile. He was holding a mold in his hands, almost like a pet, stroking it with his thumb. She didn't know how to feel about the fact

that he seemed to be rather attached to the mold of her teeth and using it as a stress ball.

"Looks great on you. You should have kept the tiara though. To complete the picture." He carefully placed the mold on the table next to him and put on his mask preparing her for the filling replacement. "You are a strange lady," Martin mumbled behind the mask squinting his eyes, possibly due to a smile.

I'm strange? Leo raised her eyebrows and met Martin's eyes as he leaned in. His forehead was shiny and tiny drops of sweat were forming above his eyebrows. With her mouth wide open she certainly hoped they wouldn't land on her.

"You didn't reply to the emails," he casually mumbled behind the mask and stopped for a second to switch tools. She couldn't reply but tried to make some sounds mimicking the word *sorry.* When somebody is drilling in your mouth and asks why you ghosted them you have to say, *I'm sorry.*

"We can talk about it later; we've got work to do." He patted her shoulder, and she gave him a thumbs up noting how awkward this all was. "I brought the mold with me, nearly grabbed the wrong one," he continued, "the inspiration for the photos." She looked at the table where the mold was and recognized it from one of the photos. "We'll have to make new ones though when we are done with this procedure. If you want Invisalign's that is."

He stopped for a second and she shook her head, "Nah, I'm good. I'll keep the plow."

Martin placed his hand on her shoulder and looked concerned, "You sure?"

She nodded.

"Can I ask that we do another mold? Maybe a few more? For practice?"

Leo stared at him. He stared back intensely. The mold smiled from across the room. Martin removed his hand but left the warmth lingering and spreading.

Leo looked away. "I don't mind if you'd like to make another mold."

"Fantastic!" Martin spun around and lined up the equipment.

Molds were made and Martin's smile grew behind the mask. The lineup of creepy toothless smiles grew until Martin exhaled forcefully with a slight moan and leaned back. "Exactly what I needed!" He squinted a new smile and placed his hand back on Leo's shoulder, "Your turn now. Let's get you fixed." Leo nodded and closed her eyes.

Martin dove back in and didn't say anything for the next hour and a half. At some point, the assistant came in and let Leo know that she had put the bag of rice with Leo's phone in it by her backpack so she wouldn't forget it, and to let it stay in the bag overnight. And oh, by the way, she could keep the rice. Still edible. Only a Brit would say that.

Leo's Friday couldn't possibly get stranger. Biking in a rainstorm with a tiara on her head, stripping down in a dentist's office, and changing to a dentist uniform. A dentist petting a replica of her teeth asking if his photoshopping skills impressed her and a bag of rice containing her phone that she could cook later. Oh, and being called strange by Mr. Strange himself!

Martin suddenly rolled his chair back, looked at the clock on the wall, and swore. "Got to go. Parking meter ran ou.t" He quickly pulled off the mask and gloves and ran out the door without even saying goodbye. The molds were left behind, sad but with yet to be filled permanent smiles. Leo waited. Thought about the kitten on the socks. Wondered if it had stopped raining.

"Hope you don't mind, miss Larsson, I'll be taking over." A tall blonde man appeared and held out his hand to shake hers. She unfolded her crossed arms, mouth still wide open, forced by the intra-oral retractor. Saliva was accumulating and she was doing her best to swallow frequently, although she would soon pull the dental saliva

pump and use it herself if she didn't get any help soon. His grip was firm and warm. His had green eyes with plenty of smile lines.

"Let's see if we can wrap this up in an hour or two and I promise we won't be sending in more strangers." He pulled down the face mask and smiled with a cheeky wink. He adjusted the retractor and offered the saliva pump. "I know, I know. Not here to talk. Let's put this in." The suction sound bounced between the walls. "I like your outfit. Do you work here?"

Leo shook her head carefully.

"Neither do I." he laughed and changed the drill head. Leo's pupils, and the drill head, doubled in size.

He continued, "As in, I'm usually in a different office, in Huntingdon. Martin asked me to help today. We sometimes do that for longer procedures." He laughed and pulled down the mask. "Sorry for scaring you, promise I'm not a random visitor. Martin should have told you, but he is a little bit…" trying to find the right words, "…strange if you haven't noticed." He winked again and pulled the mask back up. Leo laughed awkwardly with a sprinkle of anxiety as he continued where Martin had left off.

"Brian Davies is my name by the way!" He yelled as he drilled. "They call me Doctor Davie."

An hour later the loud buzzing sound stopped, and the retractor was removed. Leo had not fallen asleep this time and her mouth was sore and incredibly dry. With the chair still in motion to help her in an upright position, she lunged for the water fountain and drank two cups before she remembered she was supposed to swirl and spit, not swallow the toxic amalgam fillings.

"Don't…don't swallow that."

Doctor Davie left the room and came back without gloves and face mask and sat down looking at her as she was massaging her cheeks. Her lips had cracked in two places.

"I'd say you should rest your mouth for a while now, but you seem like a quiet person" He conferred.

She didn't respond. She was tired and in pain.

He gave her a handheld mirror and she examined the result. All her lower teeth had white composite fillings instead of the old silvery ones she had gotten as a poor student resulting from bad habits - or lack of them - as a kid with busy parents. It looked great. Sparkly. Tiara worthy.

"Wow, thank you!" She got up from the chair and stretched. It was late, and she was dying to get home and sleep. She could still catch the 9 PM train if she hurried. The phone would have to wait. She couldn't be bothered going through the bag of rice.

"One thing before you go…"

She stopped and looked at him, "Yes?"

"Have you ever noticed that your teeth are plow-shaped?"

"I've been told they are. They do their job, I'm happy with them." She folded her wet jacket and shoved it in her backpack. "No braces for me or Invisalign's." She swung the backpack over her shoulder and hurried towards the door.

"Hey! Wait!"

What now?

"You forgot your…uh… bra." Dr. Davie replied sheepily holding up her not-so-recently removed bra.

22

On Saturday, the sun woke Leo up with a slap across her face. Like nails on a chalkboard on her very eyes, Leo cursed the sun and squinted at the clock on the wall. Her jaw was aching from yesterday's procedure. She rolled to the other side of the bed and onto wet fabric. The light blue tunic stared back at her with a scrunched-up grin. Leo pulled the covers over her head and hid from her shame with a muffled moan until oxygen deprivation forced her to face the world. She picked up the tunic and let it unfold. Redness spread across her cheeks and a barely noticeable smile traveled across her face. She felt her teeth with her tongue. The lips had cracked at the corners and the tongue could barely make a swipe across the smooth fillings. But it made it, and it was worth it. Leo officially had the smoothest fillings in town.

Lion hissed and meowed loudly. It was Saturday, and Saturdays had a set schedule. The cat, the impatient little asshole, demanded to be fed, cuddled, and brushed before anything else was done. Once, and if, the tasks were approved by the furry majesty, Leo could tackle the mess that had built up during the week. And Lion would glare and judge. Leo had concluded that only masochistic or deeply mentally troubled people have cats. She had once

heard that children were like exotic animals, and you had to be rich or crazy to have them. The same goes for cats like Lion, which would be, and this is an approximation only, 99.9% of cats. With anxiety-inducing dubstep playing in the background, she would put away the few items that had been misplaced during the week, flush the toilet with shampoo, remove the mold from Betty, feed her, and maybe do a set of laundry. Betty is a sourdough, not a corpse. A sourdough that smelled like one. And Lion? He would wait by the door, a disapproving look on his face and down-turned whiskers. Once a set of laundry had been forced in the washing machine, the hairball would be carried down the stairs in a diamond-studded harness for his weekly walk around the block. Leo was allowed to join.

With a coffee in hand, from the barista around the corner, Leo walked with Lion in the sun. They settled on an old, but clean bench by a tall oak tree and they absorbed the sun while Leo stroked Lion the only way he liked to be stroked. Slow, gentle, and only halfway down the back. An old lady sat on the opposite bench, a tiny lap dog by her side. She looked sad and curled up like an old tissue on the street and the dog trembled while anxiously looking over at Lion. Leo suddenly saw herself, as an old lady on the bench, only a cat as company. Poor lady. Leo stroked Lion. Was it Old Mary?

Lion hissed and Leo picked him up and started walking. She turned to say something, but an old man had sat down by the elderly lady. He was holding her hand and she was laughing. The dog was licking his face. Leo looked down at Lion, who frowned back at her and turned away with a subtle groan.

Back in the apartment Lion disappeared in the cat tower, gates shut for the day. The sound of the door closing shut echoed in the empty apartment and the coffee had gotten cold albeit the scorching sun. Leo poured out the coffee and prepared a sourdough. She made sure the nearly empty fridge had butter and ham and verified the

milk had not expired. This was done by taking a mouthful and confirming there were no chunky bits. She looked out the window, returned to the counter, and removed the phone from the bag with rice. The rice was saved for later. The phone was left on the table, dusty and sad.

Back to the window.

Livingroom, the couch.

Staring at the wall.

Standing by the window in the living room.

Long sigh. Another fold for the sourdough.

Back to the window.

The sun crept closer to the horizon and the dough got increasingly smoother. By the time the sun was ready to set, Leo placed the dough in the fridge for overnight proofing.

There was nothing to see out the window when the sun had gone for the day. The computer beeped in the corner, a subtle call. She took the bait. Old notifications were on the screen, suggestions to improve the library. A lot of typos, a common complaint. She marked them and deleted them.

She looked at her public profile on the professional networking site. *ConsultIT!* She gagged. *Data consultant.* She selected *Edit profile* and deleted the title. *Architect.* She hit save and smiled in the darkness. *Connection requests.* She looked at the suggestions. Art professor, Faculty of Arts and Humanities. Daniel Larsson.

Her dad smiled in various photos. A book signing. A vernissage. A beautiful woman by his side, dressed elegantly in a silky gown. Lisa Larsson. *Hi mum,* Leo whispered and denied the request. She closed the laptop silently. Back at the window. Long sigh. Lion meowed for a quick cuddle. A final long sigh and Leo surrendered for the night, hairy asshole by her side.

On Sunday, the sun offered another slap, but Leo was buried under a pile of leftover hair from Lion. She got up, cleaned Lion's shit- literally. Flushed some more shampoo

down the toilet, folded the little laundry she had done
(while ignoring the massive pile in the corner) and set the
kitchen oven to maximum.

The bread was scored and baked to perfection. The
smell filled the apartment, a hidden bakery with just one
customer and one baker. Leo sliced two pieces and spread-
out butter that quickly melted. She placed the bread in a
fabric towel and opened the cupboard. Three stale loaves
of bread changed her plans and she threw the bread, and
its cousins, in the bin. She ate the slices in silence,
accompanied by an empty chair across the table. Lion by
her feet.

Back to the window.

The clouds moved slowly, the sun hid.

Livingroom. Bed.

Staring at the ceiling, then at the headphones by her
bag.

It's too far away, she sighs.

Leo drifted away like a log in a river. The tunic still on
the floor. Another regular Sunday awaiting, or so Leo
thought.

23

"Leo …" James was sitting in the lobby, tapping his pen on his laptop. He looked exhausted. Leo barely recognized him and had to take a second take. The guy with messy hair, dark blue hoodie, grey sweatpants, and worn-out running shoes was indeed James - James on a terrible day that is. He sounded tired as he mumbled her name a second time and rubbed his eyes. Leo had seen toddler parents look more rested than him.

Leo tilted her head and offered him a concerned look, "Is everything okay, James? You look tired, sick? Family okay?"

"Oh, I'm exhausted. And things are not okay. How are you, Leo?" He stopped tapping the pen and balanced it between his thumb and index finger without making eye contact.

Leo sat down across from James and focused on the coffee, "Great. Had a fantastic weekend. Martin on Friday, that was fun and weird at the same time - the usual, you know. One on one time with Lion on Saturday. Fresh bread on Sunday. Updated my profile. Almost did some networking. You?"

"Do you know how much trouble you're in?" James flashed his eyes at her as he stood up suddenly, spilling coffee on the floor. "I don't know what you were thinking and why the hell did you turn off your phone this weekend? Sick prank maybe? - but I've spent two days trying to fix your fuckup and it's not cool. David is beyond pissed, not to mention PetSockShop."

"James, I'm not following. What happened? "Leo's voice had a slight quiver to it as she grasped to process what was happening.

"The library Leo! The fucking library!" James wiped the coffee with a napkin, a useless gesture. He threw the napkin on the table and stood there waiting.

"Peterborough library?"

"No! Not the Peterborough library. Your library. The one missing. The one everybody is talking about. The one that broke the build and the site."

Leo paused and looked at the wall next to them. It was grey with scuff marks from her bike. "Oh…no…" she bit her lip, "THE library? Oh shit…I made it private…it's because I made it private, isn't it?" James nodded hard and sat back down. Leo looked at him and said the most calming thing she could think of, "I thought you thought it would be a good idea to make it private?"

"Not before deploying to production!" James was pulling his hair. "On. A. Fucking. Friday!"

Julia came running down the hallway, her flats making flat gently pounding sounds reminding Leo of her neighbor's chihuahua. A yappy little dog that Lion hated.

Julia whispered flustered, "Flower words, please? Not The F-Word? We have customers visiting." She gestured towards the table on the other side of reception where three men in suits were staring at a homeless person yelling at a young woman. Not a good look. James hadn't noticed. He lowered his head and looked at the empty cup. As a homeless person, he might as well sit outside of the corner

shop and beg for money with an empty cup. He was certain they would get fired.

"There is no flower describing how I feel right now Julia," he whispered back, "but you don't need to worry about me." He pointed at the door. "David is about to come in and guaranteed he'll be less than nature-like."

David had barely opened the door before the curse words made their way into the lobby. He was wearing a too-tight cycling outfit and tapping bike shoes, helmet still on, a packet of pull-up diapers, and a tiny bomber jacket. One could only assume the diapers and the jacket were for a miniature person and not for him.

"Julia, give these to my ex when she comes by. It's for my youngest, forgot to drop them off at kindergarten. Leo, you are coming with me. Emergency meeting, now. James, you…" James' head was tilted back, a thin strip of saliva making its way from the corner of his mouth to his chest. The laptop was resting by his feet, an empty coffee cup in his hands.

"He fell asleep," Leo whispered and focused on the scuff marks again. She could feel David's heavy breath. He was fuming like a group of vaping teenagers.

David sighed, "Julia! Can you take James to the meditation room?"

Julia came running in, apologizing to the other guests on the way. She shook James until they made eye contact. It had been a rough weekend for James. No baking for him. On the plus side, he spent more time at the library in one evening than he had spent in his school years. The downside was it had been a disaster. He had spent Friday evening trying to do a panicked rollback. He did so in front of a bunch of confused teenagers that were running around like wild geese. The internet of library-internet quality, a tribute to dial-up for those old enough to remember the pain. Meron had been fuming in a corner. Now and then Meron would let him know, as one does as a scorned lover, that he would never trust him again.

James stumbled to the meditation room and sat down on the bed. He looked at the package of diapers Julia had left next to him. How many would he need to make a shitty weekend less shitty? An unreasonably happy toddler stared at him from the package. James laid down and embraced the judgmental smirk from the diaper baby. According to the package, the baby weighed somewhere between 5-12kg. The diapers would be of no use to him. James closed his eyes and fell asleep as the sound of Leo and David orchestrated up and down. David's loud voice mirrored with Leo's timid replies.

David was pacing. Short, angry steps. "We spent all weekend trying to fix the botched deployment, Leo. And then James tells me you pulled the library right before the deployment. No cache service anymore! Crash, boom, bang! Our servers get bombarded with fucking retries in an endless loop…"

Leo moved out of the way as David attempted to make another round "…to be fair, James recommended we do exponential retries with a circuit breaker…" She ignored the fact that she had shut the idea down. How often do the requests fail? Nah, no need. Network is a reliable thing.

David's face was bright red, ready to explode, "I DON'T CARE WHAT WE SHOULD HAVE DONE!" He threw himself down in the chair and swung his legs up on the table. The shoes landed with a thud. Leo stared at them, then at David. David moaned and tried to pull them off. He wasn't very flexible and even with encouraging grunts, he couldn't get a good angle.

"Please?" He pointed at the shoes. Awkwardly, Leo helped him pull them off and remained silent as the air thickened with her sweat and anxiety. David's feet reeked and Leo recoiled. He continued, "You know how many socks couldn't be sold? How about a tiny fraction of what they usually sell! They sell socks, Leo, that's what they do! The simplest of tasks and we fucked it up for them! The requests were so slow their customers could have knitted

ten pairs before they got to place their order. The order service is still down after the failed rollback…"

"…rollback failed?" Leo interrupted still proving the difficulty she had in social situations.

"The database, Leo. The god damn database couldn't be rolled back because we don't have a plan for that!" David replied still fuming.

In his red Tour de France clothes, David looked like a balloon ready to pop. His skin tone matched his clothes, and his cheeks were puffy and hamster-like. And he was visibly furious. Which was not hamster-like. Not to insult hamsters. Hamsters are outstanding little creatures.

Leo shook her head as to make sense of the disaster he described. Her fringe joined in, swiping side to side. "What do you mean? We don't have a plan for rollbacks?" David's eyes dilated. Leo continued "Of course, we have a plan. There's a simple script you run. It only takes a couple of minutes. Why didn't you guys do that?"

David stared. Paused. Supercharged his vocal cords. Tesla charging station speed. "A script, a SCRIPT? There's a SCRIPT?"

"Yes, indeed, there is a script. Didn't you read the documentation?" Leo shook her head.

He jumped up and looked at her. Slightly shorter without his shoes. "Who reads documentation? I didn't even know we had documentation!"

Leo responded mathematically, "Don't you remember you forced me and James to write documentation? The documentathon? There is a lot of documentation, you just have to read it." She pulled up her backpack and placed it on the table, avoiding eye contact with the crazy man next to her.

"I knew that nobody was going to read it when you said we had to document everything. But hey, if you want to, now is a good time to start." Leo sat down and pulled out her computer. And within a couple of minutes she was looking at a folder with various scripts. They were in

alphabetical order, well-named, and in a big fat folder named documentation. One of the files was named How to roll back to the previous release. Leo pointed at the screen, "See, you just run this script and everything is good. Do you want me to do it now?"

David was shaking. He leaned over, looked at her computer. A silent yes echoed, like an angry but desperate whisper.

Leo sighed, "Wait, just got to finish these updates. Windows wasn't done. Only mid-update." They stared at the computer together as the computer told them no files had been touched and that they had either 2% or 99% left of the updates. David was breathing heavily behind her. It was the closest Leo had gotten to physical affection besides the dentist's visits.

A couple of agonizing minutes later, the script was run. David ordered some socks - wool and nylon, the durable kind. It took a few minutes and there were no errors. It was the first time in his life he was happy to see a performance problem. Everything seemed fine. Well, at least in terms of doing a rollback. David was not fine. He was the opposite of being fine. He was un-fine. An angry, distressed tomato in performance-enhancing spandex ready to fire Leo if he could.

Standing by the door, James scratched his head nervously. He rubbed his eyes after his long and much-needed slumber. His eyes focused on the screen, suddenly widening. "Ah. Shit. Forgot about that script…"

The tomato turned around, displaying a different shade of red, "What script?"

James stroked his wrist, looked down, then up again, "It is documented, you know."

David looked at James, got up, and walked out without a word. Leo held her breath as David's steps faded down the hallway. He was never quiet. Not like that. James shifted his weight from the doorframe to his feet and turned his stare towards Leo. David disappeared around a

corner with what seemed like a primal scream. There were also some creative swear words echoing down the hallway, eager to find Julia's ears.

James closed the door and looked intently at Leo, "Did you run the script?"

"You got to run it from the terminal server," Leo explained. "It's the T1 server. The usual password."

"Secret123!? We got to stop using that password. Didn't you say it was temporary when you made the account?" He asked.

"You know how it goes, James," Leo's lips twitched, "I mean, we want passwords that are compliant and easy to remember. It goes like this: First, you must capitalize the first letter of a chosen word. That word should describe the login or the password. For example, Secret. The next step is to add a number, I always add 1. If more are required, add them in numeral order. 123. Always at the end. That's where you put all the crazy extra requirements. More often than not, a special character is required as well. The exclamation mark is your go-to. It adds to the password birthing process frustration. Like, OKAY here is your god damn password!!!. Of course, add only one. Least effort, max benefit. If you feel frisky, try the # sign, it adds a little extra spice. Do not use a question mark, we are not doubting ourselves (OKAY here is your god damn password?). You now have what I refer to as your best-password-ever and you must use it everywhere. With the same login name. And that, James, is how I created this awesome password."

James shook his head with elation to be moving on from one of the worst weekends of his life, "That's horrible logic, Leo. Please tell me it is at least added to our password vault? Passbolt, OnePassword? Which one?"

"I emailed it, search your inbox," Leo replied.

"Oh."

"Yeah. I know." Leo sighed and closed the lid on the laptop. "I'm not a fan of email. We should have used the chat."

She looked at James for a few seconds. His face had softened, "And James, I'm sorry. Are you pissed?"

"I'm too tired to be pissed. David is pissed enough for all of us. Just make sure you fix the library and do a new deployment. Don't wait until Friday. And maybe buy me coffee and donuts. Plural. Thanks." A real smile on his face as he had opened the door to leave, Leo could hear David screaming and Julia trying to calm him down with a yelling-whispering voice. Looney tunes. Leo looked out the window and for a moment, as the reality of what had just happened settled in, wondered what would happen if she jumped. Probably not much. There was a large terrace on the floor beneath them. She would just finally meet their downstairs neighbors whom she had been avoiding in the elevator for the past ten years.

24

Leo sat in the conference room watching the battery drain slowly while waiting for David to calm down. Her charger was by her desk, which was back-to-back with David's desk. She had opened the door and moved her chair closer to the door leaning against the doorframe. It took an hour before the screaming and yelling stopped. James had sent a private message and asked if she was hiding. "I'm focusing," she had replied. "You are definitely hiding," he had replied. She was but would not admit it. James had continued, "It's an open office you know. Julia won't let him have a go at you here. You are safer here. There's also fresh coffee syrup and a client waiting for the fix."

Leo had never done a walk-of-shame. The morning after a drunken one-night stand, walking home in ruffled nightclub clothes, barefoot, heels in her hand with makeup that would arouse panda bear enthusiasts. Never. Not Leo. This, however, would be the closest she would ever get to that feeling. Barefoot, laptop in hand (dead), trudging through the lobby and the office as everybody glared. She had certainly screwed up and this was her walk-of-shame. Everybody was deployment-shaming her. Keeping her head down, she lumbered down the office. She slunk into her chair and quietly plugged in the laptop. The monitors

stayed dark as her soul. The laptop slowly absorbed some much-needed power while Leo remained drained.

Mikael walked past Leo's desk, stopped, and looked at her. He felt compelled to stop because of the pure misery leaking from her. The entire office had heard and consequently gossiped. It was unusual that Leo was the focus of office gossip as there had only been a few incidents. One of them involved Mikael.

"You got lucky, you know." he chuckled.

Leo's face turned red before she recomposed and regained her usual pale color back with sheer willpower. She pointed at her headphones and then at the screen mouthing I'm working.

Mikael tilted his head and squinted, "I can see you're not using the headphones. They're not plugged in." He leaned in and showed her the end of the cable.

Leo seemed unfazed.

"Those are just the cheap office headphones. Only managers get the wireless ones." He carried on, unfazed by her silence.

Leo took her headphones off and stared at him with a brief sigh, "I'm having a shit day."

"I heard, but nay. It's your lucky day. The front-end team is having a worse day. Urgent stuff." Mikael nodded in the direction of the frontend team.

In the back corner, there were many decorations hanging from the ceiling - a poor attempt to make it look like a tiki bar. After an Ambient Belonging and the Workplace workshop, the front-end team had decided that a 'Tiki Bar theme' would imply creative people were at work. Or at play. However, they didn't seem thrilled or creative right now. It was obvious they were arguing, and the temp product manager was waving his hands aggressively towards the deflated palm tree. The palm tree resulted from 3 months of discussions regarding the use of plastic material, the environment, and branding. Greenwashing, Mikael had called the efforts of the Green

Tribe at work. He had opted out of the various tribes but had plenty of opinions. After some compromise from the Tribe and the newly exed front-enders had settled on a second-hand bio-plastic palm tree that had to be re-inflated on a weekly basis. It was worth it, though, they claimed.

"What did they do this time?" Leo turned her chair facing the drama. The palm tree added comedy to the frantic scene of shouting.

"They messed up the bank login."

"Oh?" Leo wanting to hear more.

"Being creative and all that. Surprise feature after the hackathon last week." Mikael casually replied.

Leo hadn't been invited. It was a well-known fact in the office that she didn't attend after-work activities. She didn't mind but sometimes wished she had gotten an invitation, just to be given the option to say nay.

"They added an animated sunrise or something, only ran tests in canary, and deployed way past Balmer's peak."

"It took them two days to animate a sunrise?"

"It was a grand sunrise." Mikael looked at the office horizon with melancholy. "If it wasn't for the animation blocking the login page. Unless you are using canary which, judging by the pile of issues submitted from users, was close to none."

"I can't believe they did this again." Leo laughed for the first time in what seemed like forever. She crossed her arms, flicked her fringe to the side, and leaned back. Popcorn Moment.

Again? Mikael hadn't worked there for more than a few years and was rarely in.

Mikael continued. "They added theming. And some genius decided that to reset the font opacity they would simply set it to 0. As if that was a reverse bit."

"But wouldn't that…"

"Yes. They added invisible ink. It was a clusterfuck when they were trying to figure out what had happened.

The disappearing texts. Many screenshots from customers, 'where is my text?'." Mikael shook his head." Maybe a piña colada too many?"

Leo shrugged her shoulders. Sounded like a fair solution.

Mikael inched in, "You guys are lucky you have a mixed team…"

Leo didn't reply. James was okay. Sort of. But they could do without David.

"… because that…" Mikael pointed at a short blonde bloke arguing with the product manager while another colleague of his was pulling his shirt, "...that's what you get when you put the same sort of people on the same team."

Leo couldn't decide if, based on the scene playing out in the tropical corner next to the ping pong table, was evidence that the Ambient Belonging workshop had worked or not.

"We are hardly a team. We are three people. And that's if we count David." She was unwilling to count him in. He created more problems than he solved.

"Micro team," Mikael replied with a wink. Leo gave him a quick smile.

"There's a name for everything, isn't there." Leo sighed. "Makes it all, okay, you know. Add some jargon and it's a thing."

Mikael looked intensely at Leo. Her fringe had found its way back down and stroked her slightly raised eyebrows. No makeup, but pink cheeks and full lips, feminine contrast to her clothes. Leo looked up and immediately scrunched her face. Mikael took the hint and readjusted his focus. He picked up the cable and plugged it in.

"Just wanted to share that with you. Hopefully made your day slightly better. Happy listening." He pointed at the headphones with a smirk.

"Always happy when somebody else fucks up," Leo replied sarcastically and regained her focus on the black

screen in front of her. She ignored Mikael's last lean in to make eye contact before he elegantly drifted away from her desk like a leaf down a river.

The laptop fan announced successful startup and update installations. The monitors flickered a welcome screen. Hastily, she opened the email app and was met by a screen filled with angry unread emails, many of them from Sam00.

Scrolling through the emails she thought about how she once had decided to try for inbox zero after an enthusiastic monologue delivered by Mikael during a rare social lunch. Paper bag lunches had been David's idea, and she had been forced to attend at least one. You can enjoy your lunch while learning about something interesting! In other words, 'here is a sneaky way to get you to work for free'. David had been persistent and asked his favorite pet, Mikael. Mikael had nodded his head so hard it could have fallen off. Must be dark up there, she had thought to herself, up David's ass.

"And who would do the teaching?" she had inquired.

"We'll take turns sharing cool stuff. Mikael can do one about organizing your email inbox." David had looked at Leo as he had said that.

"I only use my inbox once a week, David," Leo had reminded him.

Mikael had laughed a tad too much at that and unprompted had rested his hand on her shoulder. "Promise, I'll show you something you've never seen before."

She shook away the memory of his sweaty hand but couldn't shake David's mandated social paper bag lunch. Social pressure made her attend the lunch after all the developers had agreed that work had to buy them lunch. Consequently, it had been the last paper bag for lunch. They never found out how many had adopted inbox zero,

but rumor has it none of the developers even checked their email to try it.

I could always simply archive them all, Leo contemplated as she scrolled to the bottom of the second page. An email from her dad caught her off guard.

Subject: Leonarda, please reply
Hello, my dear. I know it has been a while, but I'd…

She didn't open it but didn't archive it. Her day couldn't possibly get worse. *Might as well jump in that black pit in my stomach.* A loud slam startled her, and she let out a foreign squeak.

"We are not done. But one more fuckup…" David had slammed his palms against her desk, rendering the entire office into silence, the clasps against the desk echoing against the large glass windows, "…and we, or rather you, are done." He spun around and hastily left, leaving only the silence and two handprints behind. The office awkwardly returned to its usual chatter.

"Well, I guess the joy was short-lived." Mikael had magically reappeared.

"Oh, fuck off." She muttered.

He placed a hand on his chest and exhaled with a sad nod and took a step back.

"Sorry, Mikael. It's, yeah. A really shitty day." She avoided eye contact and scrolled through the next page with emails.

"No inbox zero?"

"No, not today."

He gave her a pat on the back. "You'll be okay. I mean, we all do our share of mistakes, right?" He didn't wait for a reply and walked away. Not this type of mistake, she thought.

Subject: What the fuck Leo?
Content: Join the fucking Discord server. Now.

One of Sam's epic emails. Why not? Leo joined.

Sam00: So, what the fuck was that?

LeoLoL: What?

Sky0: Why the fuck did you pull the repo?

LeoLOL: Couldn't be bothered. Too much work. The code sucked. You saw it.

Sam00: And? 99% of code on GitHub sucks. I'm not just saying that cause all the Microsoft repos are there.

LeoLoL: I've got shit to do at work. Made a big mistake.

Sam00: How bad?

LeoLoL: Pretty bad.

Sam00: Gitlab bad? As in wiping clean client servers?

LeoLoL: No. But a service went down. Socks weren't sold.

Sam00: That's fucking nothing. They can have mine. Are they giving you shit about that?

LeoLoL: Yeah.

Sam00: Who cares? You've built the aqueducts. Flush that shit out.

LeoLoL: Yeah, no.

Sam00: Seriously? Do you know how much time I've committed to your repo?

LeoLoL: Forked it?

Sam00: Fucked it.

Sam00: Put it back online. I'll make it pretty for you. Real pretty.

Sam00: Or, at least run some analyzers and let ReSharper do the work.

LeoLoL: That has never been a good idea

```
Sam00: I'm just pulling your leg. But put it
back up.

Sam00: I got to take my dog out for the daily
dumplings, but seriously, make it public
again. Add whatever improvements you've done,
and I'll get some more devs to join in on the
cleanup.

LeoLoL: Maybe

Sam00: That's a yes. TTYL, dog shit about to
fly.
```

"Wanna grab some coffee and Fika?" A cheerful voice interrupted Leo's thought. She jumped back, surprised by the new intruder. It had been a well-known fact that Leo preferred to be left alone and two surprise visits in a day were enough to induce a heart attack. Ola approached Leo's desk with Mikael in tow.

"Jumpy today?" Mikael asked and flashed his pearly whites. Tiny lines formed around his dark lashes; a charismatic trait popular among the few women in the office. Ola smiled wide and repeated his question in the warm choppy Danish accent that accompanied his fair complexion so well. Like a fairy. He brushed his blonde hair behind his ears, an elastic band around his wrist waiting to assemble his hair into a low bun. Leo couldn't decide if he looked like a front-end guy or a surfer. He was too slim and possibly frail to be a surfer. All programmers had frail wrists. He wouldn't be able to drag a surfboard around.

"I need a break." He nodded in the palm tree direction. The corner was quiet, the tropical storm settled. "Come join, we can see who broke a site the best."

"Come, as Ola said, who did better? Or worse?" Mikael beamed.

"Okay. Just give me a few minutes." It was Fika or going through emails with the possibility of another visit from David. She just wanted the day to end.

"Coolio!" Ola cheerily replied, "we'll wait by the Fat Boys."

"Not the IT support guys but the beanbags." Mikael underlined with a serious tone. Leo replied with an eye roll and a quick smile.

Alright, Sam, this is for you. Leo hurriedly located the settings for the repository and changed the Private setting to Public. Are you sure? GitHub asked. Nope. Doing it anyway, though. She sighed. One of the many emails had been from David, subject only.

Is it up yet?

She had set her status as away on Slack but suspected quite a few messages there as well. David was by the reception and kept glancing over at her desk, face red and eyes dark and piercing. She started a new deployment, copy-paste. Not her favorite way to do things, but it was better than the mandated USB transfer to an outdated client laptop they had done for a few years. "For security reasons." They had insisted. As if a random USB inserted once a week was an improvement. 'One entry point' had been the motto. How the entry was done seemed less important. Leo made a few changes to the code while on the terminal server. Felt badass. Maybe more ass than badass. She updated the repository while she was at it, some minor refactoring while waiting for the deployment to finish.

"Kom, vær med! We are leaving!" Ola waved her in, joined by Mikael and some sales guy she didn't recognize. She closed the lid on the laptop, fans angrily insisting they stay spinning, and located her sneakers by the entry door.

"Donuts?"

"Donuts!"

25

She kept the conversation to a minimum as they bought all the donuts left at the bakery. She got some for James and David. There was a hole in her stomach. A black hole, a pit. A general horrible feeling that kept sucking her in. No sweetness around it. For a moment, she almost regretted her career path. Maybe she should have done as her father had wanted her to. She grabbed three coffees and balanced them on top of the donut box, shaking her head no thanks when Mikael offered to help her carry.

"Peace offering?" He asked.

"It's that obvious?" Leo blushed.

"It's a gracious gesture." Mikael put his hand gently on her shoulder. "I would've appreciated it. Although, I'd prefer if you don't crash my site and only give me donuts." He laughed. Ola shot him a look that peeled off Mikael as if he was Teflon.

"That's not very nice of you, Mikael," he added.

"She knows I'm joking. Besides, look at her. She needs some cheering up." He tightened his grip slightly, making Leo flinch away.

Leo sneered at Mikael and made her way towards the office. She left some donuts and a coffee on David's desk.

Thankfully, David wasn't there. James, however, was. She didn't mind. She wanted to say she was sorry in person and see if he would accept the donuts as a manifestation of her conscience.

James was leaning over the desk, arms folded under his head, legs spread wide, keyboard under his chest. With eyes closed, he listened to the office ambiance and slowly drifted away mentally. The last few days replayed in his head a terrible movie that nobody wanted to see. A contemporary comedic tragedy, instead of a hopeful and inspiring movie- category unknown. Leo had highjacked the plot, even though he couldn't fault her too much. It had been a rushed fix, and he had been worried about her for a long time.

He had noticed the subtle nuances of her mood and she hadn't been happy for a long time. At first, he had tried to do something about it, but when Meron joined the plot, he had to shift focus. Even though his friendship with Meron had only existed for a few months, it had meant a lot to him, and he could not balance two relationships at the same time. But now both had gone to shit, and it stung that Meron had ghosted him. He had tried emailing, sending messages through the wide variety of social apps young kids used, but not a single reply. After the failed meetup, Meron had flipped on him.

Not because Leo had fucked up, but because of James' inability to listen. James disagreed, insisting otherwise, not wanting to be wrong.

"This is exactly what I mean," Meron had replied. "I'm telling you what the kids need, where they are at." He had raised his voice. He left James to clean up alone, as the attendees had already left. He assumed Meron just needed time to calm down. He was nowhere to be seen and couldn't be reached.

Leo approached James' desk and kicked his foot under the table.

"Sorry." She offered the coffee with both hands, the donuts tempting in a colorful box on the desk.

"Thanks," he mumbled.

"You okay?"

"No." A sullen reply.

"What's up? Besides, well, you know." Leo fumbled over her words.

"Meron is pissed at me. Guess the youth group isn't happening. I'm stuck just being a shitty consultant."

"Thanks." Leo placed the donuts on the desk.

"Didn't mean it like that," he replied.

"… it's okay. I know I'm a shitty consultant. Dunno about you, but it's safe to say I am." She paused and exhaled a laugh. Forceful and sharp. Like an exclamation mark. The end of a password. "I made the repo public again, pushed and deployed the changes. Up and running, all good. Fast and all."

"I'm surprised you made it public." He sat up and opened the box. Six donuts, four of them his favorite kind. Chocolate and sprinkles. He smiled.

"There is also an update. The security stuff," Leo said.

James took a bite and nodded. The sugar slowly absorbed and fed his energy.

"Do you mind doing a review?" Leo continued.

"Nah, don't mind." He was on his second donut.

"It's not a lot of code, just the authentication key support."

James paused. Swallowed a big bite and quickly flushed it down with some coffee and shifted his weight in the chair. Paused. No, she didn't… "Did you add the config file to the ignore file?"

"No changes to ignore file." Leo's eyebrows lifted.

James coughed and cleared his throat. "Leo, did you check in the auth keys for the client in a public repo?"

"I… I just add commit, like we always do…"

"… except it's not the same, this repo is public," James shrieked and covered his face in disbelief.

"Oh, shit." Leo gasped and met James' eyes. "Please tell me I didn't mess this up again."

"Fix, now." James pushed the donuts aside and grabbed Leo's arm. They ran to her desk and spun up the laptop.

"Are you in?" He paced back and forth.

"I'm on the client terminal server." Leo hid her shaking hands under the table.

"Doesn't matter. Rebase. Remove the file. Now!" James leaned in and took over.

"I think there is another one," Leo whispered.

"Push! Push!" James shouted.

"Done."

"Let's double-check. Clean out the repo and do a clean clone," James said intensely.

Leo's pulse was running high. Recursive delete, slow as a snail. James was checking the repo on his laptop.

"Looks good on GitHub. But we'll do a clean clone and verify the history is clean. Hope nobody saw that." A long sigh. "Got to check the fork history." James looked at Leo. She was biting her nails.

They waited. James was panting, and his hands were trembling. Leo's nails got shorter and shorter. He rubbed his eyes. "I'm exhausted."

"Head home, I've got this." Leo tapped the lid on her computer.

He furrowed his eyebrows and shook his head, his hair following the movement. "No, you don't."

They waited some more. James was rubbing his hands together.

"Cold?" Leo inquired.

"Maybe I'm getting sick."

"You should go home and sleep, James." Leo tried again.

He ignored her and stared at the terminal. "Argh, this is the slowest delete in human history."

"Go home, James. Here, have my donuts. I don't deserve them." Leo had gotten a separate box for herself, strawberry jam.

"That's true." He grabbed the box while reluctantly shutting the lid on his computer. "Keep me posted."

"I will, but get some sleep first." Leo tugged his sweater. "And James—"

"Yeah?"

"Sorry. And don't tell David, it'll give him a heart attack. The same goes for Mikael. I don't want a cheerleader full of advice." She sighed.

"Nobody wants that. We really shouldn't be checking in keys and passwords," James replied, letting the full weight of his exhaustion finally settle in.

"Tell David that." Leo echoed with a faint smile.

"No thanks. He'll just email them around and post them on post-its instead," he said with a tired smile.

Leo watched him disappear through the glass doors. She glanced at the computer. Still working. *What on earth was taking so long to delete the files?* A buzzing sound startled her. *Why am I on edge today?* The phone rattled a few inches closer to her, and she flipped it over.

Appointment changed:
Dr. Green Monday 16:00

Green? The phone number was from the dental practice. She didn't want to see a Dr. Green.

"Hi, Leo Larsson here. I'm calling about the changes to my appointment. I think there has been a mistake. Monday 16:00?"

"The doctor isn't available on that day." The blond receptionist answered.

"That's fine. I can book for a different day," she replied.

"He... errr... he requested you are transferred to Dr. Green."

Leo paused and looked out the window. Dark clouds, like last time. Maybe an omen.

"Why?"

"Green is free to see you at four on Monday. "

Why?

"Have a lovely day."

Leo had gripped the phone. She felt the blood return to her fingers as she let go of the iron grip. She rubbed them slowly while watching the pinkish color fade back to a sheer white. She felt cold and abandoned. He had abandoned her. *Was it something I said? Something I did? How could he just let somebody else take his place as if I'd let anybody in?* She caught her reflection in the window, covered in clouds. Plow mouth. She had turned him down. Indirect kink shamed him.

"Why are you grinning out the window?" Mikael walked by and offered a matching grin. Leo watched him walk away towards David. David winked him away with a half a donut, phone in the other hand, annoyed. That's when it happened. The donut dropped. David stood wide-mouthed, completely still, phone to his ear, donut on the floor. Complete silence. He slowly turned his head in her direction and locked eyes with hers. His eyes turned dark; his face followed suit with a muddy red. The phone dropped and David screamed, "LEONARDA?!!"

She jumped back. The laptop beeped. She looked down. The delete was done. Recursive from the root. Root was the main disk. Not the repo. She had Gitlabbed the server. The client-server was no more. Leo had deleted the client's server.

26

Approximately 10 years ago, 102 brown boxes arrived at the doorstep in a downtown London apartment. They were stacked, broad and high. As their own little building next to an old building on its last breath, barely keeping its balance on the cracked asphalt base. Leo had cried all the way home on the flight across the pond strapped in an iron bird in the sky, looking down at popcorn clouds and blue sea through tears.

Like a lifeless plum, her face wrinkled into a red and purple mess, and her marshmallow eyes pressed against the oval window, adding rain to an otherwise clear blue sky. As RyanAir wrapped up their third attempt at selling lottery tickets and did their famous vertical dive-landing with a bang, the crowd cheered and clapped in charter-trip-anno-2000 style. Some were happy to be alive, and a few were sincerely impressed by the straight vertical landing.

Leo did not clap.

She had hoped the landing would put an end to her misery, or preferably wake her up from the nightmare.

The nightmare would be moving from Sweden, not flying RyanAir. Although that would be perfectly a perfectly fine reason for a nightmare.

Later that day, she told herself it wasn't the move itself that was the problem. It was the removal of autonomy, even if just for a while, until she could adapt again, she concluded as she stood in her new bedroom looking out the dusty window. Could she adapt again? Until then, the room would be a cage, a prison. The walls were sticky and nicotine yellow. And the wall-to-wall carpet was moist and sticky. Like the dive pubs she used to go to in Sweden. She had been going there since she was barely 12, with a fake ID that was never shown as they did not ask her. Every step she took made this inaudible, squashy sound. Sticking to the soles of her feet, the carpet threatened to refuse her another step. A constant reminder that *you are stuck*, she concluded. The bed was too short. Are British people shorter? The queen was.

"We've talked with some connections at the art gallery, and they'd be happy to do a trial run. They need an assistant that can manage the deliveries." Leo's mom began unpacking some of the boxes.

"I'm not interested." Leo returned to the window and undid the long braid aggressively. Long strands of hair got caught in her chewed up nails, but she ignored the sacrifice and tore out the band from its strangling grip on her hair.

"Easy honey, you'll go bald if you keep doing that," her mom said softly and put down the sweater she was folding. "I know you want to work with computers, but wouldn't it be better to start with something easier and less stressful?" She placed a hand on Leo's shoulder." Last year was rough, little pie." Indeed, it had been. Leo had failed half her classes and barely got a pass after studying all summer. "It's the moving around, mom," Leo had told her mom each time she handed her the results. "It's okay, little pie," mom would reply with a poorly hidden disappointed look.

"What is happening in here? I'm a missing out on a *partay*?" A tall figure slid in through the open door. An outgrown cut and bouncy curls danced on his head. "I love your hair like that Leo!" Leo turned around for a second, shot her dad a daggering look and returned to the emptiness outside the window.

"I hate it," she said, and pulled her hair into a low ponytail.

"Your hair?" he replied and combed his curls with his fingers. Leo had the same color, same curls- albeit looser.

"Everything." Leo exhaled with an emphasis on the *e.*

Mom grabbed his arm. "She isn't keen on the assistant job."

"She isn't?" He turned around; head cocked to the side. "But honey, it's perfect for you! It's easy, pays well, and you can give that head of yours a break!" Leo sighed, dad continued. "Work with your body, instead of your head!" His laugh echoed in the room.

Leo looked at her frail stick figure arms. "This body?" she replied mockingly.

"Don't be negative! You'll get stronger! Build some muscles! Like Wonder Woman!" He flexed an invisible muscle hidden by a checkered, wrinkled shirt.

"A fictional heroine fighting bad guys in her underwear. Seems like a fitting aspiration for your daughter," Leo replied.

"A strong heroine!" he huffed.

"Why stronger, not smarter?" Leo questioned.

"Well…" he scratched his head and looked at his wife, "engineering isn't for everyone. Maybe you should try something different?" Leo's mom shook her head at him, and his voice trailed off, wrapped in defeat.

The next day, Leo cut her hair at a hairdresser around the corner. The kind of place that only knew two haircuts.

A month later Leo took her boxes, and moved to a new place, for a new job where no questions were asked. Because consultants in Peterborough were few and far

between, and Swedes, as they assumed, were tech geniuses that spoke the truth of the binary father (and mother).

Sleepily squinting at the ceiling, from her king-sized bed, 10 years later, Leo could see two of the boxes in the kitchen ready for the next move that never came. She would have to know where she was going first. Chances were, it would be programmer hell, for wiping the servers. She closed her eyes and let out a long sigh. *Ten years, but neither stronger nor smarter,* she concluded and fell back asleep.

27

By the time Leo arrived Julia had brushed out the wrinkles on her skirt at least ten times.

Leo wore the usual jeans and T-shirt reminding Julia of the first time they met, which also had been the third or fourth time. Leo came empty-handed. No folded bike, no laptop bag. She was prepared for a quick entry and departure. In other words, this was not a Ryan Air stay.

Julia stretched out her hand and gave Leo a sad smile and a head tilt. "Hi Leo…"

Leo glanced at the hand but quickly moved her focus behind Julia. Julia dropped her greeting attempt and wiped her hand on her skirt.

"I'm glad you could come on such short notice. David is waiting for us in the blue conference room." Ola and a few other colleagues approached but Julia tried to shush them away nervously.

"Is it time?" Ola asked. He seemed to be the pack leader.

"No," Julia replied and grabbed Leo's arm, "not now!"

Leo remained silent and let Julia's warm grip escort her to the conference room.

"Freshly painted," Julia said. "Blue has a calming effect."

Leo noticed David fuming in the corner, "Does he know?"

"Hi, Leo. Sit down." David pointed to an empty seat on the far end of the table. An ocean of chairs between them. No lifebuoy in sight. Sink or swim. Probably just sink.

David started, "Leo. I'll keep this short as we all know why we are having this meeting. I've got no choice but to let you go after the incident with the servers." Julia nodded slowly and pressed her thin lips together into two parallel lines. "You'll get everything in writing but for now do you have any questions?"

Leo looked at the table. Scuff marks and coffee stains, "Aren't you supposed to give me a warning at least?"

David opened his mouth, taken aback, and looked at Julia. Julia paused and thought for a moment. David tapped his pen aggressively on the table and stared intently at Julia. He gave up and turned around, facing Leo. "I can always give you a warning and demote you to support. But I'm guessing that's not your cup of tea," he said slowly and flicked the pen across the table. It rolled off the table and disappeared with a suicidal leap.

"Demoted? I thought support was the most important job at the company?"

"Do you want it?" David's eyes narrowed.

"No," Leo replied flat.

"Well then. You are fired, Leo."

Julia got up slowly and opened the door. "Leo, I'll send you the paperwork. And a questionnaire regarding the firing. How it was, what we can do better. The usual." She waved and disappeared out the door. Leo and David stared at each other for a long time.

"We shouldn't have direct access to client servers," Leo whispered into the thick air.

Shocked that she could be so brazen David air quoted, "'We', shouldn't do a mass delete without verifying that we are on the correct machine."

They spent more time in silence. The clock on the wall ticked. Soon lunch.

Leo broke the silence. "Out of curiosity, who is taking over my role?"

"Mikael," David responded with a straight face.

Leo shook her head, stood up, and walked out with a goodbye-nod.

Leo had barely made it out of the conference room when a group of people approached her. Her colleagues from earlier. With what looked like a cake.

Julia was at the forefront. "Leo! We have a surprise for you!" She held out the cake.

Ola stepped forward with a lowered head, "Leo, we are so sorry to see you go…"

Amanda joined him and gestured towards the cake, "We made you a goodbye cake!" she chirped and batted her eyelashes. The cake had a figure in the middle, a woman in a wedding dress, with decorations that made her look like she was on fire.

Ola explained, "They only had brides at the bakery. We made it look like fire because you got fired. Get it?" He smiled big and combed his hair with his fingers. "She is fire-d…"

Amanda continued, "…and she looks like you! Except for the dress, of course. But look! Like a bride Leo!"

Leo looked at the fire exit, considered making a run for it, not fully computing the gesture, "I'm not going anywhere yet. I have one month's notice."

"Oh." Frank looked around, scratched his shoulder, "We assumed you'd want to go immediately."

"And why is that?" Leo curled her lips and bit the inside of her lower lip.

"We can save the cake for your last day. It's no problem," Amanda interrupted, flustered.

Leo looked at the cake, then at the crowd.
"I'm lactose intolerant."

28

David followed Julia to the kitchen with the stack of plates clattering with busy gossip.

Julia waited for David and grabbed the plates off his hands, "Well, that certainly didn't go as planned."

David looked back at the little crowd that had dispersed and the figurine on fire left on a plate. The fire had burned out, and the cake bride was left alone in a messy dress. David threw the figurine in a bin after looking at it for a while, contemplating if he should rinse the figurine and give it to Leo.

"No, it didn't," David whispered and made eye contact with Cake-Leo in the bin.

Julia crossed her arms, "I wish you had run the speech by me first."

David had unprompted given a farewell speech during the cake cutting. As the boss of the bride.

"We are sad to see you leave Leo, and we hope you'll find a workplace as welcoming as ConsultIt." Leo had a puzzled look on her face, as if she was unsure if he was being genuine or sarcastic. Maybe genuinely sarcastic. Or sarcastically genuine.

He had continued, "And I can't believe it has been three years already!"

"Ten. I've worked here ten years," Leo had interrupted.

"Are you sure?" A flustered David had asked.

"I interviewed Mikael, remember? And he just got his five-year anniversary present three weeks ago." A too-tight workout T-shirt in the same glazed fabric David liked to wear to show of protruding workout nipples. Leo hated it. Mikael wore it at least once a week.

"Ah, if you say so. Ten years! You certainly know how to leave with a Big Bang." David laughed but went silent when Julie gave him a death glare.

"Don't hold off on the pyroshow for me," Leo replied dryly, and peeled off a corner of lactose free frosting.

Julia had stepped in front of David and, with a trembling voice, interrupted his genius outburst, "I think I can speak for all of us, David included, that we are sad to see you go and wish you all the best." She had nodded harder than a whiplash before correcting herself, "In two weeks, of course, not yet."

Julia pulled David back from his mental time-travel and cringed at the thought of the speech. "It's probably for the best, if you leave the speech part to HR, next time." She patted him on the shoulder and met his glare, "It was bad, really bad."

"Was I too harsh on her when we fired her?"

"I would say so, yes." Julia went back to her usual nodding. "I'm not sure it even was the correct choice. To fire her." Julia avoided eye contact and put away the last few glasses on the countertop.

"Brian would disagree."

"Did firing her fix the situation?" Julia prodded.

"No… but— "

"Then I don't really know why we did it. We've been struggling to hire good developers. Any developer."

"But — "David tried again.

"How do the kids call it? A *dick move*? Something like that. Don't be a dick, Dave." Julia's face was red, and she

clearly avoided eye contact and frantically cleaned the countertop with a moldy, wet sponge. It smelled like cat piss. Somebody had claimed that microwaving a sponge would like the bacteria and therefore it could be reused. To reduce waste. The bacteria had laughed a sick laughter and continued to rub its ass on any surface graced by the five months old sponge. It smelled like Cheese Doodles and rotten horse manure.

David's eyebrows helicoptered, eyes widened, and he paused for the longest time before replying, "It was a mistake, wasn't it?" He rubbed his hands nervously. "I can't undo it. I've already told Brian. Everybody."

Julia turned and faced him, "No. Yes, it can't be undone. It's a lesson for next time. It is the first time we've fired anybody. And I get it, we don't fire developers, they fire us."

Fire us? David looked as confused as a fart in a fan factory.

Julia ignored him and continued, "You should give her a call. When you are in a better place. And settle things nicely." She waited for a reply, but none came. "If not to be kind, then just to make sure the rumor doesn't spread. Like shit on a fan like the Australians say."

"I'm fairly confident they don't say that." David replied flat.

"Call her. I'll add it to your calendar. Ask James to help you with Leo, he is good with people, you… not so much." Julia left the kitchen spotless, but David's mind a mess.

29

The intercom buzzed aggressively for the third time and Leo slowly logrolled out of bed. It would minimize the engagement of the core muscles which Leo had none of. A glimpse in the window showed messy hair with a fringe that had grown too long and flat and a face that had been pressed against the pillow for weeks. It was safe to say she looked like shit but at least Lion still loved her - if fed.

"It's James." The intercom speaker sent through a raspy version of James' voice with a clicking sound at the start of each word.

"What do you want?" Leo sullenly asked.

"Your soul." Quick reply.

"I don't have one. I've been a consultant for the last ten years." She said pressing heavily against the intercom button.

"Then give me your Azure support email."

"Bye James." Not in the mood and anxious to get back to bed.

She clicked the intercom off. Half a breath later, it buzzed again.

Unsurprisingly, it was James. "Let me in, I just want to see that you are okay."

"I'd rather not," Leo hissed.

"I'll pay with donuts," James pleaded.

"I'm not a prostitute."

James laughed, "I thought you said you were a consultant?"

Leo suppressed a smile. She whispered back, "You got coffee?"

"I've got coffee. And treats for the cat." Crackling sounds through the intercom caught Lion's attention.

Leo caved. A sacrifice. For Lion. "Just a second," she moaned.

Leo ran to the bathroom, splashed water on her face - a tad too cold and forced her hair into a high bun. Only half of it made it. The rest was too short. Her fringe had gotten long enough to be reunited with the rest of the hair in a messy but trendy half-bun. A trendy latte mum in mum jeans. Her face felt oddly bare. The breath test didn't pass, and she took a bite straight from the toothpaste tube, regretting it immediately, and gurgled it around with a handful of water. It would have been easier to just brush her teeth. And less disgusting.

Back at the buzzer, she pressed the button longer than required until she heard footsteps at the bottom of the stone stairs. You could hear anything and everything in this building, except, of course, from her apartment. Nothing exciting ever happened there.

Leo opened the door, "Wow, Leo. You look awful," James exclaimed as his head popped up from the stairs.

"Thanks?" A puzzled look on her face.

"Here, life support." The donut box he offered was from an unknown shop. She lifted the lid and approved the jam donuts and some colorful donuts that came with an insulin shot. She really should have brushed her teeth first. Not that it mattered. Martin had abandoned plow mouth and had handed her over to a blind date with Green. An image of her soaked bra made her blush. Not

every day you forget your bra at the dentist. It sounded more exciting than it had been.

James pushed past her with a paper bag containing coffee. The smell filled the apartment, quickly absorbed by the odor from the cat litter pile in the bathroom.

James scrunched his nose and waved a hand in front of his face, dramatically. "What is that smell?"

"You are on a roll with the compliments today." Leo sighed.

"No, for real. Where does the smell from?" He sniffed around and ignored Leo's attempt at redirecting him. He stood in the bathroom doorway. "I see. It's like that."

"Like what?" Leo looked past him. A ginormous pile of clothes was trying to escape through the ceiling ventilation in the far corner of the bathroom.

"You aren't doing good. Is Betty even alive?" James made his way to the kitchen.

Betty had been created with only water and rye, many years ago and had been a weekly trusted sourdough contributor and pet. Betty was now a sad and crusted nail polish remover smelling creature hidden in the back of the fridge. James pulled her out without asking and jumped back as the lid came undone after much force. The smell filled the kitchen. Acetone.

"They wrote on Slack that it was a mutual agreement, that you had looked for new opportunities. But then they posted a gallery with the cake. Leo on fire. Not something you'd do volunteering, right?" James scooped out the crusty mold at the top and took a quick whiff, a moment of self-torture. He looked through the cabinets. "Do you have a clean jar?"

"Drawer to the left." Leo opened the cabinet next to the fridge where a shelf of neatly organized glass jars had been collected from dust. She couldn't be bothered recycling them, nor had the conscience to throw them, and consequently she collected them convinced that one day she'd have enough friends to share her well-kept

169

sourdough starter, Betty. James added the rest of Betty to a dusty jar and added water and some rye. Leo watched him carefully mix Betty back to life in a new jar, lid unscrewed, waiting for life signs and bubbles. They had talked a lot about sourdough baking. At first, she had been surprised that he was a sourdough artesian. But it made sense.

"I'm a hipster. Of course, I make my sourdough bread," he had said with a wink.

"It's the only long-term relationship I've been able to maintain, besides my strange, but enticing, dentist," Leo had replied. Ah, memories. Leo turned her attention to James and left the past at rest.

"Azure support was a pain. We didn't have the appropriate authorization for the resources, the client didn't have any manual backups, so we relied on whatever Azure did in the background on their failovers. David hacked your email to get a hold of support. You never check your emails, do you?"

Leo chewed down on a donut, deflecting like a true master, "How are things with Meron?"

James grabbed a chair, pulled out the other one, and gestured for her to sit. The warmth from the coffee spread to his fingers. He took a long sip and looked at the entrance where Lion lazily slept in a new corner. Lion had yet to enjoy the snacks James brought.

"Have heard nothing. He won't reply." He looked like a little boy with the sunlight as a backdrop, rounded shoulders, legs crossed at the ankle. Coffee held with two hands, looking down. Leo noticed he didn't wear a fun t-shirt under his overshirt. She had never seen him in a plain T-shirt. Hers had a fat cat on it which she had slept and lived in it for almost a week.

"I just want to apologize. And make sure he is okay." He finally said out loud.

"My dad works at his university." Leo did not know why she shared that.

James looked up. "Really?"

"Yeah. Bigshot. That's why we moved here. We don't talk either."

"Your dad doesn't want to talk to you?" He asked surprised at her candor.

"He wants to talk, I don't. I went low contact when we moved here."

"Did he fuck up royally, like I did?"

Leo bit her lip and looked intently out the window as if staring at an old photo. "We had a falling out a few years ago. He didn't like my career choice." She shrugged her shoulders.

"A few years ago?"

"Ten."

James laughed quietly, "That's not a few years. Must have been serious. What did he do?"

"He…" Leo's voice trailed off. James held his breath. "He thinks I'm stupid. A disappointment. A cliché, I know. He had bigger dreams for me, but I was never a good student. And he gave up on me. Told me to give up."

James didn't know what to say. He scooched closer and patted her on her back. "That's awful. I would have been extremely hurt if my dad had told me that."

Leo continued, "He didn't say those specific words. But he said it in other words. Computer Science, maybe it's not for you, Leo." Leo mocked her dads voice poorly.

"Why did he want you to drop your studies?"

Leo hid her face in her hands, "Because I'm stupid."

"Did he say that?"

Leo peeked between her fingers. James wasn't ridiculing her, he seemed genuinely interested. "As I said," she breathed in her hands, "he didn't use those words, but sometimes you don't have to."

"Ten years is a long time," James concluded. "Maybe he is hoping you'll reach out just like I'm hoping Meron will let me apologize." He got up and filled a glass with water and took a sip. Leo watched him, her hands resting on the table. "Just a thought," he said.

"Let's think about something else," Leo forced a smile. "I'd rather talk about Meron, work, or anything else."

"Alright. I won't push it," James smiled and accepted the redirection. "By the way, any new pushes? How's the library going?"

She knew he knew there was nothing to know, but this was her only way out of the intimate conversation.

"Nothing is happening, not from my side, anyway. Caused enough trouble. I'm on vacay."

"Staycation?"

"Yea. Staycation. Cheaper than a real vacation." She replied.

"Perfect. Then you have time to work on the library! Add some more admin maintainers, delegate responsibility, let the library live its own life. Make Sam happy." James said with a hint of forced enthusiasm.

Sam. She hadn't talked to Sam since the epic failure day.

"Maybe you should finish unpacking instead." James pointed at the boxes in the corner. "Didn't know you had moved."

"I've lived here for years." Leo shoved a diary sticking out into the box and folded the top in, shoving the box shut before it ricocheted back to its original opened state.

James leaned back, forcing the chair to lean with him with a threatening squeaky sound. Leo initially had three chairs but one of them broke during a lightbulb change. The legs had folded out into a double pancake split (the legs of the chair, that is). Leo was far from flexible. If it were to collapse, she would waggle on the floor on her back like a tortoise. The broken chair had remained in the apartment by the entrance for a year before she figured out where to throw it away. If it wasn't for the complicated disposal when you don't own a car, she wouldn't have been bothered by the loss. However, she would mind if a second chair broke. Just in case she had company again. An unlikely thought that now seemed more enticing after

James' surprise visit. "What are the boxes for?" James continued.

"Just books, don't know where to put them." She said as she looked at the boxes.

"Any good ones?" James asked.

"Nah. Unless you like to read the anxious thoughts of a Swedish teenager."

"My favorite type of reading. What does your dad do?" Changing the subject.

Leo pretended to organize some glasses in the cabinet by shuffling them. There were no matching glasses and for a moment, she thought about how that described her life right now. Messy, unmatched, and unorganized. In contrast to the life of her parents. James waited patiently, body facing her, eyes focusing on the last dying bubbles in his complicated coffee order.

"He is an art professor. Teaches, writes books, research. My mother does the same." Leo finally replied, accepting James hadn't given up on her family drama.

"I had a feeling you came from a smart family. Didn't think you came from an artistic family, though. Not with your three-color palette. If one would consider white a color," James winked.

She shook her head in response, "The pressure was there. They weren't happy with me studying computer science and failing repeatedly." Leo opened another cabinet and paused. "I think they'd rather have me be a suffering artist or caretaker of sorts, than a half-ass slave to the computer. I barely made it through uni. Wouldn't have made it without a therapist and online classes. We moved around a lot. Never stayed for more than a year. Never unpacked. I probably never will."

"I can tell. Your apartment is very empty." He said softly.

Leo closed the cabinet slowly, wiped her hands on her pants, and looked around. Yes, it is. "But it's not the same though, is it?" Leo's voice trembled, and she hid behind

her coffee. "This is by choice, not by abandonment," she whispered into the cup. She swallowed and looked up, meeting James' eyes. "Well, it's obvious I'm not that smart, right? Considering my parting events at work." A tense laugh unfolded from her vocal cords, mimicking a choking frog.

James pressed his lips together in a tight smile and nodded in agreement, "Don't let the sock shop thing get to you. If Gitlab did it, so can you." He gestured with a very warm smile. Redness spread to her cheeks, and she turned around again, looking for more things to organize. Unfortunately, there wasn't much.

"They fired me, James, that's pretty evident of my capabilities. That's how bad it is." She bit the inside of her cheek. "And if I remember correctly, GitLab never fired anybody. They just said shit happens. In theory, it should be impossible to fire a programmer nowadays, in particular a consultant. I mean, Mikael is still around but I'm not."

"Well, I guess an upside is that you don't have to deal with him anymore," James suggested as a low effort consolation. "And his code smells."

"Mikael? Already forgotten about him. I've got my smells in the library." She half-laughed.

"Then fix them. I'll even lend you my best stopwatch and gut feeling." Another kind offer.

Leo laughed and let out a snort.

"Thanks for cheering me up." She looked at him intently with a big smile.

"You are welcome." He leaned into his success, nearly tipping the chair over.

They sat in silence for a long time, both scrolling on their phone taking an occasional sip from their lukewarm coffees, interrupted by Leo's yawns. There was no awkward silence. They were programmers after all and silence was something they did well.

"No work today?" Leo stretched her legs and felt the warm fur from Lion. He had moved unbeknownst to them. Cat ninja.

"It's Saturday."

"Oh." She confirmed the day by looking at her blank calendar. She had dedicated her life as a developer to be passionate about avoiding meetings of any kind but she kind of missed standup. Or sit down. She closed the calendar app and swallowed.

James tilted his head and looked up at her, "You alright? You look shattered."

Meeting his gaze, "Compliments aren't your thing, are they?"

"I guess not." James nodded, his hair bowing with the movement like a Mexican wave.

It was an accurate observation. Leo was depleted. She had no routine now, as it had been solely based on what series she was currently binging on Netflix.

Leo rubbed her eyes, "I think I'm going to lie down and rest a little."

"Okay, cool. Do so." James didn't look up. He wasn't leaving. The sourdough was on the table, a tiny bubble building by the edge.

"OK…" Leo paused. Waited for some sort of action, not sure what to do.

"Do you mind?" He looked up at her, gestured towards himself sitting there in the kitchen as if he had become permanent décor. His khaki shorts folded to fit above the knee with busy side pockets, melted in with the walls behind him. A mint green shirt in thin cotton framed his white t-shirt like two curtains.

Mint green is a difficult color, a shout-out to the 90's with an attempt made every spring to become it fashionable again. It always failed but James had managed to put together something that worked. Maybe he could help decorate the apartment.

Leo yawned again, shrugged her shoulders, and dragged herself to the bed in the corner of the living room, which unfortunately had a direct view of the kitchen and James. She pulled the covers to her nose, immediately feeling overwhelmed with tiredness once the soft covers covered her body.

She could hear James in the kitchen and through sleepy eyes could see his outline looking for something in his backpack. Not a camera, hopefully. However, this would be the most boring video ever recorded in human history. She slept like a corpse, rarely moved a limb, made no sound, steady stream of warmth created, and blended with the covers. Something her cat loved her for. The perfect cat mattress. Unless, of course, she was drunk or hungover. Then all hell broke loose, and she would sweat and Cirque Du Soleil in her bed like a menopausal lunatic with a gymnastic flair. She fell asleep wondering if she felt oddly creeped out, or oddly comforted, that James was in her kitchen.

Lion joined her in bed. He covered half her face and they both drifted off to the humming sound of her cat's purr as Lion secretly contemplated how to best dispose of the intruder. As always, a murderous asshole waiting for the perfect opportunity.

30

She had no idea how long she had slept for. It could have been five minutes or five hours. She was just as tired as when she had fallen asleep. Some left-over cat hair tickled her face, and a few had attached themselves to her dry lips, resembling a light mustache. The familiar sound of James' keyboard echoed in the kitchen, barely heard as her stomach pleaded for food with loud rumbling noises.

"You hungry?" James' voice found its way to the living room from the kitchen. Is the rumbling that loud? "I'm starving," he continued. "There is an awesome pizza place around the corner. I'm sure you've tried it. They have sourdough pizza. I can place an order, go grab it as you freshen up."

I guess he is moving in. "Sure." She had tried the pizza place, it was decent.

"Any preferences?" He asked.

"Not really."

"Vegetarian good?"

She nodded but realized he couldn't possibly see her nodding while she was lying in the bed. The body felt too heavy to move. "Yes, that works," she yelled.

"Done! I'll go now, takes max 10. Can I grab your keys?"

He was out the door in less than five minutes and Leo rushed to take a fast shower and change her clothes. No laundry had been done since the big event and she smelled her way through the pile to identify something that wasn't too bad. It was either wearing dirty clothes or wearing the only dress she owned, a dress that had never been worn and was simply a reminder of her parents' obliviousness to her wardrobe choices and her style. Dirty clothes it is. She chucked the dress in the laundry basket, dust leaving a trail in the air as it collapsed as it embraced the loneliness among the t-shirts and jeans. She barely finished her transformation before James was back.

"You look fresh!" James exclaimed as he balanced two pizza boxes in his hand. He gave the front door a little kick to close it.

Fresh resulted from a two-minute shower, hair parted and brushed, a dab of 4-year-old moisturizer, and aggressive flossing and brushing of the plow. Fresh outfit consisted of the same pair of jeans she had worn before but in a different shade and a T-shirt that looked less worn compared to the one she had shamefully donned earlier. She promised herself that she would do laundry later that night or tomorrow morning. *Why do today what you can procrastinate until tomorrow, right? Because you're going to run out of clothes and get a surprise visitor that refuses to leave your home.* Thought ignored. Leo was the master procrastinator. Everything from laundry to going to bed. Revenge bedtime procrastination. She had read an article about the modern phenomenon. When you stay up to make up for lack of perceived free time. She had plenty of free time now but had yet to find an adult routine. There was nothing to revenge.

James walked into the kitchen, trailing with the smell of sourdough pizza. "Met your neighbors, nice people! They thought your apartment was vacant."

"No! You said hi to them?" Leo sighed and shook her head vigorously. "Now I'll be forced to say hi as well." She

bit the nail on her thumb and met James' disapproving look.

"That's not food."

"Is to me." She said and watched him slice a pizza. She grabbed two plates. One blue, one white. In a corner, James' computer buzzed happily. He had been coding.

"Work?"

James answered, big grin on his face, "Nope. Your library. I have an idea; I'll show you later."

Leo couldn't wait and had him alternate between a greasy pizza slice and his laptop, leaving sticky prints all over the keyboard. You'd think he'd care more, as a keyboard slave, but on the contrary, he had had so many laptops none of them had much value. Leo, like James, had yet to find a laptop that would last more than two years running the software she needed. Consultants don't have desktop computers, David had insisted. Even though they rarely met up with clients anywhere else than the office. That's a fact. There is something symbolic about having a razor-thin laptop that doesn't meet your needs but looks fancy and cool. Like most developers, she'd used it to RDP into her desktop computer at home to do the work there.

"It was Sam's idea," James explained and licked his fingers. "He suggested we add an interface so people can add their customized clearing logic. At first, I couldn't make it work, and I didn't know why. But now it works, and I don't know why!"

"If it works, then do not question the binary father. Or mother." Leo smiled.

"By the way, is he pissed with me?" She had to ask.

"He seemed more worried."

"Oh?"

"He asked about you. He figured we were colleagues since we both contributed to the one and only ConsultIt repo." He giggled and Leo involuntarily let the corners of her mouth pull upwards to what could be described as a

smile. The repo was a public embarrassment, but David wanted to join the Open-Source train (Microsoft does it!) and had even encouraged potential employees to do a pull with their tech interview assignment. Mikael's contribution after the hundredth interview had gathered some interesting remarks in the admin service. He had indeed simply removed the static modifier and confirmed his ego with happy path tests. It was annoying and charming at the same time, his naïvety or blind confidence. Enough to get hired and do 'zero inbox' lunches. It had been merged and celebrated with a month of debugging before it was reverted.

Leo nodded, "Nice detective work! Should I be impressed or creeped out by Sam's efforts?"

"Sam thought you'd hurt yourself." James confessed.

"Why's that?" Leo's eyebrows lifted.

"Cause you sent him a 417 HTTP request code as your last message." He replied.

"I'm a teapot?" Eyebrows still raised.

"No, that's not the I'm a teapot code."

"Yes, it is. "

"No. 418 is, I'm a teapot."

"You sure?"

"Yes", James pulled up the HTTP codes spec and scrolled down to 418.

"417…expectation failed," Leo read out loud. "Not completely wrong though, is it?"

"A bit suicidal maybe? As a final message? Leo, ping Sam. I dunno why but that guy cares about you." James added.

"He has a crush on me?"

"I didn't get any crush vibes, but then again, I'm not good with that stuff."

"Don't you have a crush on, Meron?" Leo asked.

"A nerd crush maybe, but not more. He is a kid."
James put his half-eaten slice down and looked at Leo.

"Can you see if you can get a hold of his contact details through your dad?"

Leo couldn't say no. He had fed her. And the cat, although James probably didn't notice a slice had magically disappeared. "I'll try."

"And ping Sam?"

"Maybe."

"Unless you want me to move in permanently?" James insisted with a bit of coercion.

"Not really. How much pizza and donuts can you pay with though?" Leo rebutted with a smirk.

"I don't trust consultants, they always overcharge."

"Good, I'm fired then." Leo poked James' shoulder, pretending to fire a shot.

They continued going through the code, a silent agreement had been made. The pizza got cold, the coffee had been thrown out, and the cat had shifted to a different window following the sun.

"I'm going to grab the next metro at half-past. Seems like a suicide watch isn't needed if you are a teapot." James folded the laptop and put it hot into his backpack, fans still spinning. Probably windows update. "Wanna walk me to the station? Get some fresh air?"

"There isn't any in the subway." Sarcasm colored Leo's reply. She had never been a fan of the London Underground, summer, or winter.

"Care for a walk to the station, then? Without entering the devil's hole."

"Asshole you mean?" She flashed a wide smile before quickly returning to her expressionless state.

"Just give me a second and I'll get ready."

"Developer seconds?"

"Yup."

"Alright, anything between 10 minutes and 10 hours then." James did the dishes to keep himself busy, two plates, glasses, and cutlery. Leo grabbed her laptop bag and

charger and left a dust cloud as she brushed the bag free from silvery powder. She hadn't even opened her bag since she came home that day. James interrupted the deepening pit in her stomach.

"Bringing the workhorse?" He asked.

"Rather, the donkey."

"Nice. Where are you heading?"

"Some café. Might as well get some social anxiety training today."

He nodded approvingly and opened the door, "I made a copy of your keys."

"Wha..?"

"Just kidding. Here, thanks for having me over." He said as he placed the keys in her hands.

They walked in unison down the stone stairs and met the crisp air in an embrace as the entrance door opened and revealed a beautiful afternoon. Leo had never entered or left the apartment with somebody else (besides London rats and an occasional cat, sometimes combined). It was a strange but comforting feeling.

"Just give me a second. Wait here." She turned around, went to the letter-boxes, and grabbed Mary's mail. "Be right back!" She yelled and ran up the stairs.

When she came back down, James was looking at her inquisitively.

"Don't ask." She pulled James with her. "Lounge café is pretty good", she explained, "stable Wi-Fi- not the London cloud crap and excellent coffee. Free refill if it's brew."

"That's quite American."

"Less sugary though."

"I'll walk you there, then suffer the underground on my own teapot."

They walked for a while in silence. James seemed to know where the café was located.

"Has it ever occurred to you that you guys drive on the wrong side of the road?" Leo pointed at the crosswalk ahead.

"No, this is the right side," James countered shaking his head.

They stopped at the crosswalk, waiting for the traffic light, "If it's the right side though, it's the left side, then how come the sign says, you let people know to look the other way?" Look the other way was painted in white aggressive letters.

"Because of the Swedes of course," James laughed. "It's always the Swedes." Leo didn't get it but she laughed nonetheless. The lights turned green, and she tucked her fringe behind her ears and skipped across the street. It was a fine day to be a teapot.

31

Hi Sam!

Sorry for leaving you the wrong HTTP code in the chat. James came by today and let me know that I wasn't as fluent in the spec as I'd like to think. It was supposed to be 418, I'm a teapot. As in, I'm a joke. As I'm sure James told you I got fired over my latest mistake (which is something I'd rather not talk about, let's just say I Gitlabbed a customer). My old asshole boss sent him, but I still don't know how James figured out where I live. I'll just assume that HR has some GDPR compliance to work out. James is cool though. Boss-man, not so much. Anyways, thanks for maintaining the code while I was away, I'm eager to get back to working on the lib after an inspiriting visit. Did you see the last merge? Also, apologies for sending an email. I'm too anxious to join the discord server at the moment. Having James over for a full day was more than my month's quota of social interaction. I'm sure you understand. TTYL, Leo

Leo the teapot! Email? Is this the 90's? But hey, lucky you! You sent me an email on one of

the few days I check my inbox. Glad to hear
you're doing well. Got me worried for a while.
I know we've only talked about code and cats
but is there anything I can do for you?
Looking for new opportunities? Cheers, Sam

Sam, nice to see I'm not the only one rarely
checking my email. Although, I must admit I'm
currently refreshing. The 90s? Where were you
even around then? Sam00? And how did this turn
into a chat (I don't mind, I like the freedom
to be able to pretend I got too busy to check
instead of leaving others on read haha)?

As for opportunities? I've had plenty of
recruiters asking me if I'm looking for new
opportunities. They are like piranhas,
smelling a wounded teapot. Right now, I'm not.
I'm on a break. From what? Not sure. From
David probably (annoying boss-man). James
showed me the new feature for the library that
he discussed with you (was it your idea?). Did
a live code review and all. Fancy, I know! I'm
almost proud. Looks great, merging it as we
speak. I'm going to take on the many
maintenance issues, clean up the library real
nicely. Tests and all. I'm beginning to think
this is fun. / Leo

I was around then, 00 is hexadecimal not year.
And how are you doing? You didn't answer the
question.

NUL? Clever. Binary and hexadecimal have never
been my thing although school spent some time
explaining that repeatedly. Ugh, I do not miss
school. I'm good, better. Alright, I guess.
Bruised ego, nothing was broken. James fed me;
food makes me happy. And fed Betty.

Who is Betty? And thanks, nice to hear. I'll
keep an eye out for your pull requests. And
Leo, don't go MIA again. Ping me, whatever you

need. You've got a friend here. Seems like
James is one as well, albeit in real life.

Sorry, should have mentioned that Betty is my
sourdough starter.

Hah, I sort of assumed you'd be that type of
person. A little bit hipster.

I'm not a hipster. James is.

Do you brew your beer?

No. But I do like craft beer. And wine.

Hipster, Leo. That'll be your new name. Don't
worry, I won't tell anybody.

This conversation never happened. I'm going to
code now.

See you around teapot!

32

"Having a good day?" A server smiled sweetly while picking up the black empty plates from Leo's table. Only one had belonged to Leo, but the table next to her table had been full of plates and cups.

Leo had considered stacking them and handing them over to whoever worked there, but that would consist of a) the possibility that she would annoy the server if she stacked the plates and thus greased up both sides of the plates, and b) social interaction with a stranger. She was now embarrassed she had set up camp there, next to the dump, seemingly unbothered.

The server hid her judgment, alternatively didn't care. "Good day," she repeated gently but louder with a joyous clang that perfectly matched her sunny face.

Her hair was a gingerly masterpiece with curls that surrounded her head with a glorious frizzy halo. Her many freckles made her look tan and blended in with her wide smile with equally wide dentures. *I guess that's what Martin wanted me to have.* Leo hadn't noticed she had been sitting there smiling like a crazy person but was now fully aware her oddly shaped teeth were on display. Nobody randomly smiles while by themselves. Not in Britain, anyway. And

certainly not in Sweden. They'd probably change your citizenship status. However, Leo was having a good day, a surprisingly good day. It was almost an out-of-body experience in fact.

The server eagerly waited for a reply, shining a nauseating amount of friendliness on Leo. Leo had found a seat in the corner where she had hoped to sit undisturbed but near the router. Leo gave in. "The mud cake was delicious." Her voice had a hint of shakiness to it but masked well by her genuine, joyous expression.

"It's my favorite as well," the server agreed with a hand firmly placed on her chest. "Sometimes they make it with walnuts or even macadamia nuts - my favorite! It's heaven on earth." That did indeed sound amazingly tempting. The server didn't seem to be in a rush and continued, "There is a new batch fresh from the oven now. I can bring you a tin square to taste if you'd like?"

Leo nodded, "I'd love that, thank you."

The server, Sky L. according to her name tag, disappeared with tiny but quick steps towards the kitchen with plates and cups balanced neatly on a tray, a ballerina with a mission. *Sky.* Leo reflected on the email conversation with Sam, friendly, as with Sky, although the server was extraordinarily chatty and cheery. Sam seemed chattier in terms of the repository. Oddly interested in her little library that had grown into its own ecosystem inhabited by developers from all over the world. Most of them either complained or wanted more features. James and Sam were one of the few that contributed with solutions.

Leo returned her attention to the computer screen, completely forgetting about the mud cake. James' pull request had been approved by Sam, with just a few comments and to-dos sprinkled for flavor. With her fingers dancing across the keyboard and her favorite music in her ears, she elegantly added some fixes and merged with an elevated pulse. Sky placed a slice of mud cake in

front of her with a dramatic bow and a wide smile. The cake arrived just in time to celebrate. The library had received its first major update since its release. Leo put down her headphones and uttered a *Wow* when she saw the slice.

"That's an enormous piece!"

"It's on me. I just got some good news today and the manager is not in." Sky replied with a smile.

"You seem thrilled!" That was an understatement. Sky looked like she might burst at any moment, her round cheeks barely able to stretch to accommodate her smile.

"Oh, I'm always cheery. People tell me that all the time. Makes me extra happy and brings in tips. I'm extra happy today though. I just got in at Uni. Arts. Impossible to get in!" She looked like the artsy type. Her freckles could have been a painting and her hair was out of this world.

"Congratulations!" Leo offered a fist bump, but Sky seemed to think it was a microphone as she leaned in and said, "thank you, thank you very much," she replied imitating. Leo retracted her fist bump now turned microphone embarrassed for both of them.

"University was fun," Leo encouraged unconvincingly, as clear by her flat 'fun'. It sounded sarcastic and maybe it was.

"Where did you go?"

"I studied engineering, programming." Leo pointed at her laptop. "University in Sweden, I'm Swedish." She didn't specify the city. Nobody seemed to know about the place. She pointed at her laptop and the colorful lines of code looking like children's necklaces.

"Oh, a Swedish hacker!" Sky's eyes grew bigger. "That's cool!" She leaned in and looked at the code, forcing Leo to slide her chair to the side to avoid the cloud of ginger hair. Her hair smelled like honey and coffee and Leo was certain it would feel like squeezing a marshmallow. "This is a delightful combination of colors." She inspected the code, her apron threatening the whipped

cream next to the cake. "Ah! I didn't know code was readable!"

"If it's well written and the right language. I more or less write instructions," Leo explained. Nobody could read David's or Mikael's shit.

Sky straightened herself with a little crackling sound from her back and brushed her apron down. A smudge of whipped cream disappeared into the fabric, joining all the other stains from the last few weeks. "You don't look like a hacker." Sky looked like an arts and crafts girl.

"Because I'm female?" Leo asked.

"No, well, I sort of expected you to look more goth." Sky blushed, "sorry."

"It's alright, it's popular in movies. Dark makeup, piercings, and tattoos. The lot."

Sky breathed out, "I loved the movie, Girl with the Dragon Tattoo."

"We can't all look like that." Leo brushed her hair to the side. She had never worn a lot of makeup even during her dark teenage years. Too self-conscious for that. "Dunno where they get the idea from. I don't see the point in getting a full face on when most of my day is spent in front of a screen," she shrugged but quickly continued, "but each to their own, of course."

"My mind has been blown." Sky pretended that her head exploded with a boom sound to match. They both laughed. In the corner of her eyes, Leo noticed the line of customers waiting for a cheery server and some coffee. Social hour was over. Sky looked over, "Oh! Got to run. Work work work! Enjoy your cake!"

Leo pointed towards the cake and gave a thumbs up and took a celebratory bite as Sky greeted the customers with a high pitch singing voice. She ate the cake in five large bites, each washed down with cold coffee, and a few lines of code. The sugar rush augmented the endorphins, and the music provided perfect beats for typing. She was in the flow, for the first time since...university? When she

created the library? Maybe university hadn't been that bad after all.

The latest build she triggered was green. Test coverage was up. James and Sam are going to be thrilled. And Leo…she was happy for the first time in a while.

33

David had tried for an hour to put Samuel to bed without luck. He was convinced that Samuel could sense the urgency that his dad really needed him to fall asleep fast so he could get important things done. And since toddlers are assholes, Samuel did his very best to stay awake. At least he only had one kid to put to bed. Trevor was at grandma's house, but Samuel had another one of those epic toddler colds and they didn't want to risk Elisabeth's already (but natural age you know) compromised health.

Five books, seven songs (David's full repertoire), threats and bribes, and Samuel had successfully persisted through all attempts to give in as a captured spy in an action movie. A James Bond toddler, with David as the villain.

That's why, at 9:34 PM, David was biking in the middle of nowhere with a singing toddler that seemed rather amused, as opposed to sedated. He seemed unfazed and undazed by the rattling sounds the carrier made as David pedaled like a madman in his polyester body suit on a bumpy country road.

His body had resisted the condom suit, insulting his middle-aged physique and what it once used to be, despite

the many miles he endured in rain and wind on the skinny bike that had cost him more than his last car.

He had gotten the bike to (prematurely) celebrate the bonus PetSockShop would cause when they would extend the contract for five more years and an expansion of the e-commerce platform. They had been on the fence for a while, with a rod up their rear end for parts of it. However, the domino disasters had collapsed the fence and they had pulled out quicker than David did as a horny teenager. Leo had been the sacrifice, but the contract was unsalvageable.

David glanced over his shoulder and confirmed that Samuel was dozing off just as an ambulance, one of Samuel's favorite vehicles drove by, lights and sirens blaring, almost drowning the excited shriek from Samuel. "Lance, daddy lance! See- lance!" Dave pedaled harder, regretting the money he spent on the bike and the pile of bills he would rest the bike against when he dragged himself into the apartment, leaving wet marks that looked like tears on the wooden flooring.

Trevor had always slept well, even as a newborn. David and Sarah would stay awake worried something was wrong and listen to Trevor's snores and snorts at night for the first few months until they accepted that's what babies do. Sleep all the time. It had been a breeze and they had patted each other on the back and generously handed out unsolicited advice, a parent's favorite type of advice, to other parents. So why not have another one? Another ambulance drove by, and Samuel shrieked again a mantra of 'lances'. Getting cocky seemed to be David's thing, an attitude that generally paid off- unless it was marriage, parenting, or disastrous events at work. The small things, you know.

Trevor had been small, a wobbling one and a half-year-old, when he had started at the same kindergarten as Brian's daughter. Trevor had breezed through the first day, no drama, ate like a champ, slept through panicked babies and toddlers, and socialized like a key account manager at

a networking event. Brian had complimented David on Trevor's impressive adaptation to a new life as he had brute-forced his daughter into a stroller covered in evidence from daily battles. Many pickups later, David had convinced Brian that they should develop a new version of PetSockShop.

David peaked that summer. Right before Sarah gave birth to Samuel, the literal wake-up call neither of them could foresee.

Turns out Samuel didn't sleep like a baby. Samuel fought sleep like a gold medalist. If sleep refusal was a sport in the Olympics, then Samuel would have made the Brits proud.

David couldn't help but think back to sleepless nights and zombie arguments as he stopped pedaling and went to check on Samuel. He was snoring as if he had been sleeping for hours and smelled like cotton, honey, and second-day pajamas. David made sure the covers were wrapped tight around his torso and gave a gentle kiss on Samuel's wet chin. Samuel looked like Sarah and sometimes when David looked at him, he felt a sudden pain in his heart which he couldn't quite place. He missed Sarah but there was no biking in the world that would leave enough distance or exhaustion to ease the pain. And Samuel was a reminder of how he had messed up, wrapped up in his arrogance, as his therapist called it.

He left the dishes by the sink. Sarah had sent him the article. He had blamed her for everything. The sleep deprivation, torture by a toddler, the messy house, the weight gain. The divorce. It was only when it was too late when irony would rip into his arrogance as he was the one struggling to put Samuel to bed, keep a clean house, keep the contract with Brian, that he got it.

He sat in the grass next to the carrier. He was in a rush to get Samuel to bed so he could talk to James if he was online.

David: I know it's Saturday, but I just wanted to check with you if you know how Leo is doing? Don't tell her I've asked. I'm sure she'd rather not hear about or from me.

James: I spent the day with her. She seems to do better.

David: Better?

David: Spent the day? Is she your girlfriend? FWB?

James: I'm sure HR would love to read this chat.

David: My bad. None of my business. Better?

James: Seemed kind of down at first, but cheerful when I left. I

don't think I've seen her cheerful before.

James: And no, we are not an item of any kind-besides friends. We are friends. Get your mind out of the gutter.

David: Sorry. Did she say anything about me?

James: No.

David: That's good, I assume. I'll apologize when I get the chance.

James: You what?

James: Apologies? David? You?

David: Funny. Yes. I'm not proud.

James: Going to offer Leo her job back?

David: You know I can't do that. It's not my call.

James: She wouldn't want to, anyway.

David: Understandably.

David: Hold on, my kid is waking up.

David: False alarm. I should bike back home.

James: I won't ask.

David: Don't.

```
David: See you Monday.
James: Glad to hear you asked about Leo.
David: Technically it's read.
James: ?
David: You read not heard.
James: Wiseass.
David: It's what I do best.
```

David got back on the bike. It was dark and cold, and his lights seemed to run out of battery. The evening didn't turn out as he had planned. It rarely did when he had the kids over but tonight, he didn't mind. He pedaled slowly home, enjoying the chilly breeze swiping his bare legs and the crackling sound of gravel meeting wheels. It was time to do the dishes; he had left them out for too long, always expecting somebody else to take care of them.

34

The café had closed for the evening, and Sky and Leo had left at the same time while exchanging pleasantries. Sky was eager to go home and deep-dive into her new obsession, polymer clay jewelry making. Leo, on the other hand, went to a pub where she could sit somewhat undisturbed and continue making magic on her laptop.

The pub had a musty smell of mold and pungent urine and was hidden at the end of a tiny alley. The pub was famous among locals, trendy locals in tech, but free from tourists and teenagers camouflaging as adults. There had never been a fight there, nor was it a place for single mingle.

Leo had three hours left, after making sure her laptop had charged to max at the café. She switched out coffee with pale ale, a sourdough sandwich with avocado and chips, and tucked away her headset so she could tune in to the loungy music echoing off the alley wall.

James had pushed a new pull request for the pipeline and some automated performance tests.

That should make Meron happy. She started reviewing the code.

Surprisingly well written, nothing compared to the shit they would usually produce per consultant hour.

She had felt anxious after she had sent her dad an email before she left the café. Hastily written, worried she might change her mind halfway through, she had let him know she was sorry for not replying to his previous emails with the usual lies (draft stuck in outbox, server issues, etc.), a brief update on her amazing life (omitting the fact that she got fired), and a photo of Lion. She had clicked send just as Sky had let her know she had to leave so she could close for the day. A perfectly timed send that couldn't be undone and fresh air to calm her burning skin (and laptop) from the emotions soaring through her. She had distracted herself with the library since then and it had worked well.

"Would you like another glass?" A server pulled Leo back to reality. He was pointing at her empty glass, foam resting at the bottom.

"Mmmm." She looked at the clock.

"I'll have one!" A cheerful male voice interrupted, and Leo turned around and saw a big smile worn by a young man in a suit with hair combed to perfection and glowing skin to match, "Sorry for interrupting! Just dying for a cold beer." He opened his jacket and revealed a dark patch under each armpit and laughed. "Cheap suit, I'm cooking!" Very Steve Ballmer, Leo chuckled at her thought. He seemed to take that as an invitation to start a conversation with her.

"You should have another one. I can recommend some local brews." He pointed at the menu. Perfectly manicured hands.

"Oh, it's alright, I'm familiar with the local brews." Great. I sound like an alcoholic. "I'll have another one." Leo gave the server a nod.

Her chatty guest pointed energetically at an empty bottle on his table. It had a blue label and a children's drawing of a dog. Usually means it's a fancy hipster brew, "It's amazeballs. I'm having another one. Try it!"

"Sure. I'll have what he is having." Leo acquiesced mildly.

The server scribbled something down and disappeared. Chatty stranger inched closer, demonstrating the empty bottle. "Local brewery, they only make a few batches each year." His eyes grew enormous. "Oh, I'm sorry, how rude, I'm Jack," he stretched his hand out and Leo had to lean over the table to reach it. He had a strong, confident grip that contrasted her limp and slightly sweaty palm. She shook the end of his fingers as they glided apart. Leo thought about that scene with Jack in the movie Titanic.

"Leo." She responded.

"Leo?"

"Leonarda, but I'm usually called Leo."

"Neat!" A tad over-enthusiastic response.

He sat there looking at her, waiting for something. He had slightly large ears, sticking out and giving him a childish flair that matched well with his dimples.
"Yeah." Her face turned a tad red. She escaped using her laptop, a reliable tactic. She couldn't remember what she was doing but she had to look busy. Tests. I can always write more tests.

It had barely passed 5 minutes before the new beer was in front of her and Jack saw a new opportunity to continue his Jack in a Box. He popped in with his beer and forced a cheer from her. "What are you writing on?"

Whenever somebody asked Leo what she did she always resorted to an oversimplified version of what a programmer does, often adding some extra, maybe more exciting details, to help the other person continue the conversation. "I'm a programmer, I'm coding," was always a conversation killer. Unless you could make up some cool app, preferably one that was very popular. Not Teams. And it had to be a phone app. People only care about stupid phone apps.

Leo avoided saying she was a data consultant. A title from the 80's, still popular among some firms. David wanted cooler titles and they had been code ninjas,

computer whisperers, and her favorite- cloud architect (because she clicked a few buttons and deployed to a server on Azure).

Jack was waiting eagerly and dancing closer to her by wiggling his chair in her direction. He was awfully cute and annoying. Leo had a cousin like that; however, Arthur was merely 7 years old and saw it as his sole mission in life to educate other people about dinosaurs - relentlessly. Ah, fuck it.

"I'm writing some code, a hobby project. It's not quite an app, but a useful tool for other apps that make it faster to work with data." That was the most downplayed version of what her library did that she offered, yet she had squeezed in words that were not meant for the average person. Tool. Data. Code. Well, most people knew about code and coding nowadays. Even kids were force-fed that stuff in school as early as possible. Arthur had coded his first Lego robot at 6. Coded. He had dragged and dropped some colored blocks on his tablet after his dad had fought the Bluetooth settings for two hours so the robot could take two steps forward and one to the side. She had impressed Arthur for two seconds before returning to his dino collection, leaving his dad with a lighter wallet and less hair. David coded the same way Arthur did. Drag and drop.

"That sounds interesting and vague." He took a long sip, maintaining eye contact. "What language?"

"English and Swedish?"

"No, no- what language are you writing in?"

"Usually English."

"I mean the tool. What programming language." He winked. See? I speak programmer!"

"It's called C sharp."

"Is it?"

"What?"

"Seeing sharp." He laughed like a crazy monkey and beer bubbled out of his open mouth. Leo didn't know

what to do and returned her attention to her laptop. What an idiot.

"Sorry. Sorry! Couldn't help myself!"

"No shit. Nobody can help you with that." Leo smiled and squinted.

"I'm also a programmer," he explained.

Leo eyed him up and down. There was nothing that showed he was a programmer.

"Yes, I know. Don't let this highly flammable ensemble fool you! I am indeed one of you." He leaned in and whispered, "I'm a code monkey by day, a beggar by night." He sprung back and cracked his back. "I work for a startup. This is the only suit I own, and I use it whenever I'm able to steal some time with a potential angel."

Leo raised an eyebrow.

"An investor."

"Of course." She blushed. Consultants rarely heard about angels. They referred to the customers as devils. Openly so.

"What does the startup do?"

He gestured towards her table. "Do you mind?"

She moved her laptop to the side, and he moved to her table and raised his beer. "Cheers!" The bottles met with a clear tone, and she took a long sip, feeling the bubbles tickling her throat.

"It's a payment system for e-commerce. Not very sexy, but it's my baby and I'm a proud father. We are doing well, a second round of investments and several happy customers. I should be able to take out pay in five years," he chuckled.

"I guess I don't look like a programmer either." Leo circled her head with her hand.

"More than me!" He shouted in reply.

"Well, I'm a woman. That's my fancy suit." Although she had been mistaken for a young boy occasionally.

"Meh," he shrugged, "we are 50% female devs at our company."

"Really?"

"We are only four devs though." He leaned over the table as he said this.

"Still, pretty good odds. That's almost two micro teams." She added.

"I like to think so as well. We don't micro, though, we just code."

They finished their beer and Leo ordered another and one for him. "It's on me, for your struggling startup."

"Naw, are you my angel?"

"Maybe."

"Then I'll take it!" He raised an empty bottle to the sky as he popped up dramatically. A true Jack in the Box. Jack paused for a second, tapped her laptop, "Tell me more about the library. Can I see?"

Leo hesitated. "Sure…" She opened up her laptop and slid the computer in front of him. "This is the library I'm working on. A cache clearing library that is cache agnostic."

"Wow!" Jack clicked around in the repository while muttering encouraging words, "this is very impressive! Can't believe I'm sitting next to somebody famous!"

Leo blushed, "Nah, I'm not famous. The library is, but I've kept my identity hidden."

She snapped the lid shut and Jack spun around and faced her, "Why? Why would you do such a thing?"

"Fame is not my thing. Plus, open-source isn't female-friendly."

"Have you tried?" He pressed further.

"I've had enough experience with accidentally making things public. I'd rather not go public with my name." She replied painfully remembering her latest debacle.

Jack tilted his head and looked at her, "You know what? You should. You've created an exceptional thing and people should know who wrote the library. Female open-source contributors won't get it easier if coders like

yourself don't go public." His smile disappeared and he stared intently.

"You seem very passionate about this?" Feeling more curious than before.

"I'm passionate about diversity," he replied and shrugged. "My startup wouldn't be the same without the little diversity we have."

"I just don't know if I want to be at the forefront of that change. I'm not a leader. I'm more of a reluctant follower." Leo avoided eye contact and peeled the sticker off her beer. Her nails were red from constant nibbling, and she retracted her hand and hid it under the table.

"I won't pressure you. You do you." He smiled and gestured for another beer, and they resumed talking about his startup.

"Jack!" A female voice cut through the magical atmosphere. Leo's cheeks were burning as she sought the person who owned the voice.

"Samantha!" Jack exclaimed and stretched out his arms. "My charger!"

"Well, glad you are happy to see ME," Samantha replied and poked Jack's shoulder. She was dressed in fashionable athleisure wear, hair perfectly curled and styled into blonde shiny curls, pink lipstick matching long dark lashes, and a green, winged eyeliner. She looked amazing. Leo felt like a homeless person in comparison if it wasn't for her very expensive jeans (the only brand that had jeans that fit her narrow hips and straight legs).

"This is one of the developers I was talking about! Samantha is a dev-ops guru. She makes Amazon blush with the setups she does - a wizard of the sky. And a decent programmer." Jack gladly embellished.

"It's true, my dev-ops skills are better than my programmer skills." She looked down in shame and laughed a bubbly little laugh that made her curls bob up and down. "I'm Samantha, by the way. Nice to meet you!" she shook Leo's hand and Leo replied with a meek hello.

"I've got a massive crush on this one," Jack whispered loudly to Samantha and pointed at Leo, who at this point had turned a deep red that matched the curtains behind her. "She is Swedish."

Samantha shook her head, "Apologies for my drunken colleague. He is a lightweight."

"No worries."

"I did a year in Sweden, exchange student! I loved the food there!" Samantha pinched her sides. "I've kept the memories - the UK has little to offer. Slides right off."

"The food in Sweden is pretty good, at least compared to here," Leo laughed.

"What do you mean, British food is outstanding," Jack interrupted, fake hurt.

"Really?" Samantha had stopped pinching her sides and crossed her arms instead, "Like what?"

"We have great Indian food!"

"Jack, that's *Indian* food!" Samantha pointed out.

"Oh shit. You're right." They laughed. Jack scooted closer to Leo. A risky move. It could yield closeness or a slap. Leo usually went for the latter but chose the former. *It's the alcohol.* It wasn't the alcohol. His perfume smelled sweet and spicy.

"Well, hubby is here, your charger is there, and I'll see you tomorrow morning Jackie." Samantha gave Leo a handshake and Jack another shoulder poke. "Don't forget the last train to Bristol is in 20 minutes."

Jack sighed slowly. "Ugh. Thanks." He got up slowly, head down. "Guess I've got to go as well." He put the charger in his leather bag. "Can I have your number?"

Leo hesitated. "Sorry, no pen."

"Guess what my suit pocket has?"

"A pen?"

"No, a magical device I can write numbers in. You caveman. Cavewoman. Cave dweller."

Leo tapped her forehead, "You sure you want this one's number? Not so bright."

"I guess I won't try to hire you then, maybe I'll just ask you out for a beer." Leo raised an eyebrow and wrote her number on his phone and declined his test call. "What did you save me as?" Jack asked.

"Jack in a Box. What am I?"

"Leo the lioness! See you soon, Leo the lioness!" He stumbled out between the tables, ruining his attempt at an elegant Bond exit.

Leo paid the tab and packed up. Floating on clouds and alcohol, she glided up the stone stairs to her apartment and collapsed in her bed, exhausted from the social day. With a tingling body and a big smile stretched across a radiant face. As she rolled to her side, pants kicked off and bra undone, she saw the phone lit up.

Jack in the Box: I think I had too much because I can't C#.

35

Samantha: Did you get her phone number?

Samantha had kicked off her shoes while balancing a pizza slice in one hand and her phone in the other. She had ordered the new iPhone online, assumed she wanted the big one like last time, and had received a mammoth phone. She struggled to balance it in her palm while stretching her fingers to type out the messages. Her long manicured nails didn't help. She had decorated them to match her favorite JavaScript libraries. "You'll have to redo your nails every few days," Jack had laughed when he had seen them. "You change favorites more often than I change underwear."

"Gross, Jackie. I'll just do them while I wait for your builds," she had teased back.

They had the slowest build pipeline in human history because Jack insisted they run five different analyzers on every build, triggered by every commit. The melted cheese was dripping down the sides of the pizza, but she refused to put the phone down, or the slice. She had committed to the balancing act and the only way the slice would go down would be through her throat. Her stomach rumbled

and echoed off the walls. Darian had insisted she buy them pizza and bring it home while he drove in circles, hoping for a free parking lot.

"Don't drop the pizza on the floor, love." His deep voice echoed in the hallway.

"I won't baby!" She sang back as a slice of pepperoni slid down her thigh and onto the carpet. She quickly picked it up and ate it. Five-second rule!

```
Jack: I sure did! Already texted her.

Samantha: woohoo! Go, Jack!

Samantha: quite smitten, aren't you?

Jack: she seems pretty cool. Although she is a
.NET developer.

Samantha: hey! Don't diss my favorite
platform.
```

Samantha shook her head. Never-ending sparring over languages and platforms. Not to mention editors. But he was happy to have her on the team. After all, who would do the .NET integration? She massaged her feet before shuffling to the living room where Darian had occupied the couch with his long limbs. She loved wearing kitten heels, but London disagreed. She removed her clothes in two effortless steps, mainly rolling them down from head to toes and stepping out of the ring of clothes and jiggling her stomach. "Free at last!" She liked her little pouch. Soft and round, it fit well with the rest of her body.

"Hello dear hubby-bubby." A kiss on the forehead to seal the greeting.

"Did you get me a coke?"

"Doing coke again, are we?" She handed him the bag and poked her tongue. "Got some snacks as well. Your slice is in there, can't promise it isn't mangled."

"You are an absolute angel." Darien blew her a kiss.

She twirled and elegantly landed in her chair. She had picked it out at a secondhand shop and refurbished it herself with some extravagant fabric with more colors than their apartment had in total. Darian hadn't been a fan, but he had grown to like it and it had been a conversation starter whenever they had guests over. Samantha fit perfectly on the couch; another splash of color just as sparkly as the fabric.

"Jack is interested in the girl from the pub."

"Oh? Isn't he in permanent bachelor mode?" Hubby-bubby inquired.

"I guess he changed his mind."

"So much for the monologue on focusing on the startup." He chuckled and returned his attention to the TV. Rerun of Survivor. Samantha curled up with a cover over her feet, ready to fall asleep. But not there. She had to know more about Jack's new friend. She lived, breathed, and loved gossip.

```
Samantha: So, what does she do?

Jack: she said she was on a break but had been
working as a consultant for a decade or
something.

Samantha: oh God. That must have felt like 100
years. Poor girl deserves a break!

Jack: she is doing some open-source stuff now
though, interesting stuff. Might be useful for
us.

Samantha: her own stuff?

Jack: yes. Seems popular though, at least the
way she described it. Several maintainers.
```

Samantha sat up, suddenly feeling energized.

```
Jack: okay good night.

Samantha: hey! Don't tease like that! You know
open source is my thing!
```

It was true. She had spent most her spare time contributing to open source since last year at uni. It had started with small insignificant small stuff, typos, formatting, before she took on bigger tasks. Her husband, who at the time was patiently waiting for her to come back from a long year in Sweden, had complimented her on being so confident. "Aren't you worried about nasty comments?" Open source could be a dark and nasty place. He had opted in for lower-level development and rarely even looked at open-source stuff. "I'm not. I'm as anonymous as they are online. I can bite back."

"I know you can," he had teased, "but seriously babe, I'm proud of you."

It had meant a lot to her. She had always been unexplainably confident and beautiful, two traits that weren't popular as a programmer - if you were a woman. She had kept her identity hidden and had met Darian as a beta tester for a game he had written during his first year at uni. He had thought she was a guy and unbeknownst to her had struggled with the realization that he was gay, until she confessed her feelings and later her gender.

Her phone vibrated and pulled her back to current times. It was getting really late and her curls had lost their shiny coils. She got up and slipped on one of Darian's T-shirts, it reached her knees. He was a giant and she was miniature. She loved wearing his clothes.

```
Jack: sorry, nature called.
Jack: it's a library. Manages caches. Cache
King or something.
```

Samantha nearly dropped her phone.

```
Samantha: no way! Are you kidding me?!
```

36

When the morning came, Leo had a mission. On her way home from the pub she had thought about what Jack said. "Consider it, at least. You should take credit for your work." Meeting Samantha had made a difference. Leo hadn't met many female developers and the ones she had met she hadn't been able to relate to. However, despite the obvious differences between Leo and Samantha, Leo instantly liked her. Maybe there were many more but all of them embraced internet anonymity.

Leo got dressed in new fresh clothes, gave Lion a kiss on the head, checked the mailboxes, did the usual run up and down the stairs, and headed to the café. Sky greeted her warmly with a cup of coffee and gave Leo the best spot in the café. The inner corner next to the router and power outlet.

"What are we working on today, Leo?" Sky beamed and her smile reflected in the colorful earrings that nearly touched her shoulders.

"Just a code thing." Leo smiled and pointed at the earrings. "Did you make those?"

Sky looked down and bit her lip, "Crap. They look homemade, don't they?"

"I wouldn't know, but to me, they look great. You told me you had started with polymer clay jewelry making."

Sky lifted her chin. "That's true! Colorful like your *editor*?" She pointed at Leo's computer, Leo's library on the screen. "Is that what you are working on?"

"Yes. This is a website for some code I wrote." The repository had doubled its followers in just a few days, and the traffic to the info site had likewise increased.

"Looks very important!" Samantha exclaimed but quickly waved to a colleague and whispered to Leo, "got to go. My manager is here."

Holding her breath, Leo made a few changes and pushed. The site updated. LeoLOL was now Leonarda Larsson. She waited for the dick pics overflow. And she waited some more. Nothing. Not even ASCII dicks. And those are easy to make. She logged in on Discord with her new nickname.

```
DanDorrito: Congratulations! We are proud of
you, Leonarda. What is your preferred pronoun
now, is it she or they?
```

More messages.
```
User3003: Thank you for coming out. I admire
your bravery and strength!
```

Not exactly what she had expected.
```
LeoLarsson: I haven't come out. I've always
been Leonarda.
```

```
User3003: Of course you have! Be true to
yourself.
```

Leo sighed. Well. It's out there now. Let them think what they want to think. Like that kid on the train.

The library had run loads of tests for an hour, with performance profiling in the background. The laptop was burning a hole through the café table and Leo nervously verified that it hadn't left a mark. And just as she placed the laptop on the table again, the screen went black, then blue. A very sad blue. Blue-screen-of-death blue. The sad

face was infuriating. Nothing cute about lost work. A restart later and a new performance profiling session and the blue screen returned. Her laptop died over and over but rose like a roasted phoenix every time she held down the power button. After the tenth attempt, because *the definition of insanity is doing the same thing over and over again and expecting different results (Einstein)*, she disabled the profiling and grabbed the dump file and the log. It was a long read. But the error made sense.

LeonardaLarsson: Dan, you work at PerfGate, right?

DanDorrito: Yeah, I do. How come?

LeonardaLarsson: The profiler kills my computer. I looked at the log and I think I found the bug. If the clock is manually set on the computer, then key authentication gets stuck in a loop and fucks with the memory until the computer gives up and dies.

DanDorrito: Holy shit! We've been trying to figure this out. Can you send whatever info you have? TNXT

Leo emailed the log and the dump file.

LeonardaLarsson: Done.

DanDorrito: Fantastic!

DanDorrito: By the way, Leonarda, are you London based like your profile says?

LeonardaLarsson: Yes. Looking at my rent for the month, I'm pretty sure this is London.

DanDorrito: Would you be interested in a dev position at PerfGate? We are hiring for my team. I'm the lead and we need a senior dev that is familiar with our domain and tools.

LeonardaLarsson: Tempting, I'm not going to lie.

LeonardaLarsson: Email me.

DanDorrito: No promises, it's an interview.

LeonardaLarsson: I know, I know. Don't say yay until you've crossed the river.

DanDorrito: ?

LeonardaLarsson: Ignore that. Swedish expression. I'll wait for that email.

She waited for a reply, impatiently tapping her foot under the table. Biting on the upper lip. PerfGate. That's not any company, it's the company. She opened her email, refreshed. And refreshed. What a fucking day. Refresh. Yes! An email. From…her dad.

37

Dear Leonarda,

I cannot put into words how delighted your mother and I are to hear from you. It has been too long, my dear, but I recognize you are busy as is common for the young and ambitious.

Your mother tells me you sent a beautiful bouquet with her favorite flowers for her birthday. She dried them and they have their own little corner in a vase from a local artist. We've placed them on a shelf where the cats can't reach it. Black and Grey are doing great, as cats do, and I built them a new tower like the one you bought them back home. I know it upset you when we couldn't bring it with us. When you come to visit, and I hope you will soon, you'll have to help me build an overpass for them. I don't trust myself with power tools. By the way, I tried the cat nip trick, and it did wonders. They haven't scratched the couch since then and I'm pleased to tell you I haven't had to change the upholstery on the couch for two months. If you have any advice on making them, not use the plants as expensive tropical bathrooms, please share. The orchids didn't make it and there will be more victims soon (Pete the palm tree seems to thrive though, by next year he'll be taller than me!).

Work is going great; I'll skip the details - I know it's not your favorite subject. I've been doing more teaching and your mother has written more and we hope she'll publish her book through the university by winter in this year and the children's book next year. She dedicated it to you, you know.

We are happy and doing well, but we miss you.

I won't blabber on for too long. I know you don't like that. I'm immensely happy to hear from you and I want to know everything that has been going on in your life for the last few years. I can imagine that you've done well and built an impressive career - you were always so driven and focused. Do you have a boyfriend? Or partner? How are your friends? I have thousands of questions and conversations I'd love to have with you, together with your mother, to get to know who Leonarda, my little bumblebee, has become.

Can I ask a little favor from you… please call your nana. She is now on messenger, you can video call now, she'd love that.

I'll end this email before it becomes a novel and save my words for when we finally meet again.

We've lived so close, yet so far away. But you've always been close to our hearts and we hope you know that. We miss you immensely. Proud of you my dear.

With love, ma and pa

38

James stretched his legs and wiggled his toes as he slowly forced his eyes open. Light sipped through a crack between the curtains, like a bead of sweat between two butt cheeks. Tiny but enough to fill the room and remind James that his alarm hadn't gone off. Through the haze, he tried to orient himself, but his body was heavy and resisting. *What time is it?* He patted randomly around the bed with his left arm, trying to locate his phone. There was no square brick hidden among the cotton folds and James pushed himself up with a long sigh. *You know you are old when you make sounds when you move.* Mikael had said that during a meeting and left everybody in the meeting feeling old and hyperaware of their bodies. James stumbled out of bed, stretching towards the ceiling for a couple of steps before returning to his usual banana shape. He was late. The clock in the kitchen told him so and the laptop sunbathing on the kitchen table reminded him why.

James opened the window and breathed in the fresh air, yesterday's coffee in hand. He cracked his head slowly and lifted the neckline of the t-shirt, letting the cold air sip in. Tiny bumps covered his arms as he closed the window, a Braille parade on his skin. He microwaved his coffee with no shame until it had the recognizable syrupy

216

consistency and was too hot to drink. He could either hurry and catch the next train and be 10 minutes late, or he could take it slow, enjoy his morning and be two hours late. The latter was chosen. David was highly unlikely to fire the last real developer on the team. Although he might be cocky enough to convince himself he could do it all by himself. The laptop was decorated with last night's dinner fingerprints on the lid and James wiped the lid and the keyboard. Breadcrumbs had found their way between the keys. Nothing unusual but James had tried to be more careful since the incident at work a few weeks back. He had arrived in the morning only to find that a key on his precious custom made WASDL keyboard was missing. V was missing. He had looked everywhere but it was nowhere to be found and David and he had argued about it. James was certain David had removed it to prank him. It could even have been Mikael, but Mikael claimed innocence. David jokingly suggested the hygiene engineers, AKA the cleaners, had used the vacuum cleaner on his desk because of the confetti breadcrumbs eagerly sprinkled around. They had checked the bag in the vacuum cleaner, which thankfully wasn't completely full or emptied, and indeed the V was there. Dusty, abandoned, and looking very sad. Copy and paste were saved for the day. *Who on earth thinks it's a good idea to Dyson a £300 keyboard?* James brushed the crumbs away and shook his head. Crazy. David was online and sent David a message.

James: Hi dude, sorry, late in today. Dentist appointment.

David: Up late?

James: ?

David: Dentist appointment is code for just being a lazy ass. Leo is the only one that goes to the dentist. And if one is less than an hour late, it's always the 'train was delayed' excuse.

```
James: I'll be there in two hours.
```

```
David: That's fine, I'll probably be out for
early lunch then. With Sarah.
```

```
David: heard any new fun stories from Leo
regarding the dentist?
```

```
James: unfortunately, no. I'll ask her next
time.
```

```
James: Sarah? Really?
```

```
David: y
```

```
James: That's neat! Have fun ;)
```

Work was the last thing on his mind. He wanted to finish refactoring the code he wrote last night, as well as the pull request he pushed before going to bed. Five new notifications. PR approved. That's nice. He quickly opened the PR to breathe in a green build. More performance tests and the metrics looked fabulous, at least on his machine.

That's when he saw it. It was neither Sam00 nor Leo that had approved his request. It was Meron.
"*Looks great, nice work! Check your email.*"
His cheeks turned rose, and warmth radiated as he opened the email. *Looks great. Nice work.* The words replayed, sounding better each time. It might have been the best compliment he had ever gotten and earliest in the morning he had ever opened his email.
A long email from Meron waited for him and James read it with a beaming smile like a kid on Christmas Eve eager to open a large package long awaited.

39

Mouth wide open, leaning over the bathroom sink, Leo inspected her molars in the mirror. The cold sink gave her goosebumps as it collided with the warmth generated from her right cheek. I'm cursed with rotten teeth. She rubbed her cheek and swished some cold water around while side eying herself. Half her face was a deep pink color and slightly swollen. She kept the water in her mouth and walked to the kitchen, occasionally swishing to calm her angry molar. Regret was an understatement; she had canceled the appointment with Dr. Green. She would have preferred the parking guy over him but not a second handover like some sick kink. I don't bend that way. She should have told the dentist's office that. The fridge was empty, as expected. Some fancy beer, a dead salad that always was bought but never eaten, two-day pizza, and some cottage cheese. Chewing was going to be a problem and the cottage cheese had expired.

"Damn it." Leo picked up her phone, spit out the water in the sink, and scrolled through her contact list, "hi, it's

Leo Larsson. I'm calling to book an emergency appointment."

She paced through her apartment. The smell of roses and soap from the laundry drying on a rack in the living room tickled her nose. The only dress she owned hung over the couch, slowly drying in the sunlight. A pale-yellow knee-length dress she had gotten as a present from her parents some birthdays ago. It fit. But had never been worn. She brushed some wrinkles out of it.

"Yes, I can wait." Slightly damp, she held it in front of her and felt the slightly cool cotton against her skin. The reflection in the window filled with the yellow pattern and the outline of dark hair that had grown too long, a fringe missing, hidden behind an ear. "I can do Wednesday. Yes. Please send a confirmation." She raised herself on her toes, growing taller in the window, "Thank you." She hung up and slung the phone on the couch where it disappeared among a folded tower of T-shirts. With quick movements she pulled off her T-shirt and pulled down her jeans, stepping out of them as she slid the yellow dress over her head and let her slim pasty white arms spaghetti out of the armholes on the dress. Not too bad. The dress was comfortable. The damp fabric distracted from the pain but the heat radiating from her cheek wouldn't quite let her forget. Dr. Green or the parking guy, it didn't matter. It had to be done, whatever they do with aching molar teeth's these days.

She grabbed the chair from the kitchen and screeched it across the floor until it was in the living room across from the window. Her legs trembled slightly as she climbed the chair. Crap, it's the bad chair. She found her balance and investigated her reflection. Like a lady. A strange sensation. Had she ever worn a dress? The A-line dress swung out from her hips, two pale legs grounding the slightly shimmering material. Something moved in the reflection. Leo was worried she'd tip over like a failed balancing act and break her wrists in three different places.

Anything but the wrists. Take my face instead. I need the wrists for coding. She had once listened to a podcast about a paraplegic guy who was quadriplegic. He used a combination of eye-tracking, voice to text, and sometimes his mouth to maneuver his computer and wrote code for Microsoft. I'd never be able to do that. Speech to text hates me and I can barely drink without spilling. Not that anybody will ever hire me again. Something moved again and Leo regained her balance. A person, an old person was waving from a window in the house across the street. What the hell? Leo took a step into thin air and went down like a stalk of cards with an enormous boom.

From the pile of clothes, a muffled ping followed Leo's grand dive like a frail Victorian lady. She rubbed her shoulder and pulled herself up. Her knee was red and ached but there was no blood. She went clothes diving to fish out the phone. A loud banging on the door interrupted the search. She jumped up, hitting her head on the lamp. What now?

"Hello? Police, open up."

Heart pounding, shoulder aching, and with a dry open mouth, Leo rushed to the door and unlocked it.

"Hello, ma'am. We received a call from a concerned neighbor." The police offer looked around while his copy stood still behind him, eyes fixated on Leo.

"What?"

"This is a welfare check."

"I'm well…" Leo brushed her dress down and pulled her hair behind her ears. Her mouth was dry and made speaking hard.

"What is that?" The officer pointed sternly behind Leo. A broken chair, a dangling lamp, and a pile of clothes. Leo wasn't sure what he was referring to but didn't want to talk back. "The chair? Did you attempt to take your life, ma'am?"

"The neighbor saw it," the other officer said in a gentle voice. Probably the good cop.

"Oh. No…" Leo's face was a deep red, "I… I was using the window. As a mirror. Stood on the chair to see if the dress fit. It's broken now, the chair, that is. Got them basically for free at a local thrift store in Peterborough. I've already broken one." She looked at the floor and hid her hands in the dress pockets. She hadn't noticed before it had pockets. *Didn't know they made dresses with pockets.* She had refused to wear dresses ever since she was a kid because it wasn't fair boys had pockets, but she didn't.

"It's a lovely dress." Good cop smiled.

"You sure you are okay, ma'am?" He kept looking around as if she had hidden suicidal attempts sprinkled around the apartment.

"Promise." She attempted a smile.

"Here. Take this card. Call if you need somebody to talk to." Handing her a new card.

"For general conversations? If I'm bored?" Leo added regretting the poorly timed witty remark.

"No…if life gets too hard…" The cop said sternly.

"Can I call now?"

"Ma'am, are you planning to take your life?"

"No, but you seem to mention it a lot. Is it something I should consider?" Again, the timing all wrong.

Slightly annoyed and still concerned the cop offered a, "Have a good day, ma'am. And the dress looks great."

The card was added to her pockets. She could even fit her phone there.

She closed the door and slowly exhaled. Turning around, she waved at the neighbor with four more fingers than she wanted to use. Her phone pinged again and interrupted the rebellion. It was Martin the dentist. Leo beamed and started cleaning up the crime scene.

40

In the pale-yellow dress and her best sneakers, Leo sweated her way through the entrance at the majestic building with the big PerfGate sign. Dan waited for her in the lobby as she stumbled in.

"Leonarda! Welcome!" Dan jumped up and grabbed her hand before she realized what was happening or who he was. "I'm Dan! Dorrito!"

Leo pulled her hand out of the grip and brushed her hair behind her ears. "Hi…" She looked around. The lobby was big and empty, sounds echoing off the walls. "Didn't know you would do the interview?"

"I'm going to show you around. Welcome to our castle!" He gave her a name tag that refused to stay put on her chest.

"I'll just add this to my bag instead."

They walked around the office, which was an eternity of rooms filled with computers. Each workstation was decorated with assorted toys, drawings, and masquerade clothes.

"If you are dressed up, it means you are working. We work Pomodoro style here."

"How trendy." A momentary smile flashed across Leo's face. The smile concealing her nausea.

"Here. This is it. The tech interview room." Dan opened a door and revealed a blue room with a large monitor in the middle. Two people sat at the table.

"Tech interview?" Leo suddenly felt cold and weak. "I…I thought the work was on the library and the bug hunting. I mean, you've seen my work?" The last sentence barely made it through her dry lips. She rubbed her arm and refused to budge.

"We still need to do the usual tech interview. It's easy. I promise, you'll breeze through it." Dan knocked and nodded when the two guys turned their attention to them. "This is Leonarda, the famous! Take good care of her. I'd like to keep her."

Before she had the chance to say anything, Dan had disappeared and the two Johns introduced themselves with, "Hi I'm John." And, "I'm also John."

"Have a seat, Leonarda! We had to squeeze this in, so we didn't have a lot of time. Sorry about that! But an hour is usually plenty. Here, grab the keyboard. It's US layout, hope you don't mind. Let's see, it's 12 now, so by 12:45 we'll have to wrap up."

She sat down without a word, her eyes darting around the floor, avoiding human contact.

"Alright. We would like you to create a console app, nothing fancy, and create a Minesweeper game."

Leo stared at the monitor at the far end of the table. She could barely see words in the editor. She paused, drank some water from a glass on the table. Realized it was not for her but one of the Johns glasses but remained committed and emptied the glass.

She cleared her throat, "What is Minesweeper?"

John and John looked at each other and burst into laughter.

"Oh, wait. You're serious?" John and John stared at her. Laughed again. "You've never played Minesweeper?"

"No," Leo shyly replied. "Would you mind explaining the game and the rules?"

The first John started. Explained it was a puzzle. Second John interrupted and added "puzzle game".

"You have to clear the board which contains mines. Numbers let you know how many mines are near you," the first John interrupted.

"If there are any," the second John jumped in, annoyed. They bickered back and forth while the clock on the wall did its thing. When there was only half an hour left, the two Johns had agreed on the rules of the game.

"Go for it, Leonarda!"

"Do you mind if I use internet?"

John and John looked at each other and shrugged. "Sure."

Leo grabbed the keyboard and wrote How to code Minesweeper in C#.

"What are you doing?" John1 leaned in.

"Coding?" Leo replied, fingers sweating on the keyboard.

"Let's skip the internet then." John2 pulled the network cable from the wall.

"It's connected via Wi-Fi, John." John1 added. "Just…just don't search online for the solution. We'd like you to write the code yourself."

Leo nodded. She enabled Code AutoComplete and GitHub Code Search. A few key presses later and a suggestion for the solution was shown and she accepted. John and John sat with mouth open, staring at the screen.

"And…times up!" John grabbed the keyboard and Leo reluctantly let go.

"I'm sorry," Leo whispered, "I panicked. Anxiety problems." The jagged array stared back, empty and disappointed. She hadn't gotten further than a declaration and a code search result that didn't compile. "Honestly, how did I do?"

John and John exhaled in unison. John1 replied, "Honestly?"

"Yes."

"You are not that good."

41

Leo biked back in hyper-mode while crying in the wind like a distressed lover post-breakup. She ran up the stone stairs with the bike on her shoulder, strongman style, until she made it through the door with a forceful exhale. Lion stared at the exhausted rag doll bursting through the door.

"Lion, I'm the worst developer ever. Nobody is ever going to hire me." She cried again, and bent down her beaten body attempting to steal a cuddle. However, Lion realized she wasn't bringing any goodies and consequently he merely turned around flashing his assholeness and went to the kitchen waiting for his servant. The servant did not follow. Instead, the servant stood in the hallway, laptop bag in her hand, with a defeated look on her face. If she threw it out the window, how far would it fly? With her weak programmer's wrists, it wouldn't even make it half a meter horizontally. Leo's phone vibrated and interrupted her vandalism plans.

It was James. She sat down on the floor, back against the wall.

```
James: How did it go?
Leo: It went to shits, that's how it went!
```

James: I'm sure you're only exaggerating.

Leo: It couldn't have gone worse. They had me code something called minesweeper, never heard of that, and I only got 20 minutes to do it. Complete blackout.

James:I've worked with you, you're not *that* bad. Are you sure it's not imposter syndrome? It's common, you know.

Leo: No. Not an imposter. This is the real thing.

James: Come on. It's very common for developers to feel like an imposter.

Leo: But in this case, I do suck. Nobody likes to think they are a terrible driver. If you ask a group of people to raise their hand if they are a poor driver, nobody is going to raise their hand although everybody knows several careless drivers.

James: Are you saying that you are that driver?

Leo: I know I am that driver.

James: How do you know?

Leo: Well, they told me.

James: Ouch. They really did?

Leo: Yes.

James: What about the library? I thought it would impress them?

Leo: They didn't care about the library, they wanted to see me produce, in real time.

James: I'm having a hard time believing you did such an awful job. I've seen the stuff you've done with the library.

Leo: The problem is, they wouldn't let me use Internet. And I had that available when I wrote the code for the library.

James: Well, to be fair, it's common to not allow internet use during a technical interview. Not even Mikael did that.

Leo: Oh God. You are absolutely right. I'm actually worse than Mikael. Excuse me for a second while I jump out the window.

James: You'll break a toe, at most. Just thank them for their time and move on. There are plenty of other jobs.

Leo: I seem unable to find those jobs.

Leo: But you're right, I'll thank them for their time.

Leo got up and dragged herself to the kitchen where Lion was pacing aggressively by the window. He inhaled the food that magically appeared in his bowl and disappeared with an exaggerated swagger. The light from the window poured in and warmed as she pulled a chair closer and sat down.

Dan was online.

LeonardaLarsson: Hi Dan, sorry for running off without saying goodbye. I just wanted to thank you for your time and for recommending me for a position.

DanDorrito: How did it go? I haven't had time to talk to John and John.

LeonardaLarsson: Didn't go too well, it's a no go for them.

DanDorrito: That sucks. Would you be interested in a different position?

LeonardaLarsson: Like what?

DanDorrito: What about a junior position?

LeonardaLarsson: Practically, what would that consist of?

```
DanDorrito: Smaller issues. A lot of
maintenance.

DanDorrito:… and of course…

DanDorrito:… a fair bit of support.
```

Leo made up an excuse and left the chat. She took a long shower, comprising of five minutes of hot water and 10 minutes with lukewarm water. Enough to wash her hair and to hate her life for 15 minutes. A high-pitched buzzing sound interrupted her poor woman's spa and she hurried out skating with wet footsteps. The laptop waited for her with a black screen, dark as its soul that it didn't have. It was making an unrecognizable sound. It wouldn't restart, nor would it do a soft reset. She quickly recorded a two-second video as you do as a witness to an accident. If the disk bricked, she would at least have a video to share. She hurried and frantically found a screwdriver, the tiny kind that you never have lying around, removed the lid, and disconnected the battery. It stopped and started. She exhaled and sat down and sent the video to James.

```
Leo: Hi James. Is the work laptop supposed to
sound like this?

James: You kept the work laptop?

Leo: Of course. It's my farewell present.
Picked it and packed it myself. Couldn't eat
the cake, anyway.

James: Okay… Nope, it's not supposed to sound
like that. Did you get it fixed?

Leo: Yeah, I disconnected the battery.
Basically, the turn-it-off-and-on trick.

James: Classic!

Leo: It looks kind of dusty, though. Look
here, I took a photo of the internals.

James: Leo, that battery is about to blow.

Leo: I know the laptop blows.
```

James: No, the battery is literally going to explode. It's not supposed to be that inflated. I would pull it out and chuck it out if I were you.

Leo: Explosions in apartment buildings in London is not a popular thing, James.

James: I'm serious Leo. You need a new battery. Don't use this one.

Leo: Fuck my life. This day sucks. Maybe I should just do support.

James: I'm not sure you would be a good fit for that. But I guess you could always try to see how it goes.

Leo: I'm too shit for support?

James: If you are going to give up that easily, then maybe support is better.

Leo: I never said I've given up.

James: You sound beyond defeated.

Leo: Sound? You can hear me through text?

James: Interviews are hard, you got to prepare for them. And prepare to suck at them.

Leo: I'm great at sucking. I should use my body instead of my brains.

James: I'm not sure one failed interview is enough to turn to sex work. Besides, I believe you'd still make more as a developer.

Leo: That's not what I meant. Never mind.

Leo: I'm not good at this. Software development.

James: I disagree. But you definitively sucked at the interview. I wouldn't give up. If I was you.

Leo: Thanks for the encouragement.

Back at the kitchen window Leo watched the old lady on the bench with the dog. The lady was stroking and

talking to the dog. Probably waiting for her husband again, Leo thought. It couldn't be Old Mary. Mary lived alone; Leo had concluded early on. The husband, or lover, appeared and sat down, petting the dog. Leo let out a long sigh and stepped out of the sunlight. The dusty emptiness of her apartment awaited, and she shuffled to her bed, chin lowered to her chest. She let herself fall into the bed, face first, and stayed that way until Lion came and purred.

"At least I've got you," she whispered into the covers. Lion jumped down and meowed his way to the kitchen requesting more food. Her phone pinged again.

```
Sam00: How did it go?

Leo: James told you?

Sam00: Yes. He had to help me with a broken
test.

Leo: Not well. No hire. I suck at interviews.

Sam00: Why don't you do a practice interview
instead? Apply to a position that is above
your head. Something you'd never qualify for.
And crash and burn through the interview.
After that, no interview will ever be as bad
as that one- but at least it was your choice.

Leo: That's what I did!

Sam00: Nah, you got to aim higher. Something
like Microsoft.
```

42

"Why are manhole covers round?"

It was the end of the day and Leo's sixth interview had started.

"Manholes?"

"Yes, manholes."

For a minute she thought she had heard assholes. And she did not know why the sphincter muscle was round, if not to follow the shape of the colon. But manhole? Manhole cover?

"What's a manhole?"

"I'm sorry, it's probably called something else in your language — "

"Swedish."

"Swedish, yes. It's a maintenance hole for an underground vault. The hole is round."

"And the covers are round."

"Yes! Why are they round, though?"

"Because the hole is round?"

"Yes…I guess that is true. Why is the hole and cover round?"

"It's easier to dig a round hole?" Leo smiled. "And consequently, the cover is round. To match the hole."

"Let's ignore the hole then. It's not there. Why is the cover round?"

"We need a cover if there isn't a hole?" Leo raised her eyebrows, but then winked. The interviewer laughed.

"Okay. Just play along here, Leo."

"Hmm. Well. The cover won't fall through the hole. A rectangular shape could do that, or oval. And the hole in the middle of the cover is used to prop the cover up and roll it away. Rectangular doesn't roll well. Manhole covers are very heavy! Speaking of, the compression from the surrounding earth and asphalt would be evenly distributed, making the cover more resistant to pressure."

"Wow!" His eyes lit up and leaned back with a big smile.

"I can think of more reasons."

"No, no, this is perfect!"

"There are non-round manholes out there,"

Leo added. "Some are triangular, and some have hidden hinges to avoid the cover shifting and falling in. Or simply a bigger lip."

The interviewer clapped, leaned over, and gave her a high five.

"You would make an excellent tester!"

"What about software developer?" Leo asked.

"Let's move on to the last interview. Josef is going to be the interviewer. Data structures and algorithms." He walked to the door and waved at Josef.

"Leo has done great so far. Let's see if she'll ace your questions as well."

Leo nodded a hello and shook Josef's hand before returning to her warm and sweaty assprint.

"Alright Leo! Let's talk about data structures and algorithms!"

"I'll do my best. I'm not very good with data structures, nor algorithms." Leo rubbed her hands under the table. Her thumb was bleeding at the edge of the nail where she

had repeatedly picked at the skin. She took a big breath, looked up, and smiled nervously. "Are we doing minesweeper?"

Josef wrinkled his forehead. "Minesweeper?"

"As a tech interview?"

He laughed, "I guess we could, if you wanted to. I was thinking something different."

Leo held her breath but managed to squeeze out a, "Like what?"

"Your library seems to use a decent amount of them," Josef replied with a warm smile. "Why don't we talk about data structures and algorithms in the context of your library? Tell me about Cache is King, I want to know it all!"

Leo exhaled and let her shoulders drop as he filled up her glass with water. "Where do I start?"

"Anywhere! We have plenty of time."

Leo mirrored him and leaned back with a smile. "It started back in school…"

Sam00: Tell me! How did it go?

Leo: Are you sure you want to know?

Sam00: Yes!

Leo: It went great! I got an email on my way home, and they will send an offer later this week!

Sam00: OMG!

Leo: But I've decided to decline.

Sam00: Why???

Leo: I've realized I love working with the library. I can't give that up. I'm going to try to monetize it.

Sam00: Nobody has ever made money on open-source. We are all broke, Leo!

Leo: Some have made it!

Sam00: They sold their firstborn. Or drugs. I admire your passion, but are you sure you want to take the risk?

Leo: I have some savings. I have to give it a try.

Sam00: You are insane, but an inspiration.

Sam00: Why don't you start your own consultancy firm?

Leo: I would be shit at billing. I'd be like, *oh I worked 10 hours, but 4 of them were fun, so I'll only bill for 5.*

Sam00: You should charge 15 minutes for every minute you spend thinking about a client.

Leo: Even if I'm thinking they are an idiot?

Sam00: Yes!

Leo: Where did you learn this?

Sam00: Entrepreneurship course :)

Leo: I'll take my chances with the library.

Sam00: You are cray-cray.

Leo: Thanks?

Leo: By the way, thank you.

Sam00: For what?

Leo: The website recommendation. They asked all the questions there, but I had memorized all the answers.

Sam00: Manholes covers are still round?

Leo: They sure are.

43

"Hello dear! It's Samantha!" Samantha watched herself in the mirror as she twirled a blonde piece of hair around her finger. The red lipstick made her smile bigger, and her teeth shone like little sparkly diamonds as she sang her greeting, "How are you?"

A deep voice with a strong Bristol accent replied on the other end, "I'm good, great even! Such a pleasant surprise to hear from you! Didn't know you were active on LinkedIn," he chuckled, "it still says IT consultant and cloud architect."

Samantha laughed bubblingly, "We were all cloud architects back then Tibi and IT consultants. I probably should update my profile. Maybe the startup mention would scare off recruiters."

"We need the recruiters, Samantha. I'm really struggling to find good people. It's a rough market."

"Recruiters are sharks, they can smell blood and flock to find their next victim. Circling us poor developers," she laughed again.

"That's ironic, coming from a match-maker." She could hear him smiling through the phone.

"Hah, I guess you can call me that. I like to bring people together." She looked at her nails. Painted hearts. "But it's not the same." She'd redo them again tomorrow. Deploy day. She would have plenty of time.

"Difference being?" Tibi teased.

Samantha grimaced at herself in the mirror, "I don't charge them."

"That's why consultancy wasn't for you. You should be a recruiter instead."

"I make too much as a developer. God knows the world needs more female developers." She probably counted as two, considering the amount of work she was putting in. "Besides, you know how I feel about recruiters."

"No. I hadn't noticed." The sarcasm poured through the phone.

"Sorry. Obviously joking. I mean, it got the two of us in touch again," Samantha defended herself.

"Does that mean you'd like an architect position here? AWS?"

"Unfortunately, no, not at this point."

"That's a shame."

"I like you, Tibi, and it's a good company you have rolling. But I'm heavily invested in this startup."

Tibi groaned. "You young cool people. Is it though?"

"What?"

"A startup? It has been five years if I remember correctly."

"Depends on how you see it. But if we still must play door-to-door salesmen, sorry, salespeople, we consider ourselves to be a startup." She paused. "Round two investment though. But I have somebody in mind. It would solve two problems you have."

"What would the second be? Besides the perpetual developer black hole in the market?" Tibi asked.

"Let's meet for coffee, it's better to talk face to face." She suggested.

"Very secretive. Intriguing. I like!"

"Let's just say I might speed things up for your system." She winked to herself.

"Unless you can give me a better lexical parser, I doubt that."

"Not quite that, but an add-on that could be very helpful."

"Add-on?"

"Something and somebody like that."

"Bring your husband and let's make it a beer. I haven't seen you kids in ages." Tibi added.

"You make it sound like you had him as a student in kindergarten." Samantha laughed.

"He's still a little punk though, isn't he?"

"Indeed, he is. My punk though now, mister." Samantha looked at the closed office door. Darian's keyboard could be heard through it. He had always preferred black switches, like his soul. The sound pierced through everything. Big, heavy thumps.

"Wednesday at 5PM, good for you?"

"I can make it so."

"I'll send an invitation. I'll see if Darian can leave early too."

"Take care."

"Same!"

44

I can't possibly fit another bike in the hallway. David had rearranged his bikes for the third time but could not fit the carrier in the corner with the new bike in front without blocking the front door. He slid his hand slowly down the deep red steel, feeling slightly aroused. Considering the deadness of his bedroom, comparable to a funeral home, it took little to get him aroused nowadays. Almost sparkling, promising endorphin rides, the latest addition, a classic Cannondale fitted with new Dura-ace gears, had been acquired that morning. "I'll miss you guys," he whispered and gave the other two bikes a kiss each. "It's for a good cause." He looked at his watch and felt his pulse increasing as he realized it was almost 10.

Two hours to clean the apartment. I can do it. He started the Pomodoro app. David had degraded it from his computer to an app on his phone. Laundry first. He might as well get some use out of the app, since they had abandoned it after he fired Leo. James had rarely bothered to come in and David was actively trying to avoid Mikael. All alone with

the tomato, it was depressing. The washing machine made a familiar sound and he rushed to pull out the laundry. 90% of the laundry belonged to Samuel and Trevor. Considering the size of the kids, it was an impressive pile of sandy and muddy clothes they could produce in just a week. David simply rotated the three Lycra suits and some dressier options that were rarely used. If he had a bigger apartment, he would have gotten a larger washing machine, maybe two. Trevor had learned to do his own laundry but that usually meant including stones and toy cars in the cycle. After the last attempt, David admitted defeat, fixed the broken drum and put a lock on the washing machine.

Mid-vacuuming, the doorbell rang, and David rushed to hide any evidence of recent cleaning. Palms sweaty, armpits moist and slightly shaky, he kicked the vacuum cleaner sending it rolling into the bedroom and slammed the door shut. She'd never see this room, not today. A sense of dread came over him. What if no women ever will see this room again? The bell rang once more, and he tried to rearrange his hair and wiped his face on a towel. Two sprays of perfume, a little too much, and a shirt to cover the wet marks on his back.

"Hi." He opened the door and mumbled a nervous welcome.

Sarah seemed hesitant to enter. Her eyes darted around, seemingly analyzing the state of his apartment; her hands brushing up and down the gray dress ironing it with the help of friction.

"You look great," he semi whispered. He had intended to be confident with a strong, dark manly voice, but his voice cracked, and he was reduced to a shaky teenage boy waiting for his first date.

"It's clean," she replied and took a step in.

"I'm doing my best. You never know when you get visitors." David knew he never had them. The few dates he had got via various apps hadn't been fruitful and with the kids the apartment was in a perpetual state of various degrees of mess. Never completely trashed, never completely cleaned.

"Alright. I've got an hour before I need to head to the office…" she stopped and looked at the pile of bikes.

"Still collecting?" The disappointment was palpable.

"No, no, I'm actually selling them. Except the red one. It's an old rescue bike. Cheap, but enough to get my biking done. Selling the bikes today."

Sarah smiled. "The red one suits you. Old but well kept."

David laughed and relaxed his shoulders. "Is that a compliment?"

"I guess it is." She winked and closed the door behind her. David quietly, and full of hope, inhaled the rosy scent she left behind.

I'll take it. Compliment or not.

45

"Such a beautiful day!" The lady at the ticket office handed Leo her ticket. "Sorry about the problems with the ticket machines though, should be fixed by late afternoon." Her short curls jingled joyfully as she offered a compassionate head shake.

"Not a problem, I'm early for my train." Leo smiled back. "I think the weather is going to be like this for the rest of the week." She hid her sweaty palms in her dress pockets.

"Oh, that would be wonderful! My grandkids are coming over and they love going to the park."

"Great." Leo stood there, unsure what to do next. "Well, have a nice day!"

"Thank you, dear," the curls sang, "and what a beautiful dress!"

Leo blushed, nodded, and gave a limp wave as she left.

The train had already arrived, and Leo walked slowly, looking at the carts to see how full they were. The warmth on the platform radiated from the asphalt and she pulled her hair in a high ponytail, watching her yellow reflection traveling between the carts.

"Isn't it Leo!" A loud voice made her turn her head with a

crackling sound. Fuck.

"Hi Neal, Neal, was it?"

"You remember me! My dentist friend!" He seemed genuinely happy; arms wide open, ready for an embrace that would never happen. "Is it Martin time?"

Leo nodded regretfully, "A different dentist this time."

"I'm seeing Green, mister Green," he leaned in and whispered, "can you believe they've expanded their practice? I mean, it's Peterborough! They must have found a money tree." Balancing on a leg, he showed how a tree looked like in his mind and he dramatically threw imaginary money to the wind.

Leo interrupted the circus act. "Oh, I guess I'm not sure who I'm seeing. I thought it was Green, but I got a message from Martin."

"Private?"

"Seems like it." Leo looked up the number. Private.

Neal pouted. "I got none of those." He threw up his hands. "That's alright though, Green is my man!" He grabbed Leo's hand, "Come, let's sneak in to first. You look like you belong there." Leo pulled her hand away but followed him.

"No bike today?" He pulled her like you would drag a toddler to the store close to dinnertime.

"Felt like walking today." Leo scrunched her nose as the musty smell in the cart hit her nostrils. It matched the leather seats and looked and smelled like an old person's home at a hospice.

"Bad, eh?" He shook his head and pinched his nose.

Leo nodded and sat down. Neal pulled out a laptop and a charger that looked like a brick, without the rusty color, and plugged in. "I've got some work to do. Is that cool? Not rude?"

"Not rude at all." She exhaled slowly and leaned back, feeling the cold leather against her skin. The train was moving, and she closed her eyes and embraced the

sedative movement. It felt oddly nice to have somebody there. "Wake me up when we are there?"

"Will do," he whistled for a second, "and by there you mean, Leicester?"

"What? No!"

"I'm just kidding. Train doesn't even go there. It's dentist time. Get some Zzzz and I'll get us there. Chooochooo!" Leo leaned back again. The leather had warmed up, and she drifted off before the next station.

Neal had talked about working nonstop until they made it to the dental office. She was mentally exhausted despite the nap but did her best to provide polite uhms and ahs which he enthusiastically soaked up. He hadn't even noticed that she had slept for most of the ride. That, or he simply didn't care. By the time they got there she still had no idea what he did, but she knew he had long legs and she had struggled like a little chihuahua to keep up with him while he magically never got breathless although his mouth was working without a break. *Maybe he doesn't breathe.* She had switched to nodding to preserve energy for the last hundred meters, so she'd be able to say her name once they got there.

"Hello lovely!" Neal had trumpeted his entrance. "I'm here for a date with Dr. Green!" The receptionist laughed and gestured for him to take a seat.

"Ah, Larsson, Le…" Martin interrupted "… Leo! It's been so long! Welcome! And a dress? Are we celebrating the molar resurrection?" Leo blushed and pointed at the site of pain while Neal glided past her with an exaggerated wink and disappeared smoothly through an open door. Some of the pain disappeared with Neal.

"This one hurts like a bitch."

"Then we better look at it!" He rushed her in with big, exaggerated movements. *Maybe he is on drugs.* Fleeting thoughts that had to give way for dental enquiries from overly enthusiastic Martin.

"Now, let's get another mold done, shall we?" Leo doubted her teeth had moved much since last mold but didn't want to kink shame him. The plow volunteered a bite and Martin held the result up against the light like a newly polished diamond. "Beautiful."

Martin placed the mold slowly on the desk, gave it a little pet and a *'there there'* and turned around, hands on his hips and a big smile. "Well, it's great to see you again!" *No mention of the braces?* "Yeah, likewise, I guess. It's been a while, but teeth are good. Except this. And the shape. But yeah." She stumbled over her words and looked down at her nails. They had grown quite long. Her nail clippers had gone missing.

Leo looked up, "The molar thing, really painful." *Can you say you miss your dentist? Why did he take me back?* It had felt like a breakup and now an on-and-off relationship.

"Let's have a look, shall we?" Martin leaned in and attached the bib as the sweet breath of coffee and chocolate brushed against her nostrils. He paused for a second as he was attaching the bib and looked at her. Leo could feel the heat from her face radiating, accompanied by a redness that quickly spread from cheeks to chest. "I can tell it's inflamed; your cheek is swollen and red." He leaned back. "Hopefully not infected."

Leo exhaled slowly, hoping her face would go back to its pale self. Her tell-all complexion betrayed her.

"I wish you hadn't canceled the last appointment. He would have fixed it straight away. One of my top students, as a matter of fact."

"Student?"

"We sometimes bring in students, last year only, of course. We call it two-for-one days. Cause you know what they say?"

"N..no.."

"One is good, but two is better. Double dental!" He laughed and spun around to his tools and returned with a

plate with shiny, tiny tools. "Pay for one, get two dentists. You missed out Leo." He winked.

"Oh yeah, I, I wasn't feeling good."

"Let's see if we can fix that. Open up."

Uhms and ahs later, and a sore yaw, Martin stretched and removed the bib.

"Good news, and bad news. The molar, the culprits for slightly shifting your teeth together, into a plow form, got to be removed. Surgically."

"Sounds pricy. The good news?"

"You'll be able to keep the current shape once we remove the bad molar. And yes, it is pricey." He seemed genuinely sorry about the cost. "You'll have to do it soon. Do you have dental insurance through work?"
"No." No work at all.

"I'll see what I can do to bring the cost down. I can do the extraction if you trust me, that is." Martin raised his eyebrows and offered a compassionate smile.

"I do. I just have to look over my finances."

"I'll remind you next week then."
She got up, the back of her dress was soaked in sweat, and left a butterfly pattern on the chair. They looked at it, but neither of them said anything. Martin trailed his finger along the sweat before wiping the chair quickly with paper. I never returned the uniform. She debated if she should say something as they walked out to the reception together. Martin did not wash his hands.

"Wait, just a second." Martin perked up and ran back to his office. He returned with a large box with a picture of an electric toothbrush on it. It looked very fancy. The receptionists stared at him, mouth ajar. "For you." He turned to the receptionist. "Can you find a bag that will fit the box for miss Larsson?"

"Uhm." She scrambled behind the screen and returned with a crispy white bag, "Paper, okay? We don't do plastic." She bagged the box without waiting for an answer. She scanned it but Martin interrupted and grabbed the scanner.

"It's on me." He turned towards Leo and gave her the bag. "It's a gift."

"I, thank you?" Leo accepted the bag, slowly.

"Well, got to go prep for the next patient. I'll call you next week, Leo, unless you call us first. Remember, it's urgent!"

"What's it for?"

"Your teeth." He laughed from his office.

"I mean, why?"

"A thank you." His voice was faint; she could hear him moving around. Probably prepping.

"For what?" She yelled back. The receptionist leaned in, wanting in on the answer.

Martin's head poked out from the doorway with a massive grin from ear to ear.

"For the molds, of course."

"Oh. Okay." Leo's phone pinged and a quick look at it told her she had to hurry. She muttered a thank you, leaving the receptionist scratching her head and Martin humming a song in his office.

"Hi Jack!"

"Love the dress." Jack stood by a red and blue MINI Cooper in a brown linen suit and espadrilles.

"You didn't have to come get me." She brushed her dress and smiled.

"I assumed you didn't want to bike for a few hours just to eat bread. The bakery is awesome but hidden, like most gems." He winked and opened the car door, "I think we can both squeeze in."

"I was worried I might get kidnapped, meeting up with a stranger like this," Leo laughed, "but that certainly isn't a kidnapper car."

"Hey, don't insult Miriam." He caressed the door. "She is a sensitive girl, but she can certainly kidnap a programmer or two. They are scarce nowadays."

Leo playfully hesitated by the door.

"You just want me for my code."

"A .NET developer?"

Leo punched his shoulder and got in.

"That was a weak punch. All those big objects you write broke your wrist?" He jumped in, smiled at Leo, gave a quick wink, and started the circus car. It reminded Leo of her bike. Welcome to the circus. There are two happy clowns.

46

Standing in the bright bathroom light watching herself and the puffy red cheek, Leo admitted the toothbrush was out of this world. Black and sleek, sonic, and luxurious, it was the Tesla of toothbrushes. And just like the car, she didn't have to do much, merely be present with her teeth and the brush would navigate the corners smoothly as if a Formula 1 driver was behind the wheel. For the molds. Was it worth though? She felt like she had prostituted her teeth and had been paid with the most expensive toothbrush on the market. Did she mind, though? Just a bite here, a bite there. To satisfy a rather peculiar kink. He's my sugar dentist. Leo cringed and shook her head disapprovingly at her own reflection. And Jack? Jack probably wouldn't like that. Not that they were serious. Yet.

Leo placed the brush in the sparkly charging glass and watched the pulsating green light for a second. Her right cheek and jaw pulsated in unison. It would take a large chunk of her savings to get that fixed, and without a job, that would be a problem.

The loud ring from the doorbell pulled Leo back to current time. She rushed to the door, wondering who on earth just rang the doorbell without at least making a call or sending a message. It was James' fault; he had broken

the unwritten rule of avoidance and silence and now she had to talk to neighbors. She opened the door and found herself face-to-face with a slender, cleanly shaven woman. The top of her head reflected the light from the hallway and gave and her an angel-like glow that highlighted her dewy complexion. The woman wiped her forehead with the back of her hand, sighed, and smiled. The eyebrows were drawn on meticulously but there were no visible traces of other makeup.

"Hi! Sorry to bother you!" She took a long breath and wiped her chest this time. The T-shirt clung to her petite body and each armpit had drained itself with distinctive marks on the gray fabric. "I'm Nina. Next-door neighbor. Up-door neighbor. Just moved here, well, trying too anyway! I'm sort of stuck with the sofa downstairs, my husband had a family emergency and I…" she rolled her eyes "… being miss independent and all, said I'd take care of the move."

"How's that going?" Leo replied and peeked down the stairs. She wasn't lying. A sofa was defiantly wedged halfway up the stairs, like a, 'nah f you, not today'.

"Well," she looked down the stairs, "great, if that's where I'd like to have the sofa…I'd love some help, if you can, of course."

"I'm not very strong." Leo pointed at her concave biceps on her left arm and raised her eyebrows.

"That makes two of us!"

"Just a second." Leo put on her sneakers and followed Nina down the stairs.

"Alopecia, universalis," Nina said as they rounded the first set of stairs. "In case you are wondering why I have such an amazingly smooth and shiny skull. My body hates hair and attacks it, it won."

Leo didn't reply but inspected Nina as they stood by the sofa. The shiniest head she had ever seen. Pretty cool.

"Looks cool."

"Saves me time." Nina shrugged her shoulders and slid past the sofa. "Let's see if we can get this monster off the stairs."

It took half an hour, but they made it up the stairs where Old Mary lived.

"This counts as a workout, right?" Nina laughed with the little breath she could squeeze out. "Yoga isn't exactly a cardio workout and that's all the activity I do."

"Never tried it."

"That's alright, not for everybody." Nina waved Leo further in. The apartment had stacks and stacks of boxes everywhere. "I'm a yoga teacher, I should know." She laughed and bowed. "This apartment is haunted, did you know?"

Leo shook her head.

"The apartment has been empty for years but mail would magically appear in front of the door even though nobody lived there for years. The cleaners would take care of it but the next day it would be there again. We didn't believe it but when we got here yesterday with the first boxes, our bills had made it up the stairs. Scared the shit out of my husband. I loved it, though. A bit of mystery to brighten the day."

They stood in the living room.

"Ah crap. I thought we'd gotten rid of this carpet and the pillows." Nina looked at a rolled-up carpet next to two colorful pillows with some sort of oriental design. "Don't get me wrong, these are gorgeous, bought them on one of our travels years ago, but we have so many carpets Aladdin would envy us." Nina stood silent for a moment. "Do you want them? Quality stuff! I honestly was supposed to gift them to the thrift store, but they magically escaped. I bet they'd fit in your apartment." That seems very unlikely."I...sure." Leo wasn't sure but she couldn't reject her petite Buddha neighbor.

"Wonderful! Let's get them downstairs. I don't have enough room to roll them out here. She was already halfway out the door with the carpet, "Grab the pillows! It's a set!"

They were heavier than they looked and smelled of wood and grass.

"Did you also just move in?" Nina was scanning the apartment.

"No, been living here for years".

"Minimalist?"

"Lazyist."

Nina chuckled and threw down the carpet, gave it a kick, and let it unfold in the living room. "Throw the pillows on the couch. I want to see how it looks." The oriental rug had intricate patterns with deep red, sienna, white and black, and thousands of other colors. It looked like a portal to a different planet but at the same time, oddly enough fit in. "Your apartment is a canvas. We've just added a splash of paint!" Leo nodded. Buddha had a point.

"Well, fuck me, I'm tired," Nina threw herself on the mat and grabbed her toes. "Happy baby, groin stretch."

"Oh. Does that release new energy or something?"

"Nah. Coffee in hand position is the only thing that works. And sleep. But my husband's snoring disagrees with the second option."

"Do you want some coffee?" Leo asked.

"Oh, YES please!" Nina rolled up and folded her legs neatly in lotus. Lion cautiously approached the rug while maintaining eye contact with Nina.

"He is harmless," Leo explained from the kitchen.

"Your phone is buzzing." Lion hid behind the sofa, tail brushing back and forward on the floor, refusing to be petted by Nina.

"Probably nothing important." Leo flipped the phone, face down, on the sideboard. "Coffee is ready, come."

"Let's have it here, on the rug. Oriental style."

"Oh, okay. My chairs are kind of broken anyway."

Leo returned with the mugs and sat down. The carpet was very soft.

"Nice to see somebody not prioritizing their phone over friends. We are friends now, you know, the carpet says so. Plus, I need new friends. You are my first one in London."

She took a sip and closed her eyes. The phone buzzed again, inching across the table, demanding Leo's attention, but she couldn't give in now. Nina opened her eyes and leaned forward. "Seems like most people today are obsessed with electronics."

Leo smiled politely and pointed towards her work desk where she daily worshipped the binary father and her Wify, "Yeah, about that…"

Nina stayed for one hour before her husband quietly knocked on the door, asking if Leo had seen a bald lady. "Your bald eagle is here, honey!"

Nina had leaped up and unapologetically gave him a long kiss. "I've missed you! This is my new friend Leonarda! We are going to do yoga together!"

47

Nina and Hubby had disappeared up the stairs with Nina's hand firmly placed in his back pocket giggling and talking. Leo had returned to her unrecognizable apartment. Too much color. But Nina seemed a bit too cray cray, so the carpet would stay put in case there was an inspection. The phone buzzed again demanding attention. Leo complied. Emails, not interesting. Except. A new pull request. Library acquisition request. She held the phone closer and harder. What even is that? What the ever fuck did I do this time? The phone was propelled onto the couch as Leo hurried to her desk and started the computer. Lion hissed as she swiped him down from the keyboard.

"You know you're not supposed to lie on this keyboard. Not this one. Take the Das."
Installing 2%. You got to be kidding me! Heart pounding, she went searching for the phone. It had vanished. Of course, it had. "Lion! Where is it?" Lion walked away without as much as glancing at her, tail swiping left and right, showing the asshole that he was. Yes! the computer

had successfully resurrected like a Phoenix but less elegant.

We have a proposal for you, check your email

That's it? Leo opened her email.

Hi Leo!
I sure hope I'm not bothering you with this email but a friend we have in common strongly recommended you. We've been eyeing your library for a while, and we would like to meet and discuss an acquisition and possibly an employment? I'm confident we can more than match your current salary and you can continue working on the library, which will remain open source in current form, with pay.

Give us a call.

Giorgi Gonzales had an impressive amount of email flair and a selection of phone numbers and titles. CEO was one of them. Leo looked at the oriental carpet and smiled at the memory of Buddha Nina trying to get Leo's legs into lotus position using brute force. A muffled buzzing sound interrupted the visual and Leo went couch diving to retrieve the phone from the depth of the black hole where ancient popcorn and dinosaurs had passed.

"Hello?" Leo breathed in the phone.
"Did Giorgio contact you?" A soft feminine voice asked with excitement wrapped around the vocal cords.
"Who is this?"
"Samantha!" The voice giggled. "Sorry, I tried calling earlier. Take the offer!"
Leo looked at the phone. She didn't even have her number. This makes zero sense.

"I haven't replied. Just read the email. Not to be rude…" Leo had no problem being rude "…why? Why are you even calling me?"

"To tell you, say yes! It's a dream proposal, I promise!" Samantha seemed out of breath, strangled by excitement. "You get to work on the library, PAID, and you get to work on other exciting projects. He knows about your history, he doesn't care. You won't be cleaning out any servers here. I'll monitor you." Samantha laughed loudly, forgoing her usual feminine pearly laughter.

"Did Jack set you up to this?" Leo's cheeks burned red, anger boiling under the surface "… that assh…"

"Jack? What? No! He knows nothing. It's all me, Sam."
"Sam? Who is Sam?"
"Currently your biggest contributor. Sam00."
"Sam00?"
"I thought you were a guy. Sam?"
"Isn't that ironic, Leo?"

48

"I can't believe you made me come all the way out to Cambridge for a beer." Leo dropped her bag on the floor and sat down. Cambridge pub floors were less sticky, hipster-beer seemed to produce less stickiness.

"It was Meron's idea." James pointed at Meron, who replied with a sheepish shrug, followed by a cheer.

"They've got excellent beer here. Plus, it's closer for me to get home." Meron straightened his back. Had he grown taller?

"He finally left the nest!" James elbowed Meron. "Didn't leave his brother though, well, he is too young for the pub, but they got an apartment around the corner from here."

"Scholarship," Meron replied with a proud smile.

"Why aren't we there then?" Leo prodded. The beer menu was thick as the Bible, and it would take a full afternoon to decide on a beer. She kicked her bag to verify it hadn't stuck to the floor. It was indeed a fancy pub. The floor wasn't tacky, and the repertoire was impressive. They had everything on tap. Including confidence. Confidence Ale. Ridiculous name. She was going to try it.

"Share-house, already crowded. Football today."

"There's always football." James shook his head.

"Foot what? Never heard of it. Confidence Ale, I'll have that, and crisps. Beer better work, I've got a new job in a week." Leo placed the order and watched the server as he sailed away.

"We checked out a new venue for the meetup, Peterborough library wasn't keen on having us back…"

"…understandably," James filled in.

"But we found a new one. Nerd friendly. Good Wi-Fi, mesh network all on both floors. No limit on devices, or speed."

Leo's beer didn't taste like confidence, "Sounds like a dream. Guess you guys are going big with this?"

"Yup!"

"And we wanted to ask you something."

"Oh, no don't." Leo waved her hands. "I heard your style."

Meron continued, "We'd like you to come talk about the library. I mean, considering the night at the library, it seems fitting. A continuation, part two. With a happy ending."

"I don't think you know what that means, Meron," James laughed. Meron blushed sheepishly. "And if you do, I don't want to know."

"I think you just outed yourself, James." Leo took a long sip and smiled. She kept an eye on the entrance, watching every person who entered or left. It was a busy pub, a mix of students and young professionals. You could tell them apart by their shoes. Sneakers for students, fancy for professionals. I guess that makes me a perpetual student.

"I like your hair Leo," Meron interrupted Leo's thoughts, "suits you."

"Ah this? Just maintenance cut, but I've abandoned the fringe. It's a pain in the ass with heat and humidity. And snow. Anytime, really." She brushed her hair to the side; some slight curls hid behind her shoulders and softly framed her face.

"I'll take your word for it. No experience with fringiness here. Except the node module." Meron replied.

"There is one?"

"I don't know, but at this point I'd be surprised if all the substantives hadn't been used yet." Meron grinned while James nodded with his beer.

"Is that the one and only, Sam?" James asked. A smiling blonde in a burgundy dress had made the pub freeze.

Leo lit up like a cracker on New Year's Eve and waved enthusiastically. "Sam! Jack!"

Jack and Sam waved in perfect unison and raced to the table, where Leo was ready with unsynchronized hugs.

James applauded the arrival, "Nice to meet you Sam, finally!" He shook her hand with pure enthusiasm. "Thanks for all the reviews, you sure are harder on your feedback than you look," he chuckled.

Sam placed her hand on her chest, revealing little penguins on her nails, and gave a sweet chuckle. "I thought I was lenient!"

Jack leaned in, "Trust me, she was. She tore my Pull Requests to pieces. Never skimp on that extra walkthrough before pushing. And God forbid you forget the tests."

Sam poked her tongue out. "To be fair, Jack, JavaScript is made to fuck up with. You know what they say, in C# everything is an object, in JavaScript everything is a mistake."

Jack shook his head disapprovingly and snorted. "Good one! I've got some jokes as well, but I'll callback later."

Leo sighed, "Is it pun-parade again?"

"Always!" Sam twinkled and went to the bar to make an order. She seemed to float in her long dress and small and quick steps before returning with a glass of sparkly wine.

"I've never liked beer and I'm not ashamed to admit that!" Sam boasted.

"But you are a programmer!" James covered his face.

"Balmer's peak does not discriminate. Any alcohol source will do!" Sam lifted her glass and took a sip.

James shrugged and laughed. "Fair enough."

Sam raised her glass again. "Cheers to Leo's new job!"

"You'll have to tell us all about it, your new dream job!" James insisted.

"Not much to share yet, but I'll do as soon as I get started. How's work for you James? How is David?"

"Still an asshole," James laughed, "But slightly less a gaping one."

Leo contorted her face, "Thank God I don't have to work with him again."

"His thoughts exactly." James winked. "I'm on your side though. As long as you don't get access to my servers."

"Oh, fuck off James." Leo flicked a drop of beer in his direction.

"Never going to let you forget!"

"Thanks…" Leo swung her bag onto her lap and went diving into the black hole that had swallowed her phone, wallet, and a variety of leftovers from the start of the ownership "…just a sec. My phone is ringing." The phone was successfully rescue, and she turned to the side. "Hi dad. Sorry, forgot to reply. Let me check." She looked at her calendar. Colorful blocks covered the week. "I've got yoga on Saturday at noon. How about dinner instead?"

"Yoga?" Jack whispered to James.

"She's got a new wacky neighbor; they do yoga together." James replied.

"Oh."

"There, sorry about that." Leo put the phone face down on the table and gestured to the waiter for a new beer.

"Your phone is buzzing again…" James nodded in the phone's direction "…miss popular!"

Leo sighed and grabbed the phone.

"Hello?" She got up, slowly walking away. "Oh, hi Martin."

James pulled her shirt. "We want to hear," he whispered.

"Thank you for that, yes the toothbrush is great. Yes. Twice a day. The appointment? Absolutely, let's get it done."

James and Meron listened intensely. Jack leaned in, "Should I be concerned? Who's Martin?"

"Creepy dentist, you're good." James winked.

"Sorry, it's noisy here. What did you say about the costs?" Leo waved to the table and walked away slowly.

"Dental care is expensive," Samantha chimed in, and the group nodded as they watched Leo disappear around the corner.

"Leo has a… special dentist."

"Tell me more, I love a good gossip!" Samantha's eyes widened and she tapped her nails on the table with a little paradiddle making the penguins dance.

"Linux penguins?"

"Of course," she grinned.

"Well," James looked over where Leo had disappeared, "Leo's dentist has somewhat of an obsession with her teeth."

"Obsession?"

"She can explain better. Let's just say we've enjoyed her stories from her dental visits. And I don't think I've ever been interested in that before." He laughed down his beer glass.

Leo returned with a puzzled look on her face and slowly put away her phone.

"What did your dentist say?" Samantha hoped for a juicy story.

"I got half the price of the original price…"

"Wow!"

"…through the faculty where he is apparently a teacher…"

"But how?"

"…as a thank you for providing all the molds for the students to practice on." She shrugged.

"An army of plows," James speculated.

"Indeed. An army of plow-mouths, modeled by yours truly." Leo said flashing a big, plowy smile.

49

The new bike wasn't too bad after a few minor fixes. The minor fixes consisted of replacing all moving and static parts on the bike. The cost? David didn't want to know, and Sarah would never be told. It was treated as a shameful secret, worse than the horrible one-night-stand he had last year. But he *needed* the parts. As a true enthusiast. The difference? Non-existent (except for the new brakes) regarding comfort or speed. It did, however, butter up his ego and David slid elegantly in on his bike, wearing his best coordinated outfit with made-up sponsors, and picked the parking spot closest to the entrance so his bike would get attention it deserved. Unfortunately, he was running late. This was a different type of place, probably few developers, as it was 8 AM and all the parking lots were taken, and the building was buzzing busily from every window. ConsultIt!, on the other hand, had barely woken up and only security was there to turn the alarm off and then watch YouTube videos for a few hours before people started coming in.

David watched himself in the elevator mirror, flexing his quads as a hello. The blue and yellow bike suit was his new favorite. It made him look like a Swedish bike God and was bound to impress the kids and Sarah tonight. She

was making spaghetti; he was carb loading after all and next Wednesday he would do a stir-fry for their agreed upon weekly family dinner. The elevator bounced and stopped, and David announced his entrance with his clicky shoes.

"David! Welcome! How was the ride? First time here?" A towering, gangly guy in a suit that seemed slightly too big, waved David in.

"Second time. It's nice to meet up in person again." David shook his hand and stretched himself an extra inch.

"Come with me. We'll grab a coffee and start prepping things. Big plans today! Do you want to change first?"

"Nah, I forgot to bring a set of clothes, so if it's alright with you I'll keep the skins on." David pinched the side of the top and let it snap back, demonstrating the snugness of the polyester blend carefully picked from a Chinese online store. The best Chinese online store.

"As long as you don't melt." He laughed and walked ahead of the human raclette, ready to melt onto a Swiss plate in his polyester blend.

50

On a different bike, in a different outfit, Leo arrived at her new job. Jack had offered to drive her but she had chosen the circus bike over the circus car as traffic was bound to be horrible in the morning. Not that she had much experience with early mornings, it was rather an assumption based on hear-say and she wasn't keen on taking any chances. Sam had talked up this place. "You are going to LOVE it! They do a lot of fun projects, but best of all, you can do your thing half of the time with the library. Think about how awesome that is going to be! We'll grow the project to the skies! Solve all caching problems for all, a gift to humanity. We'll save lives, gray hairs and starving kittens." She had also insisted that Leo wear a linen dress Sam didn't like the color of but that would suit Leo perfectly. It was gray. And comfortable. Buddha had agreed enthusiastically. It was the perfect dress for a fresh start, she could feel it. "It's the color of intellect, solemnity, and maturity," she had whispered wide-eyed.

"Hardly how I would describe myself," Leo had replied, looking down at the knee-length dress. Gray was emotionless, dab, and slightly depressive. Leo worthy. "I'll

take it." Nobody had warned her about the wrinkle-proneness of the dress and Leo arrived looking like a reused gladwrap with dark gray stripes where sweat had collected during the bike ride. A wrinkly zebra, ready for her first day at work.

"Leo, Leo, Leo! This must be the one and only Leo-the cache king! Or rather, should I say queen?"
Startled, Leo stopped trying to brush out the wrinkles on her dress and whispered a yes. Yes, I'm the queen.

The man, soon to be known as Keith, clapped forcefully, and whisked her in through the glass doors. His hands were warm and sweaty and insisted on a long handshake that neatly evolved into handholding. Leo dried her hand on the dress and followed his quick steps down the hallway, which felt more like a runway and Leo was modeling the latest colleague.
"I saw your bike, impressive. Brompton?" Keith asked.
"Yes, but older model. Is it okay I parked the bike indoors? Forgot my lock."
"Yea, yes. I doubt anybody in this building would know how to piece it back together," Keith chuckled. "Reverse origami is no joke. They can barely fold toilet paper here." He stopped suddenly, scratched his clean shaved chin, and turned towards Leo. "I'm not saying they are stupid; you know. Your colleagues are awesome."
"What's your role?" Leo asked.
"Oh my, sorry. I'm Keith Pearson, your line manager! And I have a superb team for you! OUR team is the best team, of course - I'm biased." Keith pointed Leo toward a second hallway, disorienting her. At this point, she was sure they had circled the offices twice, but Keith kept walking confidently in the labyrinth. Especially made so she wouldn't be able to escape.
"There. Here." He revealed an open landscape. An oasis made out of cubicle-gray boredom. Sparkly screens, a

minimum of three per desk, and blaring keyboards echoed against the spacious ceiling. They all went silent simultaneously and turned to embrace Leo's bright red face.

"Voila! This is our in-house team! Your desk is in the corner. We got you a Lenovo. Let me know if you prefer something else."

Leo nodded and waved. They all seemed unusually perky considering the time. Maybe they have small children, she concluded.

"Everybody is in early?" She counted her colleagues. 15.

"Yes! Isn't that wonderful?" Keith threw out his arms and embraced the earliness.

"I guess." Leo pulled together a smile and picked up the laptop. It was sturdy, thicker than she was used to, and the adapter was the size of a hamster cage. The docking station could fit a small dog. "We have flex hours though, if I understood correctly?" She had read the first part of the contract, scanned the pages for salary information, and returned it signed. It was 11 pages long and was written in Shakespearean or some other foreign English. As far as she knew, she might have signed away her firstborn and a batch of freshly baked cupcakes every Friday.

"Yes absolutely! Office hours are 8-16. The rest is flex. Come. And you get the day off on your birthday." Great. December 25th. "Grab your laptop, we are going in! First meeting for you but won't be the last. Let's get started!" Keith flexed barely visible biceps and hopped down the next hallway, bouncing off the walls.

"Here we are, welcome in! Let's introduce you to your extended team, we've brought onboard external consultants- but they are here to stay." Keith winked and opened the door, releasing a wall of hot stuffy air and revealing a bright room with a yellow and blue figure in the middle - posed like a statue against the stark white walls.

You got to be kidding me.

"Leo, this is David, your new colleague. Consultant from ConsultIt, but on a long-term basis. We will be working on this project together for quite some time so get to know each other as I go get some coffee for us. The rest should be in soon." Keith twirled out the door, leaving David and Leo, wide eyed and mouth open, staring at each other. Neither said a word.

"Well, hello! I see some familiar faces here!" A familiar round face popped in the open door and did a penguin walk towards the table. "Didn't think I'd see you again Leo, David told me you quit. Found a better place, I see." He winked with his tiny eyes, barely making a brief twitch. His red cheeks glowed like apples left too long in the sun, sweaty but maybe delicious. Leo couldn't quite place him. David nodded and rearranged some papers on the table, clearly sweating profusely under his condom outfit.

"Good to see you again, Bernie. It's been a few meetings since we last met face to face." David shook his hand.

Bernie fell into a chair with a large crack, and everybody held their breath. The chair survived, barely, but Bernie seemed unfazed. "You know I love a good meeting!"

The bingos. Conference bingos.

Zack glided in with a large thermos and a stack of cups.

"It's really warm in here, isn't it?" He wiped his forehead and proceeded to touch the inside of a few cups. Bernie didn't seem to mind and pulled a cup towards him and splattered some coffee around it before filling the cup.

Leo's dress slowly darkened as the sweat found its way down the thick fibers. She glanced at the timer on the wall. "Maybe we should start the air-con here, recycle some air?"

Bernie and Zack looked at the timer. "Oh, that thing? Been broken since we moved in. A window will have to do. The fan is on backorder."

AFTERWORD

Martin exists. And I only made up two stories. There was no tunic, he offered a towel. And I never found out what he did with the molds or the photos. The Philips Diamondclean 9000 Series 2 electrical toothbrush lasted me half a decade until I dropped it and broke it. I cannot replace it out of respect for Martin. Disclaimer: this is not a paid advertisement for Philips toothbrushes.

ABOUT THE AUTHOR

Iris Classon
Software Developer, Author, Microsoft MVP, Sporty Spice wannabe

Iris Classon is an appreciated speaker, author, Microsoft C# MVP, and Pluralsight trainer with a tremendous passion for programming. She has had a remarkable career path that proves that nothing is impossible. Switching from a licensed and registered clinical dietician to a software developer with a dozen certifications, applications, books, and jobs with renowned companies. She has been featured in several newspaper articles, online articles and podcasts such as Hanselminutes, Computer Sweden, and Developer Magazine. As a sought-after and frequent speaker at conferences such as TechDays, NDC, and various user groups she is known for her unique, creative, and uplifting presentation style. After bragging for half a page, she would like to say she finds the bio a tad embarrassing but an American friend wrote it, and he says it'll help her sell more books.

Plus, she'll get more dick pics. Definitely more ASCII dick art.